A Time for Singing

Carol James

A Time for Singing
COPYRIGHT 2022 by Carol James

Cover Art by *Nicola Martinez*
White Rose Publishing, a division of Pelican Ventures, LLC
www.pelicanbookgroup.com PO Box 1738 *Aztec, NM * 87410
White Rose Publishing Circle and Rosebud logo is a trademark of Pelican Ventures, LLC

Publishing History
First White Rose Edition, 2022
Electronic Edition ISBN 978-1-5223-0378-7
TP Edition ISBN 978-15223-0416-6
Published in the United States of America

What People are Saying

"Carol James tells beautiful stores that will capture your heart. She has quickly become a go-to author for me, reliable and consistent with a clear message of hope." *Stacey Weeks, award-winning author of In Too Deep.*

"One of the best romances I've read. The author's three-dimensional characters allow the reader to experience the joy, sorrow, pain, and love that Ethne and Daniel feel. I rode the roller coaster of emotions in every page of this book, through Ethne's troubled past and with each cautious step as she learned to trust. A five-star novel." *Kathleen Neely, author of The Street Singer*

"I was captured from the beginning. I couldn't put it down... I love the characters, the mixture of serious and humorous moments. Carol James did a great job of showing that God loves us where we are. I would recommend this book to everyone." *Cynthia M., Reader*

"The storyline is terrific, the characters are captivating, and the lessons learned are worth learning. Go ahead and break every chain and jump in feet first. Completely loved this story. Five Stars and highly recommend." *Dawn, Reader*

Dedication

To my partners in crime… Iron sharpens iron.
The Suwanee Critique Group: Tony, Patty, Dawn, Suzy, Cele,
Jennifer, Robert, and Gord.

And the Saturday Morning Bagel Bunch: Ruth, Donna, and Peggy.
Thanks for your wise input and encouragement.

"There is a time for everything, and a season for every activity under the heavens." ~Ecclesiastes 3:1

1

So, who would it be tonight?

From her table in the back corner, Charlee Bennett surveyed the inn's small dining room. The only empty chair sat across from her, a sure sign she'd soon have a dinner companion.

She smoothed the white linen napkin in her lap and sipped her water. Over the past few years, these monthly weekends at the Wayfarer Inn had become her favorites, times of pampering among the plodding.

A tall man who definitely wasn't from Crescent Bluff stepped into the doorway and leaned on the old oak pulpit now serving as the hostess stand. Michael presented his best maître d' smile and then consulted the reservations list. The new diner nodded. Michael gathered a menu and silverware and turned in her direction.

Perspiration prickled her face. Oh, no. Not this man. Anyone but him. Please...not a musician. She could spot them a mile away. After following Jake around for a year and then dating him for two more, she knew the look. PR. Painstakingly Relaxed.

Last month, she'd shared dinner with a trial judge from Amarillo, and the month before that, a retired humanitarian aid worker from Uganda. Not only had both men been fascinating, they'd also been safe. Both were old enough to be her grandfather. But as Michael led tonight's guest toward her table, only one word resonated within her.

Danger.

Taking a deep breath, she reached for her water glass and unsuccessfully attempted to swallow away the mass of nerves knotting her throat. She could do this.

Mr. PR turned his back and spoke to Michael. "When you said

'Charlie,' I just assumed... I didn't realize Charlie was a woman."

He probably thought she couldn't hear him...that he was speaking more quietly than he was. All those years of playing loud music had made Jake half deaf, too.

"You sure no other tables will be available soon?" the stranger continued.

"There's no guarantee, sir," Michael answered. "Friday nights are always busy."

Mr. PR shook his head. "I've got to be someplace in an hour. Can't take the chance."

Michael gestured toward the chair opposite her. "Ms. Bennett is always happy to share her table when we're busy. I assure you that you'll find her excellent dinner company. Please have a seat, sir. I'll send Joe right over to take your order. Enjoy your meal." Michael turned and walked away.

Before her, he stood tall and lanky with black hair, his face covered with a stylish amount of dark stubble. Empty piercings dotted his ears and maybe even his left eyebrow. But that one might have been a scar. She couldn't tell. The candlelight softened his features, making it impossible to know for certain.

Frayed spots decorated his tight jeans, and a black leather jacket hid all but the central portion of a black t-shirt. His painstakingly meticulous hairstyle, which could only have been achieved by applying gallons of product while primping for half an hour in front of the mirror, failed to match his relaxed wardrobe. Even the ever-blowing Texas wind hadn't ruffled his style. PR, for sure.

While she wouldn't describe him as classically handsome, he was totally attractive. Obviously, she'd failed to learn any kind of lesson from Jake's betrayal.

Despite her mind's pleading for caution, she smiled and offered him her hand. She would do this. After all, he apparently didn't want to be dining with her any more than she did with him. "Hello, I'm Charlee—with two *e's*—Bennett."

He grasped her hand and flashed a warm smile that grew until it almost covered his entire face. She couldn't help but grin back.

"Nice to meet you, Charlee with two *e's*. I'm Chance...with one *e*...Jackson. Thanks for offering to share your table with me."

She returned his firm grip. "No problem."

"Haven't been here in a while, and I didn't realize the place would be this busy."

She should let go, but for some reason, her fingers refused to obey. "It's always packed on Friday nights."

"Great news for the owner." Releasing her hand, he glanced back over his shoulder and rocked onto his toes and then back down.

"Please have a seat, Chance. With the kitchen as busy as it is tonight, you'd better get your food ordered if you're going to make your appointment."

A red flush crept up his neck and inched across his face. "I, uh, didn't know you could, I mean, I didn't intend..." He paused and took a deep breath. "Hey, I'm sorry. I'm sure I sounded petty and ungrateful, but I'm not. Thanks for your generosity." A softer smile warmed his face.

He pulled off his jacket and hung it on the back of the antique oak chair. A tattoo covered his left forearm—colorful scroll-work embellishing Greek characters. Just one more confirmation of his occupation in case she had the slightest doubt—which she didn't.

She pushed her words past the still-present lump in her throat. "Chance. I've never met anyone with that name."

Ignoring her comment about his name, he slid into the chair across from her.

"So, Chance, what brings you to the Wayfarer tonight?"

"Business. Came to Crescent Bluff to help out a buddy of mine."

"I see. And what do you do?" She held her breath, waiting to see if his reply would confirm what her intuition screamed was true.

Staring down toward the table, he fingered the folded napkin before him. "I'm self-employed. Sales."

A few years ago, she would have taken his words as truth. But no longer. His response screamed dishonesty. Or at least, a lack of transparency. For some reason, he was deliberately being elusive.

His gaze crept upward and found hers. "How about you? What do you do?"

Not shirking his scrutiny, she smiled her most innocent smile.

"I'm self-employed. Sales," she poked back.

He raised his eyebrows in mock surprise, and then his grin teased. "Oh, really? What a coincidence. Imagine that."

"Yes. Imagine that. I own a little boutique on Main Street."

Joe materialized beside their table, a pitcher of water in one hand and a pitcher of tea in the other. "Good evening, sir." He poured water into Chance's glass. "Would you care for some sweet tea? Or perhaps you'd like something else. A glass of wine? Something from the bar?"

"No, thanks. Nothing from the bar. Water and tea are fine."

Well, he was definitely from someplace around here. He'd requested the beverage of choice for central Texas.

As Joe left, Chance looked back toward her. "So, let's see. Where were we? Oh, yes, your store. Tell me, Charlee-with-two-e's, why would someone who owns a business in Crescent Bluff, and lives here—I presume—be staying at the inn?"

Her gaze never wavering, she stared straight into his eyes. They were dove gray with amber flecks. "I think you may have jumped to an incorrect conclusion. I don't believe I ever said I was staying here. Maybe I'm just having dinner."

Holding her gaze, he placed his elbows on the table and leaned forward. "Well, maybe you are. Just having dinner." As the corners of his mouth curved up, his eyes sparkled in the candlelight, and the needle on her attractiveness meter inched higher.

Refusing to surrender, she placed her elbows on the table and leaned in just close enough to enjoy the delicious earthiness of his cologne. "But I'm not." Her response was barely above a whisper. "I stay here one weekend a month when I balance the books for my boutique. I figure if I have to do something I hate so much, I may as well do it in the nicest possible setting. My own reward system."

Holding up his hands in surrender, he chuckled, and the amber flecks danced. "I have to admit, I like the way you think."

Her heart began to veer down a familiar road, one she could not permit herself to travel again, and she stomped on the brake. Easing back into her chair, she placed her hands in her lap. "You'd better order if you want to make that appointment."

"Guess so, hadn't I? Excuse me a minute." He pushed the menu into the circle of candlelight in the center of the damask tablecloth. He studied the choices, the fingers of one hand tapping against the tabletop, drumming some rhythm to what could only be an imaginary melody. The fingernails of his right hand were longer than those of his left. A guitar player.

Breathing slowly and deeply, she looked away and glanced over his shoulder toward the dining room entrance. A man with blond hair and a warm, though not magnetic, smile waited as Michael approached an older couple who now had a seat available at their table under the front window.

The man wore dress pants with a shirt and tie, topped off with one of those old-fashioned tweed jackets with suede patches on the elbows. For some reason, that style always made her picture an English lord surveying his estate. But that was certainly where his resemblance to old-fashioned aristocracy stopped. This guy could have doubled for that model on the front of this month's *Dallas Style*.

Michael motioned for him to follow. If only he'd arrived a few minutes earlier, she could have been sharing her table with him. He certainly had to be more interesting, and less dangerous, than Chance-Jackson-Mr.-PR-The-Musician. As Lord Handsome pulled out the chair, she checked for a band on his left ring finger. Nothing. Her gaze climbed back to his face in time to see him returning her look, and he winked.

Busted.

She turned back toward Chance.

He stared at her with raised eyebrows—obviously waiting for the response to a question she hadn't heard.

Her cheeks burned, and she didn't need a mirror to tell her they were bright red.

He glanced over his shoulder toward Lord Handsome, and when he turned back, a smirk covered his face.

Busted again. She cleared her throat. "I'm sorry. What did you say?"

He leaned back and crossed his arms over his chest. "I asked what your favorite thing here is. Food-wise, I mean. Like I said, I haven't been here in a few years."

The sarcasm in his voice set her whole face on fire, but the best move was to pretend she hadn't noticed it. "I'm having pork roast. It's an excellent choice, if you like pork."

"I do." He motioned to Joe. "At Ms. Bennett's recommendation, I'll take the pork, please. Oh, and you can bring me a piece of carrot cake as an appetizer."

"I'll have that right out for you, sir." Joe took the menu and headed toward the kitchen.

Chance flashed his immense grin. "You know what they say. Life's unpredictable. Eat dessert first."

His words hit her like a punch to the stomach. She couldn't breathe. The harder she tried, the more impossible it became. Clamminess crept across her face. Her heart pounded.

"Charlee? Are you OK?"

She nodded. Hand shaking, she reached for her glass, only to knock it over.

Water streamed toward Chance's lap. Attempting to stem the flow, she threw her napkin onto the puddle. But it only pushed the ice and water over the edge

Chance jumped up. The entire dining room turned toward them.

"I'm sorry," she whispered, "so sorry."

"It's OK." He smiled and shook his leg. "No permanent damage." He winked.

2

Charlee sat on the maroon velvet settee in the parlor, her stomach churning from having eaten so fast. She hadn't been able to get out of there quickly enough. Just sharing a table with Chance had been challenging. Then she'd made things worse by spilling ice water all over him. How embarrassing! But his comment about dessert had drawn her back in time, and she was sitting across the table from Jake.

That phrase had been one of his favorites. Yet he'd never actually done it as Chance did. Jake had only used it to justify doing whatever he wanted to do whenever he wanted to do it. But she'd dealt with Jake's rejection. She was over him…or so she thought. The dinner with Chance tonight proved otherwise. Ignoring something was not the same as dealing with it. And as painful as the truth was, she had to face it. She may never be completely over Jake.

She'd made a huge mistake sharing her table with Chance. She should have manufactured an excuse and had her dinner delivered to her room and eaten there. She should have obeyed the inner voice that screamed "Danger" when she saw Chance waiting in the entrance to the dining room.

Despite his evasiveness, her first impression of him had been right. He was another Jake. And although her actions might have appeared rude, she should have never let him sit down at her table. Anyone else would have been fine. Just not him.

Charlee glanced at her watch. Precious minutes slipped away. If she didn't get to work soon, Sunday morning would come and the books would still be un-reconciled.

She retrieved her bags from behind the front desk and headed down the hall toward the guest rooms. She stopped in front of the third door on the left, inserted the old brass key, and tried to turn it. Nothing. She compared the number on the key with the brass plate beside the door. Both were labeled the same: Room 5, The Nairobi Room. She tried again. Still nothing.

"So, you're the one who nabbed my room."

Jumping at the words, she turned to find Lord Handsome behind her leaning against the far wall.

"Excuse me?" Had this been a regular hotel, an unfamiliar man standing outside her room might have made her nervous. But not here, not at the inn.

He straightened and took a couple of steps toward her. "I always request room five when I come to Crescent Bluff. However, this trip, I was forced to stay in another room because someone else reserved this one first." He winked just as he had earlier.

She grinned at his feigned impatience. "Well, the reason I had to take this old room is because someone had already gotten room seven, my usual room."

His eyes sparkled. "Fair enough. So, that lock can be a bit touchy. Insert the key, and turn it as you pull the knob toward you and upward."

She followed his instructions, and the door opened. "Thank you very much, Mr…?"

"Doctor…Noah Walsh."

She offered her hand. "Charity Bennett." She hadn't used her formal name since she signed the contract to purchase her shop, but he seemed like a formal-name type of guy.

His grip was strong, but his skin was soft. Definitely not a man who made his living working with his hands…unless, of course, he was a surgeon.

He was exactly the type of man she should be interested in. Not some musician.

As he flashed his non-Chance smile, excitement tingled her stomach. She glanced down at her arms. Goosebumps.

"Charity. I like that. A lovely, old-fashioned name."

"I'd say Noah's even more old-fashioned."

"Touché. Well, since this is your first time staying in room five, I don't suppose you're a member of the SDS."

She'd heard Grandma and Grandpa talk about that. "Students for a Democratic Society? I'm a little young for that. Besides, does it still exist?"

"Not that SDS." He raised his eyebrows and smiled.

The goosebumps multiplied. "There's more than one?"

"You strike me as an intelligent woman. I'm certain you'll figure it out." Crooking his finger, he motioned her closer. "Your room is full of hidden treasure." He spoke in an exaggerated whisper. "Good luck on your quest, Miss Charity. Oh, and be certain to check the desk."

"Thank you for your help with the key." She answered his whisper with one of her own.

He made a slight bow. "To have left you standing out here in the hall all night would have been massively un-chivalrous. Will I see you in the morning at breakfast?"

"Probably. Good night, and thanks again."

She stepped into the room and turned on the light. She wouldn't have exactly described the trinkets scattered around the room as treasure. Oh well, one man's trash…

Packed with souvenirs Colonel and Mrs. Clark must have brought back with them from their safaris and other overseas trips, "The Nairobi Room" bore an appropriate name. Its dark brown and green color scheme along with the various animal skin rugs and statues gave the room a masculine feel. No wonder this room appealed to Noah. But with its white linens and delicate mosquito netting canopy, the bed provided just the proper balance of femininity to make the room welcoming to her.

After setting her overnight bag on the chest next to the small fireplace, she opened the French doors facing onto a small private patio. The primitive outdoor furniture was made of bent twigs, not white wicker like room seven. If tomorrow's weather was warm, this would be the perfect place to work.

She closed the door and placed her computer case on the desk. It was nothing special, just an old oak secretary. And yet, Noah had encouraged her to check it out.

Five small drawers and surrounding shelves at the back of the desktop would have supplied the original owner with plenty of organizational space. She opened and closed the tiny drawers. A piece of folded paper popped up from the bottom one. Removing it, she carefully flattened it. Delicate handwriting that most likely belonged to a woman covered the sheet of Wayfarer Inn stationery. Charlee read,

Welcome, member of the SDS.

The same initials Noah had used.

Last night I heard the sound of crying in the hall. When I opened my door, I saw her, Elizabeth Graham, the Lady of the House. She was sitting in the corner, her face marked by sadness. She called, 'John, where are you? Please come home.' I hated to intrude upon her privacy, but I called her name. A shocked expression crossed her face as she looked my direction and vanished. Now, in the light of day, I wonder if what I saw was real.

Well, someone had been taken in by the old myth of the ghost of the inn's original owner. The note was dated ten years earlier, and the paper was softened from being unfolded and refolded over the years. Obviously, Charlee was not one of the first patrons to have discovered the letter and read its account. Amused, she refolded the note and returned it to the tiny drawer to leave it for another guest to find. Maybe this was the treasure Noah referred to, but nothing in the letter explained the meaning of SDS.

She lifted up the writing surface to reveal the desk front, two drawers—one at the top, and one at the bottom—with a panel in between. She opened the top drawer. Stationery, envelopes, and pens. She closed it and then reached down and pulled out the bottom drawer. Empty.

She stared at the front of the secretary. No other piece she'd seen before was designed like this, without a center drawer. She pushed her hand against the panel. It shifted. She ran her fingers along the outside edges of the panel. Two latches. One on each side. Excitement fluttered her stomach. She pushed the hooks backward. The panel shifted again. She forced her fingertips into the indentations behind the clasps and eased the panel toward her.

A secret drawer!

3

Hot tears blurred the numbers on the clock beside the bed. One o'clock. Charlee had spent her entire evening immersed in reading the scores of handwritten treasures the inn guests had hidden in the secret drawer. But she now held the final letter she would read tonight. Her heart broke for the man who'd written it.

How could one person act with such insensitivity—no, cruelty—toward another? Especially someone she supposedly loved enough to marry. Charlee gathered the letter to her chest and rocked back and forth as if soothing a distraught infant. The pain expressed in the author's words resonated deep within her heart. If only she could draw him into her arms in comfort and say, "I know. I understand." But she couldn't. He was no more than block-printed letters on a yellowed sheet of inn stationery.

Hands trembling, she laid the paper beside her on the bed. Her heart ached as the memories of Jake that surfaced earlier at dinner flooded over her again. But, as much as he'd hurt her, even Jake had shown more compassion than the woman in the letter had shown toward its author.

Tonight's dinner with Chance had reopened the deep wound of Jake's rejection. She'd built walls of protection around her heart after he left. She flew from anything or anyone even remotely connected with him. No more musicians, no more music. Nothing that would remind her of him and the love she thought they shared. Although her mind whispered how ridiculous her sweeping judgment was, her heart assured her the only way to survive was total avoidance.

And then tonight, Chance burst into her tiny fortress. Everything about him so enticed her—his brilliant smile, his tall, lean build, those teasing eyes that had danced in the candlelight. Even the tattoo.

Her heart pounded as she slammed back against the pillows.

Obviously, she hadn't learned anything from her mistake with Jake. She was an idiot for feeling the slightest glimmer of attraction toward Chance. If she ever saw him again, she'd make sure she double-locked and dead-bolted the door to her heart.

She reached over and picked up the letter once more. If only she could talk with the author and learn whether he'd been able to move on with his life. Shared pain connected her soul to his. *Father, I don't know the man who wrote this letter. I don't know his present circumstances, but You do. Whatever his situation, please take away his pain and comfort him with Your love and peace.*

~*~

The well-worn oak floorboards creaked as Chance walked down the hall. Light escaped from under the door to room five. Whoever was staying in there tonight was still awake. Or maybe he or she had bought into the tale of the ghost and left the light on. Just in case.

He'd purposely switched rooms this trip. A new room for a new life. He read the plaque beside the door: Room 7, The Victorian Garden Room. A change of scenery would be good.

He stepped through the door into a lace, floral, and wicker wonderland. Definitely a chick room. Reason enough to request the Nairobi Room from now on. The guys would give him fits if they could see him now. But once he turned the lights off, it wouldn't really matter. A bed was a bed.

He put his suitcase and guitar in the closet and then headed over to the desk and checked the drawers. Empty, except for the top one, which held only inn stationery. No SDS'ers stayed in this room.

He pulled off his jacket and tossed it onto the chair facing the French doors that led out to the patio. He dropped onto the bed, pulled off his boots, and flung the half dozen or so small pillows covering the head of the bed across the room. He'd smother if he tried to sleep with that many. He leaned back.

Tonight had been more fun than he thought it would be. Three years had passed since he'd played with the guys, and things weren't as tight as they used to be. But they still sounded pretty good, mainly because of Matt. A good soundman was worth millions.

He stretched out on the bed. His mind and heart raced. The feeling was way too familiar. He was high, but the euphoria wasn't caused by any drug. It was the effect of music on his soul—he was doing what he'd been created to do.

He fingered the tattoo on his forearm. *Thank You, Father, for not being done with me years ago.*

At least one part of tonight had been great. Dinner, on the other hand, had been…interesting. He would have never agreed to share a table in the first place if he'd realized he'd be eating with a woman, especially one that attractive. And he shouldn't have flirted with her, but he couldn't help himself. She'd encouraged him.

Above all, he had to be careful. The last thing he needed right now was any kind of distraction, no matter how slight. And she was really distracting. That deep auburn hair. Those eyes like sparkling emeralds. And the freckles on her nose were really cute. Gave her a sweet, innocent look.

She was anything but sweet and innocent, though. Like a prickly pear cactus blooming in the spring, she was beautiful to look at from far away, but dangerous if you got too close.

After he'd recovered from the initial surprise of learning Charlie was really Charlee "with two ee's," their conversation had been going well enough until he placed his order. And then everything changed. He'd tried to be gracious when she knocked over that glass of water. After all, it wasn't as big a deal as she seemed to think it was. But she shut down like a power outage during a Texas thunderstorm.

Maybe she hated men and her manners had run out. But, no, she'd checked out that other guy.

Maybe she had something against him. But that was crazy. She didn't even know him.

Maybe she had some stuff going on right now. Maybe she was hurting.

Yeah, that he got.

As the adrenaline wore off, exhaustion set in. A hot shower and he'd have no trouble falling asleep, even in the middle of the flowers and lace.

~*~

The knot present in Charlee's throat last night returned. Three place settings of mismatched antique porcelain dishes decorated the small dining table in the recess of the bay window. One place for her, one for Noah, and one for…Chance? The third place could be for anyone. After all, Chance never said he was staying at the inn. Of course, he never said a lot of other things about himself, either. Maybe whoever it was would skip breakfast this morning.

She poured hot water from the rose-patterned teapot onto the strainer of Earl Gray tea in her cup when Noah stepped into the dining room. His look was less aristocratic than last night and more prep-school casual—khakis and a butter yellow cable knit sweater, penny loafers, and argyle socks. But his smile was still perfect.

"Good morning." He slipped into the chair across from her, put some English Breakfast Tea in the cup before him, and covered it with hot water. "So, how did you like my room? Did you discover the treasure?"

His eyes sparkled with anticipation, causing last night's goose bumps to resurrect themselves. Trying to relax, she took a quick sip of her tea and then leaned forward. "Fascinating. I was up way too late reading the letters."

"Welcome to the Secret Drawer Society, the SDS." He offered his hand. "So, did you contribute anything?"

She grasped his hand. "Me? No. I just read through a number of the letters."

"Ah, well, then you're only an honorary member. I, on the other hand, am a full-fledged member with lifetime benefits." He grinned, and the goose bumps multiplied.

"You've written something in there?"

He nodded. "Multiple pieces."

Although she hadn't managed to read all the letters in the drawer, she probably read at least one of his. "Well, I'd rather read than write." She released his hand. "So, Noah, what brings you to the inn? More than reading and writing SDS letters, I'm sure."

"Unlike you, I enjoy writing as much as reading. Maybe a little more. I'm a writer who's doing research on the story of Elizabeth Graham, the inn's original owner." He paused and looked straight into her eyes. "Actually, that's not entirely true. I'm certain you've heard the old saying, 'Those who can, do; and those who can't, teach.' I'm really an aspiring writer who makes his living as a college English professor."

Ah, that kind of doctor. Unlike Chance last night, Noah at least was honest.

He stirred some cream into his cup. "What about you?" His eyes sparkled.

"She's self-employed. In sales."

Charlee startled at the sound of the male voice to her right.

She hadn't even noticed Chance walk into the room. No telling how long he'd been standing there eavesdropping. His clothing looked about the same as what he'd worn last night, but his hairstyle was tousled, bed-head this morning. Spiked from being toweled off most likely after a shower, his hair looked more brown than black in the absence of product. The circles under his eyes hinted he'd probably gotten less sleep than she had. Not so PR this morning.

He ran his fingers through his hair in an unsuccessful attempt to tame it, and her breath caught. She wouldn't let herself be drawn in again. Prodded by her stomach's churning, she turned back toward Noah.

He stood. "Noah Walsh."

"Chance Jackson." They shook hands and Chance settled into the chair to her right. "Morning, Ms. Bennett."

Unlike last night, this morning she would heed the warnings in her heart. "Good morning, Mr. Jackson." Turning her gaze back toward Noah, she continued, "Chance was my dinner partner last night, Noah. He's also self-employed and in sales. Imagine that." She lifted her eyebrows in pretend amazement and slowly looked from Noah to Chance and back again. "But, to answer your question, Noah, I own a boutique on Main Street that specializes in goods from the British Isles. Bits of Britain."

"Well, I'll certainly have to drop by for a visit." Noah's eyes twinkled.

"Excuse me, Ms. Bennett." the intruder on her right spoke. "Would you please pass me the coffee?"

If only he'd overslept and missed breakfast this morning. Without breaking eye contact with Noah, she pushed the carafe toward Chance.

Noah grinned. Her gaze followed his as he turned toward Chance. "So what line of sales, Chance?"

Pouring the coffee into his cup, Chance hesitated a moment before he responded. "Music sales."

She'd guessed right.

4

Charlee stared at the date and time on her computer screen. She had to be the worst friend in the world. She'd been so wrapped up in work, she'd forgotten what today was. Ally should be home from church by now. She turned on her phone, and the message tones sounded immediately. Three messages and two texts, all from Ally. She didn't take the time to listen to the messages or read the texts but simply pushed "3." Her best friend needed her.

"Charlee! Can you go?"

Ally sure sounded upbeat, not exactly the tone Charlee had expected. She glanced at the date on her watch. Yes, today was the fourteenth, the second anniversary of Jason's death. "Go where? I didn't listen to your messages."

"An old friend of mine from high school is in town, and he wants me to meet him at The Barn tonight for a show. Please say you'll go with me. It'll be fun."

Charlee groaned inside. Ally knew how she felt about music, especially country music. Having a root canal sounded more appealing. Plus, she'd really feel out of place with just the two of them. But Ally hadn't sounded this excited about anything in a long time. "If you're really sure you want me to go." She sighed to heighten the drama.

"I am." Ally giggled.

"You're the only person in the world I'd do this for, you know."

"I know." The playfulness left her tone. "And that means a lot. You're a good friend."

Charlee sighed again. "What time?"

"The show starts at eight. Pick you up at seven-thirty. You won't regret it. I promise."

"Well, only if you promise."

"I do." Ally giggled some more. "Bye."

"Bye." Charlee ended the call and sat down at the desk. The letter called to her from the top of the leather desk blotter. Putting it back into the secret drawer with all the others felt callous, disrespectful. She'd read it twice. The first time was Friday night in bed, and the second was yesterday afternoon. Now, before she left, would be the third.

Tonight is my wedding night. What's that trite phrase? "The first day of the rest of my life." I stood with the pastor and my best man waiting for the woman I love more than anything to stand beside me. As the music swelled, I glanced down to see if my white satin vest was pulsing in time with the heartbeat surging in my ears. Once she reached me, once she took my hand, I'd be OK. I looked up toward the back of the chapel so I wouldn't miss the first view of my beautiful bride.

The doors remained closed. I waited, the music started over, but the doors never opened.

The arms that should be full tonight are empty. The heart that should be overflowing with joy is a dry, dark well. The woman I loved with no restraint, the woman I'd given my heart to, had taken hers back. Or maybe she'd never truly given it to me.

I'd known our wedding day would change my life. But not like this. My mind tells me to pray. I should, but I don't want to. I have no words beyond, "Why?" If God loves me, why would He let this happen?

So tonight, as I spend my wedding night alone with empty arms and a broken heart, I ask, "Is this really the beginning of my new life?" If so, I don't want to be a part of it.

Holding the sheet of paper in her left hand, she traced the words with the fingertips of her right, as if touching the ink would connect her to the letter's creator. She closed her eyes to envision the face of the author, but she saw only one image. Jake. Three years of unconquered agony flooded her heart. *Father, why do I have to relive all the hurt?*

She looked back down at the handwritten words. To feel such a strong bond with someone she'd never met, someone who might not even be real, seemed impossible. After all, this letter might be a work of fiction, nothing but a cruel joke played on the SDS by its author.

Certainly, some of the pages in the drawer were products of their writers' imaginations, little more than amusing anecdotes. But then others, like this one, were heartfelt confessions. Whether it was truth or fiction didn't matter. The possibility alone of the letter's authenticity was enough for her to take a chance. Thirty minutes remained before she had to leave.

She pulled a blank piece of stationery and a pen from the top drawer. Noah would no longer be able to tease her about being an "unofficial" member of the Secret Drawer Society.

~*~

Charlee ran down the driveway, the evening mist dampening her hair and clothing. She jumped in Ally's SUV and slammed the door behind her.

"I'm so glad you agreed to come." Ally radiated excitement. "I really didn't know if you would."

Charlee hadn't seen this much sparkle in her friend's eyes since before Jason's death. Maybe this renewed friendship was just what Ally needed, after all.

"The sacrifices we make for those we love." Charlee added just enough "poor me" to her tone to hopefully make Ally feel sorry for her. Then she winked and smiled. "Of course, I did have to postpone cleaning out my refrigerator, and you know how much I love doing that. But anything for you."

"You're such a saint." Ally laughed. "Seriously, I know this is a big step for you, so I hope you'll just relax and enjoy tonight."

"Breathe in, breathe out, breathe in, breathe out. I can do this." Charlee sighed. "So tell me about this old friend."

"His name's Trey. I had a crush on him all through high school. Toward the end of our senior year, he finally realized I was alive, and we went to prom together. We dated that summer, and in the fall, he went to Tennessee, and I went to TCU. I met Jason, and the rest is, as they say, history."

Tennessee. A knot rose in Charlee's throat. She took a deep breath. Just because Trey moved to Tennessee didn't mean he was a musician.

"Anyway, I ran into him at the dog-park once when he was home visiting his parents."

Dog-park. Maybe he was a vet. "Really?"

"Yeah, last fall. We've been talking and e-mailing back and forth since then."

"Last fall. As in a year ago?"

Ally nodded.

"And you didn't mention it to me?" Charlee grinned hoping to lighten the weight of the secrecy dividing them.

"I'm sorry. I…I wasn't sure how you'd react." Ally's eyes filled. "It had only been about a year since…"

Charlee's heart broke for her friend. For her inability to trust. "Oh, Ally, grief and loneliness can't be measured by the risings of the sun and the revolutions of the earth." She placed her hand on Ally's shoulder. "I'm your best friend. Of course, I understand. I'm happy for you."

Ally reached over and squeezed Charlee's hand. Then she brushed away a tear. A smile crept across her face. "He called and invited me to dinner Friday night. Just as friends. At first, I turned him down, but he persisted. Then I figured, what could it hurt? So, I agreed. And I'm so glad I did. It was as if he'd never left." The smile grew. "I can't wait for you to meet him."

And Charlee couldn't wait, either.

Ally put the SUV in reverse and backed down the driveway.

Too soon, they pulled into the gravel covered meadow that was the makeshift parking lot next to a large red-painted wooden structure. The September rain had stopped, and the temperature had dropped ten degrees. At least one thing about tonight—the cooler temperature—would be enjoyable.

Farther down the lane sat the old two-story farmhouse that had been converted into a restaurant and bar. This unremarkable farm out in the middle of nowhere often hosted big names in country music, but Charlee had never heard of tonight's group.

The gravel crunched underfoot as they made their way to the building. Portions of the side walls had been removed to make it an open-air theater and allow the Texas wind to rush through the structure. A stage dominated the far end of the building. Swagged from rafter to rafter and upright post to upright post, strings of soft white bulbs danced in the evening breeze. She and Ally stepped onto the concrete floor.

Ally handed the usher two tickets and practically skipped as she led the way down the center aisle through the mass of people and turned into the second row on the right.

Charlee glanced at her watch. Ally's date should be here any minute, or he'd miss the beginning of the show. "Will Trey be able to find us up here? Maybe you should text him and tell him where we're sitting."

Ally giggled. "Oh, I'm sure he will, but texting him's a great idea." She pulled out her phone and tapped in the message.

Ally chatted on about their dinner the other night. She was beginning to heal, to move on. Charlee leaned over and hugged her friend. "I'm so happy for you."

The house lights dimmed, and in the darkness, featureless silhouettes moved across the stage. The band was loading, and the seat next to Ally was still empty. If this Trey guy stood up her best friend, she'd get his phone number and give him a piece of her mind. No, forget the phone. She'd hunt him down and do it in person.

Ally trained her gaze toward the dark stage, a smile warming her face. If she was upset, she hid it well.

The stage lights came up and the music began. Charlee leaned over toward Ally. "You think he got lost?"

Ally turned toward Charlee, her brow knit in confusion. "What?"

Charlee leaned in closer and spoke loudly into her friend's ear. "Do you think Trey got lost?"

Ally grinned and grasped Charlee's hand. "You're so funny. There he is. The guy in the denim shirt on the right playing guitar." Turning back toward the stage, Ally waved, and the blue-shirted guitar player nodded.

Dread blanketed Charlee. Now she understood Ally's secrecy, her reluctance to share about Trey. It wasn't caused by the length of time since Jason's death, but the depth of pain Jake's betrayal had caused in Charlee's heart. Trey was a musician, just like Jake. Charlee couldn't change what had happened in her past, but she could prevent Ally from making the same mistake she'd made. She could not let her be fooled and hurt by Trey.

~*~

The songs droned on, one blending into another, all sounding the same. Rather than waste these precious hours, Charlee decided to make the time productive. The lights were low enough that she could search on her phone for unique "Made in the British Isles" products that might be good additions to her store's inventory. Ally sat on the edge of her chair, completely absorbed in the music, or more likely the musician. No one else was paying attention to Charlee, either.

After what seemed like forever, the final song ended, and Charlee followed as the crowd jumped up. The band left the stage, but the applause continued ensuring there'd be an encore. After an appropriate amount of time and cheering, the band came back out and began playing the intro to an old love song.

This was one classic country song, maybe the only one, Charlee truly liked—or used to, anyway, before Jake.

She dropped her phone into her pocket and stared at the band.

Trey stepped up to the mic to sing lead, his gaze trained on Ally.

Charlee turned toward her friend, and for the first time in two years saw unrestrained joy covering her face. She wanted to be happy for Ally. She deserved to find love again after losing Jason and living through these lonely months. But shared love, not the kind of one-sided love a relationship with Trey would demand.

~*~

Chance sure hadn't expected a packed house in this remote venue. Performing with the band again felt good, and the gig had gone really well. But even with all the faces in the audience, he hadn't missed hers. He would have never figured Charlee to be a country fan. Something about her, no everything about her, screamed classical music.

"Hey, buddy. Thanks for playing with us." Trey grabbed him in a quick bear hug. "The keys were awesome tonight. Sure you don't want your old job back?"

Chance pulled off the straw cowboy hat and sunglasses and ran his hand through his hair. "Thanks, man. Naw, but I had a great time. I'll be glad to sub in some, but nothing permanent."

"We can always use a good sub." Trey stuck his hands in his front pockets. "Did you see her out there? She was the cute blonde near the front."

He'd been so distracted by Charlee that he hadn't noticed any of the other women in the audience. In fact, at times, just knowing she was there had made concentrating on playing tough. The keyboard was at the back of the stage, out of most of the wash from the spots, so he was pretty sure she hadn't seen him. Plus, whenever he'd glanced her way, she was staring down toward her lap. "Sorry, man. I was so wrapped up that I missed her."

"That's OK. You'll get to meet Ally and her friend in just a few minutes."

Suddenly, Chance wasn't feeling too social. The last thing he wanted was to make small talk with a blind date. He would have backed out, except he was the only other unmarried band member, and he couldn't let Trey down. Besides, it wasn't exactly a date. More like babysitting so Trey could spend some time with his date without having to worry about her friend feeling left out. Nope, he couldn't leave Trey hanging. "OK. I'll meet you in The Farm House as soon as I pack up."

5

The old fashioned, clear light bulbs in the chandeliers filled the Farm House with a soft glow, helping soothe Charlee's throbbing head. The combination of the loud music and the lack of sleep this weekend had birthed a pounding headache. She popped a piece of gum into her mouth. Sometimes the chewing motion helped loosen her jaw and alleviated the pain.

Ally had chattered continuously about the show since they'd stood to walk up the path from The Barn.

Charlee smiled and nodded, but her mind was far away. The next hour or so promised to be awkward. A part of her felt like a chaperone...protective. Ally had struggled through the heartbreak of Jason's death, and Charlee didn't want her to suffer the same pain of rejection as she had at Jake's hands.

But then another part of her felt like an intruder. Ally was an adult. After an appropriate time, after she got a feel for Trey, maybe Charlee would excuse herself and go to the ladies' room for a while, or even go sit in the car and nurse her headache.

She could hardly keep her eyes open, and had she realized tonight's plans included dinner afterward, she'd probably have turned Ally down, or at the least come in her own car so she could leave at any time. Right now, she just wanted to wrap herself in the dark cocoon of her comforter with a pillow over her head.

"Now, don't be upset, Charlee, OK?" Ally grinned as if ready to burst with excitement.

"About what?" She couldn't help but return Ally's smile.

"Trey's bringing one of the other guys with him. He says he's really nice. His name's Ace." Ally bit her bottom lip.

Not a blind date on top of a headache. "Ally, I wish you'd said something earlier. You shouldn't have done that. I would have been fine with the two of you."

"No, you wouldn't. I know you. You'd have felt like a third wheel. I thought it might be good for you to have someone to talk with, that's all. Not a date or anything."

Right. Not-a-date-or-anything.

"Ace is safe. Trey says he's completely into his career with no interest in dating. Just relax and enjoy yourself. You never have to see him again after tonight."

Ally meant well. If Charlee hadn't spent so much time on her phone, she might have been able to recall the faces of the other band members, but the best she could do was remember the instruments—drums, a bass, two other guitars besides Trey's, and a keyboard.

"There's Trey." Ally stood and waved toward the entrance.

Charlee looked down to confirm her friend's feet were touching the ground. Then she turned back toward the doorway to see the band's lead singer strutting toward them.

"Hello, gorgeous." Trey grinned.

As he bent down and kissed Ally on the cheek, she giggled. "Hi, Trey. The show was wonderful!"

"Thanks." His gaze locked onto hers. "Glad you came. It means a lot."

Ally gestured toward Charlee. "This is my best friend, and boss, Charlee."

Trey turned toward her.

Charlee looked into Trey's soft blue eyes and found a gentleness she hadn't expected, not a self-centered hunger as in Jake's. "Nice to meet you, Trey."

"Same here, Charlee. Glad you could come. Ace'll be along in a minute." He slipped into the chair next to Ally. "I took the liberty of pre-ordering the brisket platter for four. Hope that's OK." Trey motioned to the waiter and then placed his arm on the back of Ally's chair.

The two began rehashing tonight's show.

If they asked for Charlee's impressions, she'd be in trouble because she'd only be able to discuss the new flavors of English tea biscuits she'd found online.

Trey raised his hand. "Here he is."

As her "not-a-date-or-anything" made his way across the restaurant, Charlee recognized the lanky silhouette of the keyboard player, the brown plaid shirt, the straw cowboy hat, the sunglasses. Good grief, it was eleven o'clock at night. What was with the glasses? She took a deep breath and smiled.

"Ladies, meet Ace. We go way back to my first days in Nashville. Ace, this is Ally." The two shook hands. "And this is Ally's friend, Charlee."

"Hello, Charlee with two *e's*."

His voice sent shock waves through her body. The keyboard player removed the glasses and hat and transformed from Ace into Chance. How could she have not recognized him? He'd been on the stage in front of her for almost two hours. But she hadn't really been looking at the stage much. Plus, the stubble he'd worn the other times she'd seen him was gone, and the glasses and hat camouflaged his appearance. Dismay replaced shock as she realized Chance was to be her partner for the rest of the evening.

"Hello, Chance. Or would you prefer Ace?" She held out her hand. "How many names do you have, anyway?" Her words dripped with all the honey she could muster.

"Enough." A smirk covered his face. He grasped her hand briefly and eased onto the chair beside hers. He scooted her water glass toward the center of the table. "I didn't bring a rain poncho tonight."

Charlee rolled her eyes. "Funny."

"What?" Ally asked.

"Private joke," Chance answered.

"You two know each other?" Ally's eyes opened wide.

"We had dinner together at the inn Friday night." Chance answered for both of them.

"Oh, I see." Ally raised her eyebrows and grinned. "That's an interesting coincidence."

The waiter delivered their dinner, and as the other three rehashed the show, Charlee slowly withdrew into her fortress of self-preservation. She would have felt less like a third wheel if Chance, or Ace, or whoever he was, hadn't come.

While the other three talked and laughed as if she weren't there, she contributed nothing to the conversation. If she could have snapped her fingers and disappeared, she would have. But she loved Ally too much to desert her.

Her headache raged, and her stomach churned. She moved the food around on her plate. She wanted to go home and climb into bed. Anxiety coupled with the nausea from the headache prevented her from eating much, if anything. She pushed her plate aside and placed a fresh piece of gum into her mouth. The first one hadn't helped, but maybe this one would.

She glanced at her watch. One fifteen. The Farm House bar would be open for a while longer, but the other dinner patrons left ages ago.

Late nights like this hadn't bothered her when she and Jake were together. But her body was no longer on this schedule. Plus, she'd spent the whole weekend working. Well, working and reading the SDS letters. She leaned forward and closed her eyes. Moving in slow circles on her temples, her fingertips worked to ease some of the pain. Surely, they'd be ready to leave before too much longer.

The sudden silence was oppressive. She peeked up and saw the other three staring at her.

Ally reached across the table and gently squeezed one of her wrists. "Headache?"

Charlee nodded her response. "Sorry. It's been a long couple of days. I hate to break up the party, but it's after one, and we've got to work tomorrow, Ally." She sounded like Ally's mother instead of her best friend.

"Oh, sure. Of course." Trey stood. "How about we walk you ladies out to the car?"

Ally and Trey led the way, hand-in-hand, still talking. She and Chance followed in silence with a gulf between them that could accommodate a Texas longhorn. Even if they'd both stretched out their arms, their fingers couldn't possibly have touched.

Good, at least they were on the same page.

~*~

The colonel had been nice enough to let him move to the room he'd originally requested, the Nairobi Room, for his final night at the inn. He'd lain in bed for almost an hour, but sleep still eluded him. Maybe he needed to perform his ritual. Reaching over to the nightstand, he flipped on the monkey lamp. He swung his legs over the side of the bed and walked across the stiff fur of the Zebra pelt rug to the oak desk. He sat down, opened the secret drawer, and removed the stack of SDS letters. Glancing quickly through them, he saw several new ones. But his was missing.

He opened the other drawers one at a time. In the top one lay an envelope addressed to "The Bridegroom." He turned it over and lifted the unsealed flap to remove the contents—two folded sheets of stationery. He opened the top sheet first. The letter he'd written years ago. He unfolded the second one. Precise, feminine cursive covered the page. A woman had responded to him. He carried both pages to the bed to read.

Dear Friend,

I call you Friend, not because we know each other, but because one of the components of friendship is caring that springs from shared experiences. Although we've never met, my soul is filled with compassion for you.

Your letter broke my heart. I, too, was rejected by my fiancé. Not for another person, but for something I could never compete with. His career. However, my rejection happened days before, and not the day of, my wedding. My private suffering was painful enough. For it to have happened publicly is unthinkable. I am so very sorry.

The pain dulled with the passage of time, and I thought I was free, until I stumbled across your letter. I don't know if someone ever completely heals from such a hurt. It's always buried deep in my heart. The days come and go, time moves on, and life covers the pain. But does the hurt ever completely go away? I want to believe that, as hard as the betrayal was, God used it to save me from a lifetime of unhappiness I might have otherwise experienced.

As I read your letter for the first time the other night, I prayed for you. Wherever you are, whatever you're doing, I hope you have been able to move on with your life and that you're happy.

My dear friend of the heart, I'm sure that if we ever met, we would become true friends.

Blessings to you,
The Bride

~*~

The brass bell jingled just as Charlee stepped into the office after opening the shop. Either Ally was coming in through the front door, or Charlee had her first customer of the morning. She stepped out onto the main section of the floor. A tall, blond man browsed through a selection of coffee table picture books of the British Isles.

"Noah, what a pleasant surprise!"

He smiled. "Good morning, Miss Charity."

No one ever used her formal name, mainly because Charlee seemed to fit her better. But when Noah said it, the syllables were musical.

He quickly scanned the store. "Lovely boutique. Reminds me of a shop in Swindon."

"Swindon?"

"My mum's hometown. It's as if I've traveled back to my childhood. Even the mustiness. You must have modeled this on a shop you visited."

"No. I've always wanted to visit England. Never been, though. I had a trip planned once. But, I…it didn't exactly work out. I had to cancel it for personal reasons." Yes, not wanting to go on a honeymoon alone, even if it was to Britain, was certainly a personal enough reason. "Anyway, I guess you could say I'm kind of an Anglophile."

He crossed his arms over his chest and smiled. "Let's hope that plays to my advantage."

Her cheeks burned.

He stepped further into the shop. "I had no idea your store was this large. It looks tiny from the street. I'll have to stop in again when I don't have to be back in Arlington for a class and have the time to browse more thoroughly."

"Is there anything specific you're looking for? Something I can help you find?" A date, perhaps?

"My mum adores English marmalade. I hoped you might have some I could take to her. A little reminder of her homeland."

"Your mum?" She raised her eyebrows in teasing skepticism.

"Yes, my mum." He punctuated his response with a nod.

"Of course." She smiled. "Well, I have several varieties, but let me show you my favorite." She picked up a jar and held it out toward him. "It's the perfect blend of sweet and tangy. Any additional women you might want jars for?" The words popped out before her mind could rein them in. As perspiration prickled her upper lip, she tried to retract her statement. "I'm sorry. I didn't mean that the way it must have sounded." She was so out of practice with this flirting thing.

Noah grinned and held up his left hand, fingers splayed. "No wife. But I think you determined that Friday night." He winked. "And currently, no other women, either."

"One jar of marmalade coming up." She turned away from him, took the marmalade, and strode toward the register. "Let me wrap this for you. Is a simple gift bag with tissue and ribbon OK?"

"Perfect." He followed her and placed a credit card on the counter.

She processed the transaction and then handed the card back. She turned to wrap the marmalade for him. He leaned on the counter, his gaze burning holes in her back.

"I'll be coming back to the Wayfarer the second weekend of next month. Maybe I can stop by and see you again. I'd love to check out some of your other products."

She tied rainbow strands of curling ribbon onto the gift bag handles and turned to face him. "I think I'd like that."

He grasped the gift bag. "Until next month…good-bye, Charity Bennett."

"Good-bye, Noah Walsh."

The bell jingled as he walked out the door. She liked him. For years, she hadn't wanted anything to do with men. The fear of being so deeply hurt again convinced her marriage shouldn't be in her future, and that had been OK. She had her work, and her business was thriving. If being single was God's plan, she could be content.

But maybe she'd been wrong. Noah was an attractive, mature man. And best of all, he wasn't a musician like Jake and Ace, or Chance. Or whatever his real name was. Probably Aloysius.

6

Laden with the heavy scent of musty leaves and loamy earth, the October breeze swirled around Charlee as she rolled her suitcase up the walkway to the inn. Normally she dreaded the weekends she had to balance the books. But not this month. This weekend Noah was due back.

Colonel Clark held the door open for her. "Good to see you again, Charlee. How've you been?"

"Very well, thank you." Although more than ten years had passed since he'd retired from the army and purchased the inn, the colonel still sported his military haircut. She smiled. Some things in life never changed. "How about you and Mrs. Clark?"

"Fine, young lady, just fine. Your room should be ready in about thirty minutes. I can keep your bags here at the desk if you want to relax and have some tea in the parlor while you wait." He took her bag and computer case and placed them behind the desk.

"Thanks. I'll do that. By the way, has Noah Walsh checked in yet?"

"Not yet." The colonel grinned. "But it's usually around dinnertime when he gets here. I'll let him know you asked about him."

"Thanks, but that's really not necessary." Her face warmed, and she turned toward the parlor before he could see.

A porcelain tea service brightened the old mahogany butler's tray table beneath the front window. She grasped the teapot and then looked out through the glass and across the meadow. The autumn sun cast a golden glow over the browning grass. Although cool, the afternoon was too beautiful to spend inside. She set the pot back on the warmer and made her way onto the front porch.

She pulled her Shetland wool cardigan around herself as

protection against the wind. Today's weather felt more like December in Texas rather than October. These same winds blew in a cool front last night, transforming the skies from drab summer slate to brilliant winter periwinkle. The crispness enlivened her. She should have plenty of time to walk to the lake and back by the time her room would be ready.

Across the meadow, in a stand of trees along the banks of the lake, sat Travelers' Rest. The rustic wood and stone chapel, built by the original owner as a place of peace for visitors, had become the most popular wedding venue in town. Her heart ached as thoughts of The Bridegroom welled up. More than likely, that was where the love of his life had betrayed him and left him at the altar.

A sweet piano melody greeted her as she wound her way down the path to the chapel. She tried in vain to resist, but its beauty drew her closer. She recognized the old hymn from her childhood.

This is my Father's world, and to my listening ears

All nature sings and 'round me rings the music of the spheres.

She grasped a wrought iron handle, eased one of the antique carved doors open, and tiptoed into the intimate foyer, silently closing the door behind her. On the stage, the rounded end of the mahogany grand piano case jutted out toward the center of the chapel. The keyboard and its player were hidden back in the recesses of the piano alcove.

The pianist continued.

This is my Father's world. I rest me in the thought

Of rocks and trees, of skies and seas. His hand the wonders wrought.

Although the melody was simple, the additional harmonies and the irregular, but fluid, timing confirmed the talent of the musician. Whoever played was a gifted pianist—not some sort of rock musician like Jake.

The music stopped, and her soul yearned for more. She was empty and had been for such a long time. Before she could decide whether to make her presence known or quietly slip back out, the music began again. This time the song was a classical composition.

She knew the piece, but its grandeur seemed out of place in this primitive country chapel. Hearing it in such a simple setting captivated her. As the haunting melody gripped her heart, she slipped into the back pew and sat, eyes closed, letting the majestic chords seep into her soul. The beauty of the melody and the pain of the memories it evoked filled her eyes with tears.

Music hadn't moved her like this in a long time. She hadn't allowed it. She'd told herself she hated music. It had ruined her life by stealing her future. She'd had nothing to do with anything musical after Jake. Until that night at The Barn last month.

And now she was sitting here inviting the possibility of more pain. She should leave, but her body wouldn't cooperate. Maybe this was what addiction was like—wanting something so badly, even though it would ruin her life and her future, but being powerless to overcome that desire.

The music stopped again and silence filled the room. The stone walls began to squeeze in on her. She had to leave. But she couldn't. Her need to know the identity of the musician overpowered her desire to go. Silently, she stood.

Not wanting to startle whoever it was, she tiptoed down the center aisle far enough until she could see the pianist. The head of spiked, dark brown hair was bowed, the gray eyes closed. She gasped, unable to control her shock. Her heart raced. How could he, of all people, create such beauty?

Obviously startled by the noise, Chance lifted his head and opened his eyes. They glistened. The music had moved him, too. His gaze dropped toward the piano keys and then crept back to meet hers. The impatience she expected to see was missing. His face held a mixture of embarrassment and sadness. "I thought I was alone. Didn't hear you come in."

A knot rose in her stomach as sympathetic embarrassment filled her. "I'm sorry. I shouldn't have intruded. I was on a walk when I heard the piano, and I just had to see who was playing. I...I didn't intend to interrupt. I only wanted to let whoever was playing know how much I enjoyed the music. How beautiful it was."

"Thanks." A soft smile warmed his face.

She clasped her hands together and pulled her gaze away from his. "Well, I guess I'll head back to the inn."

"Wait." He scooted the bench back from the piano and stood. "I'm finished here. Let me close up, and I'll walk back with you. That is, if it's OK."

"Sure. I guess so." Now she wouldn't be able to finish her trip to the lake. Not waiting for him, she turned and headed out the back through the double doors.

The trees surrounding the chapel moaned in the wind.

Chance came out and slipped on a brown leather jacket. He turned toward her and cleared his throat. "Feels more like February than October."

"It sure does."

They hiked up the path toward the inn. The space between them, now filled with awkward discomfort rather than an imaginary longhorn, was smaller than the night when they'd walked back to the car after the show at The Barn.

"Doesn't usually get this cool this quick." His voice broke the silence, but his words in no way lessened the awkwardness.

"No, it doesn't."

He jammed his hands in his jeans pockets and stared forward toward the trail before them. "Wonder if this means we'll have an early winter."

"Could be." Enough. She refused to participate in more mundane conversation about the weather. "Chance, the Mussorgsky was magnificent. Words can't express how it made me feel."

He stopped and turned toward her. A slight half smile brightened his face as he raised his eyebrows. "You know Mussorgsky?"

"'The Promenade' from *Pictures at an Exhibition*? Don't look so surprised. Yes, I know it quite well." But she wouldn't tell him it was the wedding processional she had chosen. The wedding processional that was never used.

He nodded his head and grinned. If he was attempting to remove the surprise from his face, he was unsuccessful.

"Where'd you learn to play like that, anyway?"

Walking on, he looked away from her and then stared down toward the tips of his cowboy boots. His face reddened as he turned back toward her. "Juilliard." He shrugged his shoulders.

"Juilliard?" She stopped short and stared at him.

"Don't look so surprised." Sing-song-ish, his voice echoed her earlier words. "My mom had this whacko idea I should be a concert pianist. She made me take piano lessons before I even began going to school. Her dream was always for me to go to Juilliard. She would've loved for me to spend most of my life in a suit of tails in a philharmonic hall somewhere." He looked up at her and smiled. "That's not me."

She studied him from head to toe. The leather jacket, jeans, and boots transformed into a white bow tie and black tails with his hair combed back away from his face. She could see it.

"What?" He returned her stare.

"Oh, nothing. It's just that I think that could be a good look for you." She gently shrugged her shoulders and walked on.

He caught up with her. "You're kidding, right?"

"If men only knew how attractive they look in tuxes, they'd wear them all the time." That thought probably should have remained unspoken.

"Really?" He pulled his phone out of his pocket and held it up to his mouth. "Note. Buy a tux."

The path that led to the lake was just ahead. He stopped. "Hey, I planned to take a quick walk down by the lake after I finished practicing. Want to join me? Or do you need to get back?"

She looked at her watch. Her room should be ready by now, and she really wanted to freshen up for dinner. But she should have plenty of time before Noah arrived. Plus, the lake had been her original destination, anyway. She looked back up into his face. A musician's face. "Thanks, but I've got to get back up to the inn. Maybe another time."

He shrugged his shoulders and flashed his sparkling smile. "Sure. See ya around."

~*~

Chance inched his way down the steep path to the water. He

stepped out onto the damp earth that bounded the lake, turned left, and headed to where two trees stood side by side. Their lakeside roots, exposed by years of erosion, had knit together to make a rustic bench. The trees swayed in the autumn wind as he settled onto the damp wood where he'd sat many times before.

So, he'd been right. She was a classical girl. Not many women he knew, except maybe those he'd studied with…and one other, would have been able to name that piece or the composer. But she knew both. Not many women his age liked, much less knew about, classical music. Her knowledge intrigued him.

Plus, she was beautiful. Tall and slim, and those freckles did a number on his heart. Her makeup hid them some, but in spite of her efforts, they were visible. Mighty cute.

In the chapel, she shed those prickly thorns just long enough for him to get a quick glimpse into her heart. When she surprised him at the end of "The Promenade," he saw the shimmer of tears in her eyes. Music spoke to her just as it spoke to him. If God were ever to bring another woman into his life, he prayed it would be someone that could share his passion for music. Someone with the same sensitivity as Charlee.

Maybe it was good she hadn't come with him. He wouldn't have been able to concentrate.

He closed his eyes as the wind raced across the surface of the lake and covered his face with a cool mist. He'd come to talk with his Father and to pray about this Sunday—for wisdom and guidance for himself and the church. If everything went well, his life was about to take a turn down a new path.

7

Charlee placed the key in the lock and followed Noah's instructions from last month. The door opened on the first attempt. She had a couple of hours before dinner, plenty of time to soak in the tub and do something she'd been waiting a month to do.

She pushed her suitcase into the closet and dropped her computer case onto the chair on her way to the desk. Before she did anything else, she had to check. Opening and closing each drawer, she rummaged through the old oak desk. The SDS letters originally confined to the secret drawer were scattered throughout the desk, and her envelope wasn't there. Surely, no SDS'er would take it, or worse throw it away after all this time.

She studied the top of the desk. An ivory corner peeked out from under the leather blotter covering the writing surface. Holding her breath, she slipped the envelope out. Her handwriting covered the face of the envelope. Her heart raced as she stared at the outside, unable to make herself open the flap.

How ridiculous to think her letter might have been answered. The chances that the man who wrote the original letter might have just happened to come to the inn within the last month, and might have just happened to stay in this room, and might have just happened to read her letter were "slim and none," as Dad would say.

She kicked off her shoes, dropped onto the bed, and pulled the leopard throw over her feet. Her hands trembled, the paper rustling as she eased the two sheets of stationery from the envelope. She unfolded the papers. The Bridegroom's original letter was on the outside, and her reply was on the inside. Just as she'd left it. She turned over her letter and gasped. The same block printing that formed the words of the original letter covered the back of her reply. He had come, and he had responded.

Dear Friend,

Thank you for your letter. After all this time, I was surprised to see a response. Yes, I think we would be true friends if we ever met.

For someone who makes his living through words, though, I'm suddenly finding it difficult to put the thoughts that have been in my mind all these years onto paper.

Over time, I've come to realize that as painful as the rejection was, it was the best thing. My life was a shipwreck, and God allowed her actions to pull me from a deep sea of self-centeredness in which I might otherwise have drowned.

I did love her, but it wasn't enough. True love means sacrificing for your partner, and I wouldn't have been able to do that. I was self-absorbed and could never have been able to love her as a husband should. She deserved much, much more than I had to give.

And you're right. With time, the pain does lessen. But, to answer your question, it has never gone away. Yet that's OK, because through everything, God has taught me that life is not all about me. This experience has made and will continue to make me a better man.

God's mercies are new every morning, and sufficient for each day. And I will be forever grateful for the new work He is doing in me daily.

Your New Friend

She sank back against the mound of pillows, closed her eyes, and clutched the letters to her heart. After Jake, she stopped looking for a husband, but if God ever brought a man into her life, she wanted it to be a man like this. Someone who could understand what she'd gone through with Jake. If only she could meet him. She held the letter up to read it again when her gaze fell on the second paragraph: *For someone who makes his living through words…*

Only one man came to mind who made his living writing and would have stayed in this small inn within the last month. Her breathing quickened. He had stayed on that Sunday night after she'd checked out. Maybe he switched rooms to stay in "his" room. He had no wife. Or girlfriend.

Her heart raced. Noah…it had to be. Noah was The Bridegroom.

~*~

"Are you ready to order, Ms. Bennett?"

"I think I'd like to wait a few more minutes, Joe."

"Sure thing." He refilled her water glass. "Just wave when you're ready."

"I will." She drummed her fingertips on the table top. It was after seven, Noah wasn't here, and the dining room was full. The restaurant was even busier than when she'd stayed last month. While she was happy for the Clarks, all these patrons meant she wouldn't be able to hold the seat at her table for much longer. It was the last available one, and Michael was already putting names on the waiting list.

Another hopeful diner arrived. Chance. His gaze scanned the room, obviously searching for a possible seat. When Chance saw her, he smiled and raised his hand in a slight wave.

She smiled back. Maybe Noah had cancelled his plans and wasn't coming tonight. Sitting here with an available chair while Chance waited would be selfish. But then, Noah might be here any minute. Or he might not.

Of course, if she ate with Chance, she might lose it again over the dessert issue. But he hadn't ordered dessert first at The Farm House last month. Plus, simply knowing to expect the possibility eliminated the shock factor. Decision made, she held up her hand and motioned for Chance to come.

As he nodded, he spoke to Michael, and the two made their way to her table.

His outfit was a carbon copy of the one he'd worn last month. A limited wardrobe, the sign of a struggling musician. But then maybe his closet at home held two dozen pairs of jeans, twenty black tee shirts, three black leather jackets, one brown leather jacket, and, oh yes, the brown plaid shirt and straw cowboy hat he'd worn at The Barn. Or perhaps he was color blind. Fewer choices certainly simplified wardrobe coordination.

Whatever the reason, black was a really good color on him.

"Hi." He smiled his big smile. "Thanks for letting me share your table. I was afraid I'd have to head to the Burger Bin. I've got to be someplace at eight thirty."

That's right. Trey's band was playing again at The Barn tomorrow. They were probably rehearsing tonight. "No problem. Have a seat. So, how was your walk to the lake?"

He slipped into the chair across from her. "Good. You would've enjoyed it if you'd come."

Her stomach fluttered at the warmth of his gaze. Maybe having dinner together wasn't such a good idea after all. "We'd better order if you're going to get to your appointment on time."

As she signaled, Joe approached the table with an order pad in hand. "Ready to order, Ms. Bennett, Mr. Jackson?"

"Yes, Joe," she replied. "I'll take the spaghetti with a Caesar salad, please. No croutons."

Joe nodded. "And you, sir?"

"Ditto. Except for the croutons." He caught her eye. "I'll take all of hers, too."

As Joe turned to leave, Chance continued, "So, you don't like croutons? How can someone not like croutons?" Playfulness colored his tone. "I'm pretty sure they were created on the eighth day. So, they've gotta be good. Right?"

"I'm pretty sure you're confused." She waved her finger at him.

He grinned, and the golden specks in his eyes sparkled. "About what?"

She had never seen eyes like his.

He lifted his eyebrows, waiting for her answer.

She sighed. "It's not so much that I don't like them. I don't want the extra calories. That's all."

"Well, I wouldn't worry—"

Joe interrupted him by setting the salads on the table. "Your spaghetti'll be out in a few minutes. Can I get you two anything else?"

"This is great, Joe. Chance?"

"Tons of croutons. Perfect." He nodded his head.

As Joe walked away, she spoke. "What were you about to say?"

His face reddened as he studied his salad. "Uh, nothing."

His cheeks contradicted his reply. "You sure?"

"Positive." He popped a crouton into his mouth.

~*~

As a series of soft raps sounded on her door, Charlee glanced at the clock. For over two hours, she'd been plodding through the books. Band rehearsals usually went on into the wee hours of the morning, so it couldn't be Chance. Goosebumps prickled her arms. Maybe it was Noah. Taking a deep breath, she pushed the desk chair out and walked to the door. "Who is it?"

"Why don't you open the door and find out?"

The door muffled his voice, but no doubt who it belonged to. "Noah!" Her hands couldn't get the door unlocked quickly enough.

"Hello, Miss Charity. Don't you look lovely tonight."

He wore classic preppy from head to foot.

"Colonel Clark said you were looking for me earlier. He's got a spectacular fire going in the parlor, and I wondered if you be up for a nightcap." He flashed his model-perfect smile.

"Well…" She paused for a moment and glanced back at the desk to avoid appearing too anxious. "I think I've earned a break. A cup of tea would be perfect about now."

"I hoped you'd agree." He crooked his elbow so she could entwine her arm with his. "Shall we go?"

"Can I meet you there in a couple of minutes? I need a few seconds to finish up something in here."

"I don't know…can you? As far as I'm concerned, you may if you can." He winked. "I'll be waiting."

Her gaze followed him as he turned and walked down the hall toward the parlor. Even though he'd spoken with a smile, that little exchange felt a bit awkward. The whole "can" or "may" quandary was one of Mom's pet peeves, too. Most people nowadays didn't even pay attention to that. But, then again, Noah was an English professor. And although she wasn't a student of his, he'd sure made her feel like one. Going forward, she'd watch her word choice more carefully.

She clicked the door closed and then slipped into the bathroom. She pulled a brush through her hair, gargled with mouthwash, and put on some lip gloss. She smiled. Not too shabby, except for one thing. She snatched her makeup brush out of her cosmetic bag, dusted a little concealer across her nose, and the freckles faded. Better.

She grabbed her room key and headed down the hall.

The golden glow from the fireplace painted the antique furniture in the parlor with soothing warmth. An arrangement of candles on the old upright piano in the corner provided the only other light source in the cozy room.

Noah sat on the settee facing the fireplace, the glimmer from the fire making his hair shine like molten gold. She soaked in his handsomeness before she spoke, "Hey."

He turned and looked at her. "That was quick."

"I didn't have too much to do. May I get you something to drink?"

"Yes, you may. I'll take coffee, black, please."

She walked over to the coffee service on the buffet next to the door into the dining room and prepared their drinks—coffee for him and tea for her. Herbal tea would be perfect for this time of night. No caffeine to keep her awake. She picked up the two cups and saucers. The front door opened and Chance came into the room. Band practice must have ended early.

"Well, hi there." The tone of his voice reflected a warm familiarity.

"Hello, Chance. How was your appointment?"

"Great. Thanks for asking." He glanced toward the parlor and then turned back and smiled. Or maybe it was more of a smirk.

She stretched to her full height and raised her chin. She had nothing to be embarrassed about.

Chance held out his hand. "Can I help you with one of those?"

May I help you with one of those? "No, thanks. I've got them."

"All right, then. See you around. Night."

"Good night." As he headed down the hall toward the guest rooms, she walked over to the sofa and handed Noah his coffee.

"Thank you." He patted the seat next to him, and she sat down. "Wasn't that Chance? How coincidental that all three of us are here together again this month." His lips smiled, but his eyes were unreadable. "By the way, I'm very sorry I missed dinner. I had to stay late at work. I was really looking forward to spending time together."

"Not a problem. Those things happen." She hadn't exactly eaten alone.

He rested his arm across the back of the sofa. "I'd like to make it up to you, Charity. Would you do me the honor of having dinner with me tomorrow night? But not here. I have someplace special in mind."

He was asking her out on a date. "I'd love that."

He draped his arm across her shoulders and caressed her upper arm. And there they came again—goosebumps.

8

Charlee's eyes popped open as the bright sunlight flooded through the French doors and warmed her face. She rolled over, looked at the clock, and then jerked straight up. It couldn't really be ten thirty. The last time she could remember sleeping in like this was after those late-night concerts when she was dating Jake. No wonder, though. She and Noah had stayed up talking until after two.

In reality, he'd been the one doing most of the talking while she stifled yawns as she concentrated on listening. The hours of conversation had been politely superficial—built mostly upon what he did, a little bit of what she did, but not much about who they were. Maybe tonight they would go deeper until she could break through his exterior defenses and peek into the beautiful heart of The Bridegroom who had written the letters—the man she hardly knew, but for whom her heart cried out.

Breakfast service had been over for half an hour, so she slipped out of bed to brew a cup of Earl Gray in the pot on the console. That would have to do until she could get an early lunch.

She walked over to the patio doors and flung them open. The breeze ushered in the musty scent of fall, but the temperature felt more like summer. Yesterday she'd needed a wool sweater on her walk to the chapel, and today, in true Texas fashion, she could wear shorts and be comfortable.

The weather was perfect for outside work, so after a quick shower, she'd move to the patio. If she finished everything before her date with Noah tonight, she'd be able to relax and enjoy dinner without anything hanging over her head.

~*~

Chance settled into the white wicker rocker on his patio. Today was too beautiful to stay inside. Scooting forward, he rested his guitar on his knee. He'd stumbled across this song barely a week ago, and he needed to practice the chords and words before he sang it in public for the first time.

The keys were an extension of himself. When he sat down at a piano or stood at a keyboard, he didn't even have to think. He just put his fingers on the keys, and they played. But not the guitar. He did fine if all he had to do was strum chords, but anything more involved was still a challenge. He sounded a lot better than he had a few weeks ago, though, and he would master the guitar, no matter how much time and effort it took.

He closed his eyes, his fingers plucking the individual strings while he hummed the melody. This song was quickly becoming one of his favorites.

He made it through with no mistakes, so now it was time to concentrate on the lyrics. Unlike many of today's worship songs, this old hymn had tons of words to memorize. As his fingers moved back over the strings again, he closed his eyes and sang softly, the words flowing from his soul to his Heavenly Father.

I am resting, resting, in the joy of what Thou art;
I am finding out the greatness of Thy loving heart.
Thou hast bid me gaze upon Thee, and Thy beauty fills my soul,
For by Thy transforming power Thou hast made me whole.

Not too bad for the first shot. Maybe on the last verse, he should stay on the two-chord at the end, repeat the chorus, and then tag the last line. He'd give that a try. He played and sang through the next three verses and then repeated the chorus and tagged it. Yeah, that sounded great.

When he opened his eyes, he jumped in spite of himself. Charlee's face was about five feet from his, peeking around the fence that divided his patio from the one next door—obviously hers.

She giggled and covered her mouth. "Sorry. Didn't mean to startle you."

His first impulse was to downplay his reaction, but she wasn't stupid. She'd know he wasn't being truthful. So, he grabbed his chest.

"You trying to give me a heart attack?"

She rolled her eyes. "Whatever. Shall I call the paramedics?"

He grinned. She looked amazing. The copper highlights in her hair sparkled in the morning sun. The wind swirled it around her head, and she tried to tame a couple of strands by tucking them behind her ears.

Eyebrows raised, she stared, obviously waiting for his response.

"Nah. I'll live." He was sitting. No self-respecting Texan male would still be seated while a lady stood. Mom would have skinned him alive. "Sorry." He jumped up and gestured toward the other wicker chair. "Have a seat?"

She looked over her shoulder toward her patio and then back at him. "Well…I…" She paused. "OK, I guess." She walked over and sat on the chair.

He set the guitar on the loveseat and dropped into the rocker. Her face was scrubbed clean, no makeup, and the freckles made her look even younger. Today she was more the girl next door than the successful businesswoman down the street. "So, this is your weekend to balance the books, right?"

"Yes, I make myself do it the second weekend of every month. The first year I was in business, I put off reconciling the books until the end of the year. If my parents hadn't bailed me out, my business would have gone under. Right then I promised them I'd balance the books every month." She smiled. "This month, I should have my folks all paid back. It's a good feeling."

"I imagine so." The gaze that had been locked on his crept away. She began to run her fingers through her hair, and his chest tightened.

She looked back. "I didn't realize you were a guitarist, too."

"I think you're being generous. I'm still learning. Been teaching myself for the last few months, and I have a long way to go. That's why I practice with my eyes closed. Helps me concentrate. But I sure won't be doing much of that around here anymore. That is, unless I wanna have a heart attack."

A slight smile warmed her face. "That was a lovely song. I've never heard it before."

"It's an old hymn from the 1800s. Words are the same, but the tune's been changed." Her eyes were much greener when she didn't wear makeup.

"Did you write the music?"

"Me? No." As she nodded, her hair shimmered in the sun, and his mind transformed into a black hole, devoid of words. Grasping his hands together he raised them over his head and stretched. "Well…"

"Can I…?" she spoke at the same time. "Oh, sorry."

They both paused, and he smiled. "Ladies first. Please."

"Can I ask you a question?"

"Sure. Your quota's one a day, though. And I'm afraid you just used it."

As she wrinkled her forehead and pursed her lips together, he looked down to see if she was tapping her foot like his sister would have done. "Just kidding. You can ask me as many questions as you want. Ask away."

"Why did you lie to me?"

No further explanation was necessary. He knew exactly what she was talking about. "I don't consider it a lie, Charlee."

"OK, then. A misrepresentation. Sales? Really, Chance? So is all this music, this playing with Trey's band, really just a hobby?"

"I think of it this way: everybody's selling something whether they're getting paid for it or not. So, basically, we're all in sales."

Her gaze locked onto his. She obviously waited for more.

He continued, "Look, when I first meet people, if I tell them I'm a musician, they generally start asking all sorts of probing questions that I may not want to answer unless I get to know them better. Plus, they treat me weird. Like I'm some celebrity. I loved that when I first started in the business because that's what I wanted. But not anymore."

She stared in silence and then slowly nodded. "Sold." The slight smile from earlier was back. "How about one more question? If it's too personal, just tell me, OK?"

She could ask him anything. Just because she asked didn't mean he had to answer. "Sure, although you must be up to five or six by now—way over your quota."

Her smile grew to a grin. "What does your tattoo mean? Or is it just a design?"

He'd definitely answer this one. He loved explaining about the tat. He'd gotten it as a personal reminder, sure, but also for a chance to share with other people. "It's the Greek word *poema*. We get our word poem from it."

She cocked her head to the side and rolled those eyes again. "Oh, well that certainly explains it."

He suppressed a grin as some more of her sass surfaced. "There's this verse in the Bible, 'For we are God's handiwork, created in Christ Jesus to do good works, which God prepared in advance for us to do.' The Greek word used there for handiwork is poema."

He held out his arm. "These letters remind me that my entire life, who I am, is being written by God. Each moment of every day is a new line of the poem that's me. And if God's the perfect poet, can His poems be poorly written? Can the meter be off or the rhyme faulty?"

He paused, although he didn't really expect an answer. "Nope," he continued. "Each one of us is His workmanship, a masterpiece, no matter how our lives are written, how they play out."

Her gaze left his and looked up into the sky as if processing all he'd just said. Then she looked back at him and gently shook her head. "Each one of us, as in all of us? I'm going to have to think about that."

"Good idea." Mission accomplished.

Glancing at her phone, she stood.

He followed suit.

"Well, I guess I'd better finish my accounting. Keep up the good work on the guitar, Chance. It really sounds great."

"Thanks. See you around."

She disappeared behind the fence. If anyone had asked him, he wouldn't have been able to tell them exactly what made her so interesting. Certainly, she was attractive. But there were lots of good-looking women out there. Besides, he'd grown past being charmed by the exterior. Or at least he thought he had.

Something more than physical beauty made her attractive. Like her feistiness. He'd seen it at dinner last month and now today. Could be that was her personality. Or maybe a defense mechanism. Time would tell. Either way, he kind of liked it.

Whoa. The reason God had brought him to Crescent Bluff had nothing to do with a woman. This was the first time in years he'd even been the slightest bit intrigued by one. Maybe this attraction proved he really was stupid after all.

Plus, thinking about Charlee would only confuse everything, and he needed to keep his mind focused for tomorrow. Reaching over, he grabbed the neck of his guitar. Better go inside if he was going to be able to concentrate enough to finish practicing.

~*~

Charlee's laptop was open to last month's spreadsheet, her gaze trained on the screen. Her fingers rested on the keys, but her mind was miles away. Or at least a few feet away. Chance had gone back into his room right after she'd left, and maybe that was good. She would have been even more distracted knowing he was sitting just behind the redwood divider between their two patios.

Poema. The symbols in the tattoo spelled poema. His response to her question had even sounded like poetry. But he was a musician, not a poet.

So, Chance had revealed a facet of himself she hadn't expected. Surprising. He'd been playing a hymn yesterday when she'd run into him in the chapel. Other than that, she hadn't seen any evidence that he might be a believer. Yet, she hadn't seen any evidence that he might not be.

But then, Jake had started going to church when they began dating. He even became the back-up worship leader right before they got engaged. And the debris he left behind had revealed one truth she'd missed while they were dating. Jake had been all about Jake. Self-centered and egotistical. And she hadn't been able to see it. Or she'd simply chosen not to.

Chance seemed different, though. His comment about being God's masterpiece might have been interpreted by some people as arrogant, except he'd said it with such humility. And if he'd been boasting, it hadn't been about himself but about God.

Plus, she couldn't get that song he'd been practicing out of her mind. The melody haunted her and made concentrating on her work impossible. And the words. Something about God making us whole. How did that happen? Jake had taken a part of her heart when he left, and no matter how hard she tried, she hadn't been able to get it back.

In the end, Chance was a musician, too, and she would never stop reminding herself of that. She'd been deeply hurt and made a fool of once by one, and it wouldn't happen again. Nothing or no one would ever convince her that turning her back on music and musicians hadn't been the right decision, the only way to protect herself. That assurance resonated deep within her heart.

The wind blew and rustled her stack of receipts. If she wanted to be finished by the time Noah came to pick her up for dinner, she'd better get back to work.

Noah. Now, he was the kind of man she should like. Safe.

9

A knock sounded on her door, and Charlee checked her look one final time in the mirror. She surveyed her khakis and sweater. She had no idea where they were going and no idea if she was appropriately dressed. But as far as she was concerned, they could drive through at the Burger Bin and eat in the car. The location of their date didn't matter as long as they got some time alone. Tonight was her chance to confirm what she already knew with ninety-five percent certainty—Noah was the Bridegroom.

She grasped the doorknob, took a deep breath, and pulled.

He smiled his perfect smile. "Hello, Miss Charity."

Noah looked as if he'd stepped out of one of those old 1940's movies Mom loved. Corduroy jacket, ivory turtleneck sweater, leather driving gloves, and a little camel colored wool cap with the front smashed down to the bill. Those hats must have a name, but she had no idea what it was. An old-fashioned look for sure, but also timeless and classic.

"Hello, Noah." The goosebumps tingled. At least she had on long sleeves. "I hadn't really planned on doing anything but working this weekend so I didn't bring clothes for a fancy date. I hope my outfit will be OK."

"You look lovely tonight. I've never been to this restaurant before. But I imagine it will be fine. And if it's not, we'll go someplace else." Stepping into her room, he turned back toward the door, sidled up to her, and leaned against her. "In fact, with my sweater and khaki pants, we look like bookends." He held out his arm. "Shall we go, my dear?"

They walked out to the parking lot in front of the inn. The sun had begun to set, and this morning's summertime temperatures had once again cooled to fall. Noah led her to a small antique-looking, dark green two-seater convertible with right-hand drive. "Is this your car?"

"One of them. It was my dad's, and my mum wanted me to have it after he died." He stopped at the driver-side door and motioned for her to walk on around to the other side. "It's an MG. They don't make them anymore."

As she settled into the passenger seat, the engine of the car rumbled to life. Definitely a classic movie come to life. "It's so cute. I've never ridden in anything like this before."

"Cute? That adjective is not a proper modifier for a man's car." Noah's voice rang with offense as he shifted the car into gear and pulled out onto the highway.

She'd insulted him. "Sorry. I just meant that I really like it."

He turned his head slightly and grinned. "I'm teasing. Feel free to describe it any way you wish." He reached over and squeezed her knee.

Butterflies joined the goose bumps.

As the speed of the car increased, the wind noise prevented any further conversation. A nice car, though not very conducive to a date, especially a first date. But they had the whole evening to talk. Besides, most of her time was being spent trying to prevent the wind from turning her hair into something that looked like an experiment for static electricity.

Intent on driving, Noah kept his gaze trained on the road. He could have been a model rather than a college professor. His classes were probably some of the first to fill up, at least with women.

From time to time, his gaze left the road and found her watching him, and he'd smile. She couldn't understand why his fiancée had left him. He was such an attractive man.

Before long, the car slowed as they turned off the highway onto a small country road. An old wooden sign painted brick red was posted at the corner. In familiar large white letters it read, "The Farm House and The Barn." An arrow pointed toward the right. So this was their dinner destination.

Noah spoke above the now soft purr of the engine. "Here we are. I've heard this place has delicious food. Homestyle, 'Just like Mom used to make.' But in my case, probably better. I love my mum, but the culinary arts are not her forte. A family tradition, so I'm told."

"I've eaten here before. Last month, in fact. The food was good." Her mind returned to the concert she'd attended with Ally, and then the dinner. Maybe she should have only said she'd been here before. Between the headache and being distracted by Chance, she hardly ate anything that night.

Ally had been excited all week because Trey's band was playing here again tonight, which, of course, explained why Chance was back at the inn. Surely, she and Noah would be gone before the concert started. Noah didn't look like the country music type, thank goodness. The last thing she wanted tonight was another headache.

Noah pulled the convertible into the same meadow where she and Ally parked last month. After getting out of the car, he removed his hat and gloves, dropped them onto the driver's seat, and walked around to her side. He opened the door and offered her his hand. When she grasped it and stepped out of the car, he moved her hand into the crook of his elbow.

A couple dressed in western attire, complete with hats, boots, and jeans, walked by them toward The Farm House. Noah leaned over. "Well, I must say, I'm a bit relieved," he whispered. "It appears we're appropriately dressed or maybe even a bit overdressed. I was somewhat concerned. I knew my turtleneck and jacket would be acceptable even if most men had ties and suit coats on, but if dresses were the norm for ladies, there isn't much we could have done about your slacks." He laughed.

She pushed down the defensiveness fighting to creep into her voice. "Well, if I'd known we'd be going out, I would have brought something besides casual clothes with me to the inn."

"Yes, I guess I didn't give you a proper warning, did I? Forgive me?" His free hand reached over and gently squeezed the fingers that were cupped around his arm. "But it all worked out quite well. Oh, and you may want to make your first stop the ladies' room. I hope you brought a hairbrush with you," he whispered again.

She could have taken his comment as demeaning, but surely that wasn't his intention. After all, if she'd had some left-over lunch between her front teeth, she'd hope someone would tell her so she could remove it. Surely, his words were spoken out of thoughtfulness to save her from potential embarrassment. She ran her fingers through her hair as they made their way to the Farm House.

"Charlee, wait up," someone called from behind them.

She stopped and turned.

Ally, Trey, and two other guys from the band were coming up the path behind them.

Charlee scanned their faces. The feeling of disappointment at failing to see Chance surprised her.

Noah turned toward her, confusion covering his face. "Charlee? Who's Charlee?"

She returned Ally's wave. "Me. That's my nickname. When I was born, my brother couldn't pronounce my name. 'Charity' came out 'Charlee,' and I've been Charlee with two e's ever since."

"So, no one calls you by your proper name?"

"Only you." She smiled up at him.

He grinned back and squeezed her fingers again. "Well, let's leave it that way, shall we? I like having something only the two of us share."

She squeezed his arm back.

"Besides, for a woman of your age and position, 'Charlee' seems rather juvenile, wouldn't you agree?"

An image of Grandma Bennett popped into her mind. Age and position? No matter how hard she tried, she had no idea how to turn that phrase into a compliment.

"Charlee, I didn't know you were coming here for dinner tonight." Ally looked radiant once again. Being with Trey transformed her.

"I didn't either. Noah surprised me." After Ally hugged her, Charlee looked up at Noah. "Noah, can I introduce you to my best friend? This is Ally Grant. Ally, this is Noah Walsh."

"You may if you can." He raised his eyebrows and smiled.

Chance hadn't corrected her grammar this morning when she'd asked him about his tattoo.

Ally grinned and cast a sideways glance at Charlee. Then she held out her hand. "Very nice to meet you. Charlee's told me a lot about you."

A satisfied grin covered Noah's face. "She has, has she? *Enchanté*." He grasped Ally's fingers, leaned forward, and kissed the back of her hand.

Charlee's cheeks burned. And for some unexplainable reason, she was relieved Chance wasn't here.

"Hey, why don't we all have dinner together?" Trey spoke up.

"Yes, and then you can join me for the concert afterward. I have connections and can get you some free tickets." Ally winked.

Charlee restrained herself from laughing out loud. Noah definitely wasn't the country music type.

"Noah, I'll bet you're a country music fan, aren't you?" Smirking, Ally cast a sideways glance at Charlee.

"As a matter of fact, I am. The whole idea sounds delightful. What do you think, Charity? Shall we join them?"

Frustration mingled with dismay filled Charlee. Now she'd have no chance to have a private discussion with Noah. Yet, she had no choice. Saying "no" would offend people she cared for. Maybe eating first would prevent her from getting a headache like last time, but if it didn't, she had a new pack of gum in her purse to use as a defense. "Sure. That'd be fun."

Ally smiled in triumph. "Great." She reached over and brushed a strand of Charlee's windblown hair to the side. "Why don't you boys get us a table while we girls visit the ladies' room?"

Charlee's relief at Chance not being here just doubled.

~*~

Facing the fireplace, Chance sat in one of the old wingback chairs, its leather softened over time by the inn's patrons. His Bible was closed on his lap, the glow from the fireplace now too dim to read by. If he didn't get up and put another log on the fire, it would die away soon. Brahms played softly in the background. He closed his eyes and pushed his head against the back of the chair, settling into the wings. No more reading and no more logs. He just wanted to "be." As sleep called him, he closed his eyes.

The creaking of the front door opening behind him startled him awake. He blinked and yawned as the door clicked shut.

"Thanks so much for dinner and the concert. I had a nice time."

Charlee had gone to dinner with someone.

"The pleasure was all mine."

Walsh. This could become awkward. Maybe he should cough, or stand, or something to let them know they weren't alone.

"I hope we can do it again," Noah said. "Just the two of us next time. I..." He paused. "I'm sorry. Gum-chewing is a pet peeve of mine. I'm distracted by your constantly moving chin, adorable as it is."

Too late. It was dark enough that if Chance sat still, they'd never know he was here.

"Sorry. Loud music can give me a headache, and if I chew mint gum, it often helps ease the pain. Let me get rid of it."

The conversation stopped. Chance didn't have to see them to know Noah was kissing her.

She giggled. "Want to sit in the parlor and talk for a few minutes?

Uh-oh.

"As much as I'd love to spend more time with you, I really can't. It's quite late, and I have some work to complete. I'm a bit behind after last night. May I walk you to your room?"

"Thanks, Noah. But I think I'll sit in the parlor for a few minutes."

Oh, no.

"Good night, dear Charity."

Charity?

"Good night, Noah. Thanks again."

"Sweet dreams. I'll see you at breakfast."

Silence. He was probably kissing her one more time.

Charlee giggled again. Heavy footsteps moved down the hall to Chance's right, lighter ones toward the sofa behind him on his left. The room was dark enough and big enough that if he continued to sit still, she'd probably never know he was there. He pushed his head back against the chair and concentrated on stealth breathing.

Movement. Charlee entered his field of view as she neared the fireplace. Her back toward him, she removed the wrought iron poker from the stand, opened the screen, and jabbed the coals until flames rose up. She picked up a couple of small logs and placed them on the embers. As the flames met the dry wood, the fire crackled back to life, and a warm glow illuminated the area where he sat.

The fire enhanced her hair's copper highlights, like this morning. Her style tonight was tousled, more relaxed. Very nice.

After placing the poker in the stand, she turned toward the sofa. As her gaze met his, she jumped and clamped her hand over her mouth. A small yelp escaped. "What are you doing here?" she demanded.

He stood. "I was sitting."

She pursed her lips together and gave him a drop-dead look. "I thought I was alone. You practically scared me to death."

"Gotcha back."

"What's that supposed to mean?" She lowered her eyebrows and cocked her head to one side.

"For this morning. On the patio. Gotcha back."

A smile crossed her face.

"Join me?"

She dropped into the wing chair on the left side of the fireplace, and he sat back down. Her face was pinker than usual, but probably not from the fire.

"So, how long have you been sitting here, Chance?"

He wanted to say, "Too long," but he'd better not. "A couple of hours. I read for a while and then dozed off." He wouldn't offer any more information unless she asked.

"Oh." She smiled. "Hey, where were you tonight?"

"I just told you." She knew enough.

"No, I mean, why weren't you playing with Trey's band at The Barn?" She ran her fingers through her hair and rearranged the tendrils. Then her fingertips began to move in small circles on her temples. "I thought you were back in town for the concert. If you're not, then why are you here?"

"I was only subbing for the regular keyboard player last month because he was sick. I'm here on business again."

She leaned her head back and closed her eyes.

"Headache?"

Peeking over at him, she nodded.

He stood and reached into his front pocket. "Gum?" He held his hand out to her.

"Thanks."

"Peppermint can be a good headache reliever. Also, herbal tea. I'll get you some." He walked over to the butler's tray and dropped a chamomile teabag in a cup. If nothing else, this might help her relax and sleep when she returned to her room. He filled another cup with hot water. He could use that, too. Tomorrow was a big day. "Here you go." He handed her one of the china cups and saucers.

She lifted the cup to her nose and breathed in. "Chamomile." Her eyes sparkled in the firelight as she smiled up at him. "That's very thoughtful. Thank you."

He eased back into his chair. "Sure. Hey, I like the new 'do. Looks good. Relaxed and deconstructed."

"My hair?" She ran her fingers through the copper strands again. "Styled by Mother Nature and an MG convertible."

"You've got an MG? Awesome. I'd like to see it sometime."

"It's not mine. It's Noah's." She stopped and narrowed her eyes. "Exactly when did you wake up from your nap? When I put the logs on the fire?"

"Before."

"How much before?" The same demanding tone as earlier colored her voice.

Time to leave. "It's getting a little hot in here. If you'll excuse me, I think I'll head to bed." He picked up his tea and stood. "I've got to get up early tomorrow."

"Church?"

"Job interview."

"A job interview? On Sunday? What kind of a business conducts job interviews on Sunday?"

He shrugged his shoulders.

"Wait. You didn't answer my first question, either."

He had no intention of giving her a straight answer. He picked up his Bible and headed toward the hall. He couldn't help himself. "Good night, Charity."

"Charity? Chance! Get back over here."

10

Charlee pulled her car into the church parking lot. Today was the first time in over a year she'd been able to attend church on her accounting Sunday. But Noah's invitation for dinner had motivated her to get her work done yesterday afternoon.

Last night at the concert, Ally had practically begged her to come to the service this morning and then go for a picnic lunch afterward. She'd offered no clue as to why it seemed so important, but Charlee wanted to be a good friend. So, here she was.

Noah hadn't been at breakfast this morning, and she missed him. She'd hoped to speak with him about the SDS letters last night—to tell him she was the Bride and she understood his pain. But the timing hadn't been right. Plus, they'd lacked the privacy needed for such a discussion.

She remedied that, though, before she went to bed. She wrote an invitation on the SDS letter to meet her in a secluded place next month when he returned to Crescent Bluff. A place away from the inn, away from Ally, away from Chance. A place where they'd be able to talk in privacy. The root-bench by the lake.

She glanced at her watch. Five more minutes before she could go into the auditorium. By then the music should be over and the sermon beginning.

Charlee stepped out of her car into the bright sunlight and meandered up the curved path toward the auditorium. Another warm, sunny, fall morning. The complete opposite of the frigid weather on Friday when she ran into Chance at the chapel.

Chance. He hadn't been at breakfast this morning, either. He was probably sleeping in. Last night, he'd deliberately avoided answering her questions about the exact moment he woke up. But he called her Charity. Proof he'd overheard her and Noah when they were at the door. He just hadn't wanted to admit it. He could be so infuriating.

She didn't buy his story about a job interview today. His comments about his work were always elusive, uninformative. Yesterday's admission on the patio certainly confirmed what she'd known from the beginning. Sales wasn't his occupation.

His life was none of her business, though. She really shouldn't be concerned about what he had going on. But then, Crescent Bluff was a small town, and if he did get some sort of a job and move here, she'd more than likely run into him regularly. But not today.

She stepped into the foyer and headed toward the doors into the sanctuary. Mr. Williams grinned, reached into his pocket, and presented her with a peppermint, as he had every Sunday for as long as she could remember. "Ally told me to watch for you, but I was beginning to think you weren't gonna make it today, Charlee, and I would have to save this for next Sunday." He winked and then whispered, "But I'm sure glad you came. It's a great day." He held the door open for her.

She accepted the candy and returned his wink. She stepped into the dimly lit sanctuary and paused while her eyes adjusted. Dr. Lewis stood on the stage behind the lectern. He closed his Bible. He sounded as if he were summing up rather than beginning. She looked at her watch. The sermon couldn't possibly be over this early. No, all the music, except for the closing song, should be done, and he should be starting, not ending, his sermon.

Ally sat a few rows up, an empty seat beside her on the aisle and Trey on the other side. Trey in church. That was unexpected.

Charlee tiptoed up the aisle and slipped into the open seat next to her friend. Ally smiled, reached over, and squeezed her hand. As Charlee leaned forward, Trey grinned and nodded.

Charlee turned her attention back to the pastor.

"So, as I said earlier, we're doing things a little differently today. We've saved most of the music portion of the service until now to give you an opportunity to respond to the sermon in worship. Let's stand as we pray."

Charlee bowed her head. The pounding of her heart drowned out her pastor's words. Memories of Jake flooded over her, and she gripped the back of the seat in front of her. She wanted to leave, to be anywhere but here. Ally's hand rested on her arm as her friend read her mind. Leaving when she'd just arrived would be ridiculous, no matter what the reason. Even though she hadn't sat through the musical portion of a church service since Jake, surely after these several years she could do it this once.

"Amen."

Raising her head, Charlee focused on the circle of soft light bathing the person on the stage. The musician today was most likely one of the members of the worship team filling in until the church found a new worship leader.

He sat on a stool, a guitar resting on his knee. He was dressed all in black, his face unshaven, his hair rough, not smoothed back. And if he smiled, she'd see the grin that had become too familiar. Her heart rose up into her throat. Chance was the last person in the world she would have expected to see here—up there—leading worship.

The fingers of his right hand moved across the strings as the song he'd played on the patio yesterday morning emerged from the guitar, and he began singing. The tone of his voice was clear, the words haunting. At first the sanctuary was silent as the congregation listened, but by the third verse their voices had joined his, singing the words on the screen above his head.

O, how great Thy loving kindness, vaster, broader than the sea!

O, how marvelous Thy goodness, lavished all on me!

Yes, I rest in Thee, Beloved, know what wealth of grace is Thine,

Know Thy certainty of promise, and have made it mine.

They sang the fourth verse, and then the sanctuary grew silent except for the gentle melody of his guitar as he transitioned to another song.

She wasn't familiar with this one, either. The lyrics sounded more like a love song than a church hymn. The words proclaimed the beauty of God.

Around her the congregation began to stand in reverence, their voices again joining his.

Ally and Trey stood, and she followed suit.

The song began as a sweet love song, but then it built in intensity and volume as the drums and other instruments joined the guitar. Perspiration covered her brow. Nausea knotted her stomach.

Although she tried to push them away, the walls of the church bore down on her just as the ones in the chapel had when she'd stumbled across Chance in Travelers' Rest.

She struggled to breathe. Her head swam. She had to leave before she passed out. She leaned toward the aisle.

Ally reached over and grasped her arm. "Don't go. You can make it," she whispered.

But Charlee couldn't. She didn't want to. She pulled loose. "I'll meet you at the lake." She turned and headed up the aisle toward the exit as quickly as she could without being disruptive. Walk, walk. Don't run. Walk.

Mr. Williams held open the door. Concern shadowed his face. "Charlee?"

Passing him in silence, she burst through the door and into blinding sunlight. She dropped onto a nearby concrete bench. By now the nausea had overcome her, and the pounding of her heart throbbed in her head. Closing her eyes, she willed herself to breathe and not throw up. Before today, the only time she'd felt this way was when Jake called off the wedding.

Even outside, she could hear the music. The song had changed to one that was upbeat and fast paced rather than slow and contemplative like the other two. The sound of a piano pounded out the melody, and she imagined Chance had set down his guitar and moved to the keyboard.

She eased to standing, steadied her legs, and crept to her car.

~*~

Charlee sat on the root-bench. A breeze skimmed across the surface of the lake, cooling the warm tears that streaked her cheeks. A sense of betrayal filled her heart. Why did Chance, of all people, have to be there today? None of this would have happened if he'd been honest last night rather than making up some story about a job interview. She'd known all along it was a lie.

She brushed the tears away with her fingertips. As much as she wanted to place blame, the real problem wasn't Chance's dishonesty. It was Jake's rejection. She'd loved him, trusted him, wanted to spend her life with him. But her love for him hadn't been enough to overcome his love for his career.

Dad had assured her she'd get over him…in due time. Yet days had grown into months and months into years, and she hadn't. The pain of Jake's betrayal—of feeling unworthy and unlovable—ran deep. How long was long enough?

He had stolen her trust and her ministry, but worst of all he'd stolen her heart. And she couldn't figure out how to get it back. She'd tried to move on, attempted to forgive Jake's treason. And maybe that was the problem. She hadn't done either. She'd run away from rather than confront the agony.

And no one she knew could really understand her misery. Except maybe one person. The Bridegroom.

She closed her eyes. The words from the song Chance sang today echoed within her. "For by Thy transforming power, Thou has't made me whole." Wholeness. She wanted to be a whole person again.

And wholeness could come from only one place.

Father, I need You.

The wind rustled the leaves overhead, and a still, small Voice whispered her name.

~*~

"Charlee." Ally's words broke through the darkness.

Charlee opened her eyes. The long minutes she'd spent in prayer seemed only a breath's time.

Her eyes round with concern, Ally rested a hand on Charlee's arm. "Are you OK?"

Spreading a blanket, Trey squatted nearer the lake.

They were both far away, dreamlike. "I'm fine. I was praying, and I don't know…"

Ally rested her hand on Charlee's arm. "You want me to drive you home?"

Embarrassment warmed her face. She squeezed Ally's hand. "Of course not. I'm fine," Charlee replied with more confidence than she felt. "I'm just tired. I didn't sleep much this weekend. I'm sure that's it." That was true, but it wasn't the real reason. And Ally knew that. "Lunch should help."

The brush behind them rustled, as Chance inched down the steep trail. He carried a gallon of sweet tea and a bag of chips.

Charlee shot Ally a killer look. "You didn't tell me he was coming," she whispered.

Ally shrugged. "Trey invited him, and I couldn't exactly uninvite him, could I? Besides if you'd stayed for church, you would have known."

She was right.

Chance reached Trey and the two men began unpacking the picnic basket.

She could do this. After all, she and Chance had an interesting chat yesterday morning and a friendly one last night…until he'd called her Charity.

She followed Ally to the blanket.

When Chance looked up, a smile lit his face. "Didn't see you ladies over there." He stood and drew Ally into a hug. "Hey." When he turned toward Charlee, she thrust out her hand. As he grasped it, his eyes danced. "Good to see you, too…Charity." He winked.

Ally and Trey sat on one side of the blanket, and she and Chance sat toward the corners of the facing side.

Trey grinned at Chance. "Great service today, dude. You've come a long way with the guitar. Didn't know you had it in you."

"Thanks, man." Chance looked down at the blanket and then back up at Trey and grinned. "I wasn't sure I had it in me, either."

Ally handed Charlee and Chance plates of chicken salad, hummus and vegetables, and grapes. "So, when will you find out the church's decision?" Ally asked.

"Dr. Lewis said they'd let me know something by the end of the day," Chance replied.

The nausea from earlier crept back into Charlee's stomach. "So, the church is considering hiring you for the worship pastor position? I figured you were just filling in today."

Chance turned toward her, a smug grin covering his face. "I told you last night I had a job interview this morning." Exaggerated impatience filled his voice. "But you didn't believe me."

"It wasn't exactly that I didn't believe you."

He leveled his gaze at her. "Yeah, right."

Trying to defend herself was ridiculous when he knew the truth. "I was curious, that's all."

He'd caught her in a lie. And he knew she knew it.

"Ace, would you bless the food?" Ally spoke up.

"My pleasure."

Ally and Trey grasped hands, and then Ally held her free hand out to Charlee, and Trey grabbed Chance's. The only break in the circle was between Chance and her. Chance held his hand palm up in invitation. Had he been Noah, she would have grasped his hand in a second, but he wasn't.

"Come on, Charlee," Ally pleaded. "I'm starving."

Charlee took a deep breath, placed her hand in Chance's, and bowed her head. The warmth of his touch overpowered her other senses. She couldn't concentrate on the words of his prayer. She peeked through her eyelashes. His hand encircled hers. She'd never noticed the largeness of his hands or the length of his fingers. A musician's hands for sure.

Silence. She looked up to see the other three staring at her. They'd dropped hands, but she was still holding on to Ally and Chance. Charlee cleared her throat and let go. "Amen." Grabbing her plate, she crammed a huge bite of chicken salad into her mouth.

"I guess you wonder why we called this meeting." Trey grinned and looked over at Ally. "Baby?"

Ally hadn't radiated this much joy since before Jason's death. Reaching into her purse, she withdrew a small black velvet box and opened it, revealing a sparkling diamond wedding set. "Last night, Trey asked me to marry him." She leaned her head against Trey's shoulder. "And I said yes. We wanted to tell you both first, before anyone else." A rosy blush painted her cheeks.

Trey laughed, and Ally giggled.

Charlee struggled not to choke.

Chance jumped up and clapped Trey on the back. "Congrats, buddy. I'm happy for you both."

This was happening way too fast. The two had been back together only a few weeks, and they needed more time, or at least Ally needed more time to get to know the real Trey. The last thing she wanted was for Ally to be hurt like she'd been.

Ally seemed to search for something Charlee couldn't give—an excited response. Her best friend had suffered enough. Jason had been a wonderful husband, but she'd lost him. And now…to join her life with a musician. Trey would bring her pain. Maybe not right now, but eventually.

Ally's gaze still asked, probed. "Aren't you going to say anything?"

Charlee chewed and swallowed with care as she took Ally's hand. The last thing she needed was to choke and force Chance to have to grab her in a Heimlich-maneuver-hug. "I'm just surprised. That's all. It was quick. You're sure you're ready? That this is what you want?"

Confusion wrinkled Ally's brow, and then she nodded. "Absolutely. I love him so much. When it's right, you know. And I know."

Trey put his arm around Ally, drew her close, and kissed the top of her head. Then he removed the engagement ring from the velvet box and placed it on her finger. "Love you, baby." He turned back toward them. "So, as I said, I guess you wonder why we've called this meeting." He winked. "We want to get married in January. We'd do it before then, but I'll be on the road the whole month of November and the first part of December. That wouldn't be fair to my new bride." This time he kissed her hand. "Ace, would you perform the ceremony?"

Chance wrinkled his forehead and then smiled his magnetic grin. "Guess I could, couldn't I? Honored to, man."

"And Charlee…" Innocent trust filled Ally's face. "Of course, I want you to be my maid of honor."

Refusing wouldn't help the matter. She still had a few weeks to try to change Ally's mind. "Sure. You know I will."

Chance pulled his phone out of his pocket and looked at the display, and then he stood. "Excuse me just a minute."

~*~

Chance walked away from the blanket and toward the lake. He took a deep breath. This was it. "Hello."

"Chance? Josh Lewis here."

"Dr. Lewis." Chance's heart pounded like a bass drum. He hadn't realized how much he wanted this position until now. Music had been his life—so much a part of who he was, and for years he'd used it only for personal gain. To now have the opportunity to glorify his Father through his music was humbling.

"Great service today, young man."

So far, so good. "Thank you, sir."

"The elder board had a quick meeting, and we'd like to make you a formal offer."

His first impulse was to pump the air with his fist and shout "Yes." But out of respect for the other three, he controlled himself. "That's great news, sir."

"Let's get together tomorrow morning before you head back to Austin."

"Sounds great." He'd never thought he'd want to live in a town as small as Crescent Bluff, but everything about it felt right. And if God had a place for him here, not only would it feel right, it would be right.

"You know where The Wayfarer Inn is?" Dr. Lewis asked. "Let's meet there for breakfast, say about nine."

He looked back toward the inn. Yep, he knew exactly where it was. "That'll work. See you then. And, thanks again for the opportunity, sir."

He dropped his phone into his pocket and turned toward the other three. He studied their faces. Ally and Trey were animated and smiling. Charlee, on the other hand, was less than enthusiastic. Something about this whole situation was off. She didn't know Trey well enough to dislike him, but she sure had something against him. She definitely was unhappy about the engagement. Maybe she was being protective because she thought it had happened too fast. But they were adults, capable of making decisions about their lives and their relationship. She could have at least been supportive and glad for their happiness.

Chance wasn't surprised they were getting married or even that it had happened so fast. Trey had never gotten over Ally, and he wasn't letting her get away again.

But Trey's request for Chance to marry them had shocked him. Now that he was licensed, he could do that stuff. He'd just never thought about it. So what exactly did the minister say during the ceremony? Maybe there was a book or something. Seemed like he'd seen some officiants holding a little notebook in addition to their Bible, but he couldn't remember if the preacher at his wedding had one or not.

Anyway, he could probably download some stuff. Anything could be found on the Internet.

He walked toward the blanket. He'd missed the weddings of most of his friends because of the choices he'd made, and he wouldn't miss this one.

"Everything OK?" Trey took a bite of his sandwich.

"Yep. Everything's great." Chance dropped back down onto the blanket. "That was Dr. Lewis. He and the elders want to meet tomorrow for breakfast. To make me an offer."

Ally giggled and clapped her hands.

Trey raised his hand for a fist-bump.

Charlee sat there stone-faced.

She was a tough one to figure out. Friday at the chapel, she'd radiated vulnerability. Later at dinner and Saturday morning on his patio, warmth, even lightheartedness. Last night in the parlor she'd been demanding. And now today, withdrawn and sullen. He never knew which way Wind Charlee would blow.

~*~

"Is Noah Walsh still here?" Charlee's face warmed. She'd changed her mind about waiting until next month to find out if Noah was the Bridegroom. She had to know now.

The colonel grinned. "I believe he's in his room. His new room, that is. He moved across the hall to the Safari Room after you left, and we got it cleaned up."

"Thanks. I missed him at breakfast and need to check with him about something." She walked past the desk down the hall toward room five.

Facing the door, she held up her fist to knock but stopped in midair. She didn't want him to think she was chasing him. Plus, she hadn't even thought through what she was going to say. *I just wanted to see you one more time to find out if you got left at the altar.* That was ridiculous. Besides, he might even be taking a nap or worse…a shower.

She had to stop overanalyzing things. Before another excuse entered her mind, she rapped on the door. Done.

The door eased open. "Hello there, Charity. What a nice surprise! You look lovely today." Noah leaned against the door frame and smiled. He wore an Oxford University t-shirt and sweatpants. His face was unshaven, his hair uncombed. She'd never seen him any way but totally neat with every hair in place and his clothes perfectly pressed. This look wasn't nearly as attractive on him as it was on Chance. Her heart thudded at that unbidden thought.

"Hi. I, um, meant to speak with you at breakfast this morning but missed you." She looked toward the floor.

"I'm working on mid-term grades. They're due next week, and I'm a bit behind after the concert last night. So, I decided to sequester myself until the job was completed." He raised his arm and leaned against the doorframe.

"I probably should go then. I'd hate to interrupt you." She stepped back from the doorway.

He grasped her right wrist before she could move any farther away. "You already have. But it's a very welcome interruption, I assure you. Please come in." He smiled.

She looked over her shoulder. The hallway was empty. She

ignored her mother's old-fashioned admonition about entering a man's hotel room. She'd be careful. "Well, maybe for just a minute. I, uh, think I may have left something outside on the patio. Do you mind if I check?" What a lame excuse. Though truly, she hadn't been able to find that one receipt for office supplies. She certainly could have dropped it out there.

He stepped back and gestured toward the patio. "Have a proper look around." He closed the door behind her.

She walked across the room, stepped through the open door onto the patio, and made a show of looking around. "No, it's not here." Then she turned and walked back inside. "Maybe it's on the desk."

As she moved toward the desk, he stepped in front of her. "Let me move my paperwork out of the way. Grades are confidential." He reached down and picked up a stack of papers and held them to his chest. An envelope dropped onto the floor. "Oops." He bent over and retrieved it, but not before she read it. The lettering on the outside of the envelope was in her handwriting and read, *The Bridegroom*. Her heart began to race. She was right. Noah was the Bridegroom.

"What is it you're looking for exactly?" Impatience strained his voice.

You. Now was the perfect chance to ask him, to confirm her suspicions. She could confess she was the Bride.

But no. Telling him now would be inconsiderate. The moment should be special, planned. He should have the chance to be emotionally prepared. She'd wait.

"I was afraid I might have left a receipt here, but I must be mistaken. It's probably in the stack with all the others." She looked up into his eyes. "So are you planning to stay here again next month?"

"And what if I am?" He winked, set the papers down on the bed, and stepped toward her. "Yes, I'm certainly planning to come again next month. I hope that's acceptable to you." He smiled.

Next month would be great. She shrugged her shoulders. "Of course. I was thinking I could stay here the same weekend so we could see each other again. That's all." She smiled back as he inched even closer.

"Lovely. I could arrange to come the weekend of the tenth.

Would that complement your schedule?"

The rate of her breathing increased. He'd read the letter. That's exactly the date she'd written.

By now he was so close she could have counted the individual whiskers on his chin if she'd wanted. "That would be perfect. I'll confirm my reservation today before I leave."

"Come here." He drew her close in an embrace and bent down to kiss her.

Gentle guitar music floated into the room through the open patio door. Chance. He was out on his patio practicing again. He couldn't see them, and they couldn't see him. But the presence of his music intruded as much as if he'd stepped through the door.

She pushed away, stood on her tiptoes, and kissed Noah's cheek. "I refuse to be responsible for you not completing your mid-term grades in time."

An amused smirk crossed his face. "Thank you for your concern. You are indeed a thoughtful woman."

She walked to the inner door and opened it. Looking back, she waved. "See you next month, Noah."

"Oh, and, by the way, proper grammar would be 'you're not completing' not 'you not completing.'" His words followed her out into the hall.

11

Chocolate ranked low on Chance's list of favorites. But last night he began craving a particular candy bar from his childhood. Doing a quick search on his phone, he found the address for the nearby store he hoped would have them. He drove the few blocks from the inn and parked in the gravel lot beside the small building that obviously had been someone's home a century earlier.

A forest green painted sign embellished with gold letters spelling out "Bits of Britain" hung from chains under the eave. Two ferns flanked the front door, and flower boxes full of pansies and snapdragons rested on the top of the wooden porch railings. Gardening wasn't his thing, but Mom had planted those two every fall for as long as he could remember. They were some of her favorites.

After walking up the stairs and across the porch to the entrance, he grasped the brass door handle. If her behavior yesterday was any clue, the shop's proprietor probably wouldn't be happy to see him this morning. He shrugged. They'd just have to make it work, if only until after Ally and Trey's wedding.

He took a deep breath, pressed down on the thumb latch, and pushed open the door. A brass shopkeeper's doorbell announced his arrival. He stepped inside and closed the door. The haunting notes of Celtic music together with the combined scents of old-house mustiness and warm vanilla gave the shop an inviting feel. The worn pine floors creaked as he moved toward the old wooden shelves along the left wall.

"May I help...?" Charlee stepped through the doorway at the back of the store.

He nodded. "Good morning, Charlee."

The smile on her face faded. "Chance. This is unexpected."

Shelves full of merchandise rimmed the room while large, antique wooden tables stationed throughout the space held a variety of products from books to porcelain to clothing. In the back corner was a small seating area facing a fireplace. "Nice shop…boutique."

"Thanks. Is there something I can help you find? Or do you just want to browse?" Seeming distracted, she kept glancing past him toward the front door.

"Actually, I'm looking for a particular candy bar, and I thought you just might carry it. A ChocoCrumble bar."

She looked back at him and smiled as she slipped into salesperson mode. "Not many people know about those, but they're my favorite. Right over here." She led him toward a shelf near the back counter.

"That's them. I love these things. The first time I had these was when I was a kid and my dad took me to London on one of his business trips. I've never been able to find a store in Austin that has them. Just thought I'd take a chance on you." He picked up a bar, and then put it back as he changed his mind. One wasn't enough. "I'll take six."

She raised her eyebrows. "Six bars? Are you sure? They're four dollars a bar, Chance."

"Really? Then I'll take a whole box." Who knew how long it would be before he had a chance to get more? He hadn't had to buy breakfast this morning because Dr. Lewis had done that. And he'd skip lunch today to help pay for them. "I've got a four-hour drive home to Austin, and it's going to be several weeks before I'm back in Crescent Bluff. Better stock up." He smiled at her, but she turned away.

"I'll step in the storeroom and get you an unopened box. Please feel free to look around, or have a seat in the back, if you'd rather. There's a selection of teas back there and some coffee. Help yourself to a cup."

Coffee sounded good. She disappeared through the doorway, and he walked to the sideboard along the back wall. While he studied the flavors, his fingers drummed in syncopation to the ticking of the clock on the mantel. The bridge for a new song he was learning played through his mind.

China tea cups and saucers. He chuckled. The absence of Styrofoam cups was no surprise. She was definitely a classical music and china teacups kind of girl.

He poured some coffee into a cup and added some cream. She came through the storeroom door with a box of candy bars. "Here you go. I'll set these over here on the counter until you're ready to pay."

"Thanks. Nice store. It has a warm and welcoming vibe. Feels exactly like someone picked up a shop from an English village and dropped it here in Crescent Bluff."

"Really? Thanks. I've actually never been there, but I've studied lots of pictures. One of these days, though, I will go."

Even in the subdued lighting, her freckles were visible. "Can I fix you a cup, too?"

She set the box of candy bars on the counter. She leaned her head to one side, and her hair gleamed. "I'd love a cup of currant, but I'll get it."

While she walked to the sideboard, he browsed around the rest of the store.

"There's a new variety of tea biscuits on the counter. Help yourself, if you'd like to sample some."

Her salesman's hat was still in place. "No, thanks. Just came from The Wayfarer. I'm stuffed."

She spun around toward him. "That's right. You met Dr. Lewis for breakfast. How did everything go?"

Chance walked back to one of the overstuffed chairs facing the small Austin stone fireplace. "Good. No, great. Surprisingly, the elders made me an offer. And I accepted. I start mid-November."

She sat in the chair facing him. "I don't know why you're surprised. You're an excellent musician."

He sank into the other leather chair. "Thank you." He was working hard to be a new man. He didn't want to get into old issues right now with her. Maybe he never would. The past was the past, and every day he moved a step farther away. "Let's just say that they're taking a big chance on an inexperienced person. I've subbed on the occasional Sunday at my home church, but I've never been responsible for planning the music for worship services on a regular basis." He smiled at her. "The first line in a new stanza."

She wrinkled her forehead.

He held up his left arm and pointed to the tattoo. "Poema."

She smiled and nodded. "Poema."

The bell on the door jingled, and her gaze left his to find the new customer. Her smile increased and a pink blush almost obliterated her freckles. "Excuse me, please." She stood and set her cup on the sideboard.

He turned to look over his shoulder. Walsh.

~*~

Charlee moved toward the front door. "Noah. What a pleasant surprise!" He was back in his English lord's jacket.

"Good morning." His gaze crept toward the chairs at the back of the store, and he waved. "I see I'm not your first customer this morning."

"No." An irrational feeling of guilt prodded her to explain. "He stopped by on his way out of town to buy some ChocoCrumble candy bars."

"ChocoCrumbles? Ghastly things."

She glanced back over her shoulder. Nothing in Chance's demeanor indicated he heard Noah's comment. "Well, some people really like them." She kept her voice low.

"I'm sure there are a group of people with unrefined tastes who find them enjoyable." He leaned in and whispered in her ear. "Chance, for example." He winked and then chuckled.

The musical clink of porcelain sounded from the back of the store. "Well, Noah, I—"

"Hold still. You have something on your face." He moved close, his eyes almost crossing as they focused on her nose. His index finger began brushing the bridge, and the image of monkeys at the zoo grooming one another popped into her mind. "Oh, sorry. It's just one of your freckles that's a bit darker than the others. I thought it was a speck of dirt." He laughed again.

She responded with a smile she didn't feel.

"Well, Charity, I'd best be on my way. You left so abruptly yesterday I didn't get to tell you good-bye. I'll see you in about a month." He pulled her into a hug and kissed her quickly on the lips.

She drew away. "Please, Noah. I'm at work," she whispered.

He grinned and winked.

"Have a safe trip home. I'll see you the second weekend in November."

Noah walked out the door. When she was around him, he always made her feel inferior. Not intentionally, surely, but every time they were together, he seemed to point out one of her flaws. Something she said or didn't say. Something she did or didn't do. Some way she looked or didn't look.

She turned toward the back of the store. Chance had moved to the far corner and was staring with pretended interest, she was quite certain, at her selection of toast racks. "Would you excuse me a moment, please, Chance?"

"You bet."

She stepped into the office behind the counter and pulled her purse out from the bottom desk drawer. Rummaging around in it, her fingers found the small makeup pouch. She removed the compact and carefully dabbed her nose with powder. She held the mirror up and turned her face toward the light. Better.

She stepped through the door back into the shop. She jumped at seeing Chance leaning on the counter.

"Gotcha again." He grinned and held up a credit card between two fingers. "Guess I better pay and get on the road."

She reached out. "Debit or credit?" Her fingertips accidentally brushed his. The tips were calloused from playing the guitar. She hadn't noticed that yesterday when they'd held hands during the blessing at the lake.

"Debit."

She moved toward the register, keyed in the transaction, and then handed him the receipt and his card back.

He stuck the card into his wallet. "You didn't need to do that, you know."

"You didn't want a receipt? It isn't a problem. I just figured you'd want one for your records."

"That's not what I meant." He looked down at his hands and then back up at her face. "You didn't need to try to cover up your freckles. I don't see anything that could be mistaken for dirt."

So, he'd been able to hear Noah's comment, and he'd guessed the reason she slipped back into the office.

"They're actually kind of charming." His face flushed bright red, and he picked up the box of candy bars. "Well, I gotta go. See you next month."

Her cheeks warmed in response to his words. "Wouldn't you like a bag for those?"

He called back over his shoulder while he strode toward the door. "No. Thanks. This is fine. Bye."

As the brass bell jingled and the door slammed shut, she giggled. He'd embarrassed himself. Her face grew warmer. He'd embarrassed her.

She walked back into the office and grabbed the compact from her purse and a tissue from her desk. She should have thanked him for his kind words, but they caught her off guard. Plus, he left so quickly she hadn't had the chance.

Again, she looked in the mirror. "Charming," she whispered. He actually used that word. She brushed the tissue across her nose and cheeks and the freckles reappeared in the mirror. Chance seemed to have a kind heart.

The bell on the front door jingled again.

She dropped her compact into her pocket and hurried out. Maybe he'd forgotten something.

"I just saw Ace pulling out of the parking lot." Ally made her way to the counter. "He sure was in a hurry, but I flagged him down and he stopped just long enough to tell me the good news. The church hired him, but I guess he already told you that." She put her purse in the office and returned to the counter. "I hope he's not sick or something. His face was really flushed."

Charlee turned away and began straightening the gift bags.

"Wait a minute. Look at me."

Charlee turned her head slightly toward Ally. "What?"

Ally grinned. "If there's a virus going around, you've come down with it, too. OK, I get it now."

"Get what? There's nothing to get." Willing in vain for the blush to disappear, she turned toward Ally. "He just bought some ChocoCrumbles, that's all."

"Yeah, right." She planted her hands on her hips. "I can't remember the last time I saw you blush over a man. I know what's going on here."

"Ally, nothing's going on. You can't possibly believe I'd be interested in Chance—Ace—whatever you want to call him. Have you forgotten he's a professional musician just like Jake? Do you think I'm crazy? Jake was nothing more than an actor. He spent his life trying to make people believe he was something he wasn't. And I bought his lies. He walked the line between truth and falsehood so much, eventually he stepped over and never looked back."

Ally gave her a quick hug. "You're making generalizations based upon one person who hurt you. One musician. You can't really believe they're all that way. That Chance is that way. That Trey is that way."

Her face must be scarlet by now if the temperature of her cheeks signified anything. She took a deep breath, pulled the compact out of her pocket, and dusted powder across her nose again. "Noah. I know he's made me blush. A lot."

Smiling, Ally pulled on her apron and twirled away. "'The lady doth protest too much, methinks.'"

Charlee was literally saved by the bell as a jingling signaled the opening of the front door. She turned. "It's Mrs. Jensen. I'll get her."

~*~

Today had been so busy she and Ally hadn't even stopped for lunch. But now the afternoon lull had set in and the shop would be quiet for the next hour or so until people stopped by on the way home from work. Time and customers had reined in this morning's emotions. Now was a good opportunity for a serious, calmer conversation.

Ally picked up a clipboard. "I think I'll go in the back and inventory the tea towels. That is, unless you have something else you'd rather I do."

"Don't worry about that today. Let's just prop up our feet and take a break. I'm starving." Grabbing a box of tea biscuits, Charlee moved toward the back of the shop and dropped into the chair facing the entrance.

Ally followed and sat in the chair Chance had occupied earlier.

"Ally, we need to talk." She held out the cookies. "You know I would never do anything to hurt you."

The diamond engagement ring sparkled as Ally reached into the box. "Of course. I would have never made it after Jason's death without your love and support. You gave me a job when no one else would, and I'll be forever grateful for your friendship. Yet, for some reason, I feel a 'but' coming on."

Charlee reached out and squeezed her hand. "All I want is your happiness." She paused and took a deep breath. *Speak the truth in love.* "But—"

"There it is." Ally raised her eyebrows.

"I'm concerned about how quickly you and Trey have gotten engaged. You've only been dating a little over a month. It's fast, Ally. Too fast."

"Charlee, it's not like we just met. I've known him for a long time, but it's been a few years since we've been together. When I'm with him, though, it feels like no time has passed." She smiled. "Thanks for your concern, but you have nothing to worry about."

Ally was so innocent, so trusting. "All I ask is that you wait a little bit longer before getting married. Just slow things down. Take time to make sure you understand what life with Trey will be like. Having a relationship with a musician can be rough. His career will take precedence over any other part of your life. He'll be on the road and leave you alone a lot of the time."

"Not any more than a Marine." Ally's smile was gone. Frost stiffened her words.

It wasn't the same. A soldier's actions were selfless. He sacrificed himself and his relationships for the good of others. A musician's motives were selfish. He sacrificed others for his good only.

Charlee's response begged to be spoken, but she clamped her mouth tight. Her words had already, although unintended, erected walls of defensiveness between them. Maybe Charlee needed to analyze her motives to determine whether her words had their origin in selfless love or selfish pain.

No, the root didn't matter. Truth was truth, and Ally needed to hear it.

But not now, not yet. With the wedding a few months away, Charlee would have other opportunities to complete this discussion. And since Trey was moving to Crescent Bluff, Ally and he would have more time together. Why, she might even reach the same conclusion on her own without Charlee having to say anything. "You're right. I'm sorry."

Ally grinned as the bell on the door jingled. "Thanks for being such a good friend. And Maid of Honor."

~*~

Slipping below the horizon, the setting sun striped the slate western sky in fiery orange as Chance pulled into his parents' driveway. When he left Crescent Bluff, he thought he'd be home long before now. But he'd stopped to cash the check Dr. Lewis gave him this morning and then bought some strings and picks at the guitar store and a new plaid shirt and some jeans at Rancher's Depot.

After bringing Mom and Dad so much pain over the last few years, his life was finally back on track. He hadn't told them about the possible job offer. With his history, he hadn't been sure it would work out, and there was no need getting their hopes up. They'd assumed he was going back to Crescent Bluff to sub with Trey and the guys, and he hadn't corrected them.

He was stoked. He hadn't been this excited about anything in a long time, and he couldn't wait to share the good news with them.

He stepped through the gate into the backyard. Mom sat in a

redwood chair facing the fire pit he and Dad had made this summer. Well, he'd made—Dad had supervised. Dad was crouched down preparing to light a small pile of kindling in the center of the brick ring.

Through it all, they'd been the perfect picture of unconditional love. Even when Chance had been so far gone he'd wanted nothing to do with them, they'd waited patiently, lovingly, and welcomed him home with open arms when he'd finally come to his senses. *Thank You, Father.*

"Hey, guys." He walked over to them.

Dad stood and pulled him into a big bear hug. "Hello, son. You made it just in time for the inaugural lighting of our fire pit. It's a might too warm, but your mother insisted."

Chance bent down and kissed Mom on the cheek. "Hi."

"Hi, sweetheart. Don't pay your father any attention. He wanted to try it out as badly as I did. He couldn't wait to show off your handiwork." She squeezed his hand and smiled.

Dad turned and grinned at Mom. Chance had always thought he'd have the kind of marriage they had. After thirty-five years, they still loved each other dearly. He'd taken their relationship for granted and assumed his life would be a duplicate of theirs, but the older he got, the more he doubted it. The love they shared was rare. He knew that now.

She pointed to the chair to her right. "Have a seat, and prepare yourself for blast-off. Well…not literally, I hope." She winked.

As the flames danced around the kindling, Dad stacked on some small logs and then sat next to Mom. "That's a mighty fine fire, even if I do say so myself. Good job on building the fire pit, son."

"How was your trip?" His mother reached over and patted his hand.

"Good. No, great. I have a surprise. I should have told you this earlier, but I wanted to make sure everything worked out before I said anything." He took a deep breath. "I've been offered the worship pastor job at the largest church in Crescent Bluff."

Silent, his parents glanced at each other and then turned back toward him. Their reaction was underwhelming. Not exactly what he'd expected. He'd thought they'd be ecstatic.

Finally, Dad spoke. "Is this what you want, son?"

Chance had thought a lot about this over the past several weeks. "Yes. But more than that, I believe this is what God wants."

"And this will make you happy?" Mom's eyes were warm.

"When I'm up there in front of the church, I feel like that's what I was created to do. I can't really explain it. But yes, it makes me more than happy."

His parents looked at each other again and then turned back to him. Dad shot out of his chair like a rocket and shouted, "Yee-haw."

Mom jumped up and began clapping. "When do you start?"

"In a month. They gave me time to tie up some loose ends at the Hope House. I'll start the second Sunday in November."

"Time to celebrate. Sweet tea all around!" Mom turned to walk toward the back door, but she paused and leaned close to him. "We're thrilled for you. Your daddy and I have prayed for this moment for a long time…a very, very long time." She cradled his face in her hands and kissed him on the forehead. "Hopefully we'll be able to check off the next item on our prayer list before too much longer." She winked. "A special young lady. We'll just keep working on that one."

12

The November wind blew, and Chance closed his eyes and listened. The rhythmic sound of the water lapping against the shore of the lake behind the chapel calmed him. He'd come early so he could pray. This little root-bench was his "place" in Crescent Bluff. Here he felt a special closeness to his Heavenly Father. Creation filled his senses with peace, and right now he needed that to counter his pounding heart. Whatever happened in the next few hours, days, months, a new line in this poem of his life was being written, and he prayed for the strength and grace to handle it.

Something rustled in the brush. He opened his eyes. Charlee was making her way down the trail. She was the last person he would have expected to see. Yesterday's rain had made the steep path slipperier than usual, and she was struggling to keep her footing. He jumped up to help her before she fell and hurt herself. "Hang on. I'm coming."

The last time he'd seen her had been when he'd left her shop after the freckle comment had popped out without his thinking it through. Seemed like Walsh was pretty critical toward her, and he'd wanted to make her feel good about herself. Besides, her freckles really were cute. The one thing he hadn't figured was that his words would embarrass both of them. Anyway, it had worked. When he'd left, she'd been smiling.

Today, however, her face registered surprise at the best, annoyance at the worst. That final comment in her shop last month apparently had been forgotten, or maybe it hadn't affected her in the first place.

He jogged over to her and held out his hand. "Careful there. Let me give you a hand."

"No, thanks. I'm fine." She refused his help and steadied herself by holding on to a nearby sapling. She turned around to come down backward.

"You sure?" He kept his hand extended.

She glared back over her shoulder at him. "Positive. Would you please just move out of my way?"

Her refusal had become comical. "Yes, ma'am. Happy to oblige." He stepped to the side and folded his arms over his chest. This should be fun to watch.

"Really, do you have to stand there and stare at me?" Her face was scarlet.

"No, ma'am." He turned his back. A juicy plop sounded.

"Oh, no!"

He turned back around. She stood with her hands straight out in front of her covered with mud up to her wrists. She must have slipped off the hill and caught herself. Some of the mud had splattered up onto her face leaving dots that obviously weren't freckles.

She stamped her feet and tromped toward the edge of the water. "I can't believe it."

He would have laughed out loud, but that would only make matters worse.

~*~

Charlee stooped down and began washing the mud off in the cold lake water. Of all people to be here now. Chance. Noah was bound to be along any minute, and Chance's presence would spoil everything. "I can't believe it. I'm such a klutz, and on today of all days...and now he's here." Her muttered words were for her ears only.

"What? Did you say something?" The brown autumn grass crunched as Chance came closer.

She kept her back turned so she wouldn't have to look at him. "No. I was simply voicing my private thoughts." He had such a talent for showing up in the wrong place at the wrong time. She stood and shook her hands trying to get as much water off as possible.

"Well, if they were private, maybe you shouldn't have *voiced* them."

He was mocking her.

By now he'd reached her side. "Here, use this."

She turned to face him. He pulled his burnt orange sweatshirt with the longhorn on the front over his head and held it out to her. "I don't need it. It's not nearly as cool out here as I thought it'd be."

He wore a gray t-shirt underneath rather than a black one. That was a change. "Thanks, but I don't want to get it all dirty."

"Believe me, it's seen much worse over the years." He grinned and nodded his head once. "Take it."

"Well…only if you'll let me wash it and bring it back to you."

His arm was still extended. "Deal." His gaze focused on her cheeks rather than her eyes.

She drew the shirt to her. It smelled of his cologne and fresh air, and the fleece on the inside was warm from his body. It felt good on her cold, wet hands. "Thanks, Chance. It's very kind of you." She turned to walk away from the lake.

"Uh, hold up. You've got some…splatters on your face." He held out his hand. "Come here. Give me the shirt."

She handed it to him, and he squatted and dipped the cuff of the sleeve into the lake. Then he wrung it out and handed it back to her. "They're on your cheeks and nose."

So much for her makeup. This was not how she wanted Noah to see her. As she began to rub, Chance's gaze bored into her face. "Did I get them?"

"A little more to the right." His face flushed.

"Here?" She rubbed her right cheek.

"No, *my* right. Sorry." He grinned. "My bad."

"Oh, the other right…" She smiled back, her earlier impatience at finding him here had disappeared. He really was trying to help. "Better?"

He opened his eyes wide. "It's kinda smeared, and now it's up under your eye." He pointed his finger toward her cheek and got it as close to her face as possible without touching her. "There, right there."

"Could you just get it for me?" She held out the shirt to him.

His pink cheeks deepened to red. "Well, I…"

Just like last month at the shop, he was boyishly cute when he was embarrassed. "Please?"

"OK." He moved close to her. Very close. She could hear his breathing, and she could see her reflection in his eyes as he leaned down. "Close your eyes."

He cradled her chin with his left hand and began rubbing her cheek with his right. His touch was gentle. By now her face was burning, and the cool water felt good.

"You can open your eyes now."

His face was close to hers, his eyes dreamy. She tried to move away, but she couldn't. Her stomach swirled as some unseen force tethered them together.

Chance blinked and suddenly stepped back. He cleared his throat. "That should do it."

"Yeah, thanks." She grabbed the shirt from him. "I'll wash this and bring it back to you."

"Great. Great. That's good. I'm staying at the inn until I can find an apartment or something to rent. Room five." He jammed his hands into the front pockets of his jeans so that only his thumbs showed. "Well, uh, guess I'll see you around."

"Sure. See you around." She waited for him to leave, but he stood rooted to the ground. "Weren't you going to leave?"

"No, I thought you were." He pulled his phone out of his pocket, glanced at the screen, and looked back over his shoulder toward the trail.

"I just got here." She placed her hands on her hips.

"Oh, yeah. Right." He laughed but stood firm.

He looked toward the sky for a few seconds and then shook his head. Unexplained tenderness covered his face when their gazes met again. His nervousness had disappeared. "Hey, I want to show you something special. Come on."

He led her further down the shore to the root bench where she'd sat after church that day Ally and Trey announced their engagement. He smiled and held his hand out toward the root-bench. "Have a seat."

"I love this bench." She dropped onto the far end. "One of my favorite places in all the world."

"Really?" He sat apart from her. "One of mine, too." The wind whipped through the trees and dipped to paint the surface of the lake with small snow-capped peaks. They sat in silence for a moment. The fingers of his right hand tapped his thigh, pressing the keys of an imaginary piano. "Can you hear it?"

"The wind?" Maybe her original assumption that his hearing had been damaged by the years of loud music was correct. "Yes, I'm not deaf. Can't you hear it?"

"Of course, I can, but that's not what I mean. Not the wind. The music. Do you hear it?"

"What are you talking about? I don't hear any music." Maybe he was delusional rather than deaf.

"Sh-h-h-h. Close your eyes and listen."

He would probably pull some joke on her. Whatever, she'd play along. Anything to get rid of him before Noah came. "OK, I'm closing my eyes."

"Quiet."

With both her eyes and mouth closed, she waited. Nothing. Maybe he'd sneaked away. Maybe that was the joke. If so, it would be just fine because Noah should be here any minute. She peeked through her eyelashes. He still sat beside her with his eyes closed. His fingers continued tapping some melody only he heard. She closed her eyes again.

The trees moaned like cellos as they resisted breaking against the force of the November wind. The water was a snare drum as it lapped rhythmically against the rocks on the shore. Like cymbals, the branches overhead crashed together. And from somewhere far off came the piccolo trill of birds. Her breathing quickened. The sounds around her were symphonic. And she'd never heard them before. Not like this.

He must have sensed her excitement. This time his words were a statement, not a question. "You hear it," he whispered. "I knew you would."

Very softly he sang. "'All nature sings, and 'round me rings the music of the spheres.'"

Her eyes fluttered open to see his. They were gentle, and his smile was warm.

Awe tempered her response. To have spoken above a whisper would have been disrespectful. "I've never heard it before. I guess I've never really listened. It's beautiful." She closed her eyes again as the concerto of nature continued.

Her pulse began to race as that same feeling she'd had when he'd led worship last month overcame her. Places in her heart that had been dark for a long time began to flicker with light once again. The music she'd banned from her soul was trying to needle its way back in, but she wouldn't permit it. She'd never let it hurt her as it had before.

She jumped up, and the music stopped. She'd almost fallen prey. He'd probably think she was crazy, but she had to leave. "I've got to go. I've got to get back."

"But I thought you said you weren't leaving because you just got here." He stood.

She gathered the burnt orange sweatshirt. "No, I'm done." The last thing she saw was his confused expression as she hurried toward the path back to the inn.

"Wait, Charlee. Stop."

But she wouldn't. She tied the sweatshirt over her shoulders. Then she grabbed a sapling and fought her way back up the hill.

~*~

Chance knew her secret. The truth hit him when they were standing on the shore and she refused to leave. He'd read the SDS letters and the invitation to meet at the lake today. That's why he'd come. But he hadn't expected to see her of all people. Yet as he thought back over the timing of the letters and her reactions after church last month and again today, everything made perfect sense.

Ally had shared some of Charlee's past with Trey. And before they met at The Farm House after the concert in September, Trey had told him that Ally's friend had been engaged to some musician several years ago, but the ceremony had been cancelled. Ally's "friend" ended up being Charlee. He'd assumed she'd been the one to call off the wedding. But his assumption had been wrong. Her confession in the letters proved that.

That other guy had broken her heart, and now Chance had caused her pain, too. Unintentionally for sure, but it couldn't have hurt any more if he'd done it on purpose. All he could do now was try to redeem himself.

One of his college professors had told him that the area of the brain that governs creativity is the same area from which all strong emotions originate. That musicians and artists in general often felt things more deeply than non-musical or non-artistic people. He'd never checked that out to see if it was a scientific fact, but he knew one thing.

Music moved him in a way nothing else could. And when used in worship, it brought his soul to life. He'd fought against the emotion of those feelings for years. Tearing up in church as a sixteen-year-old wasn't cool, so he'd rebelled and made fun of the hymns as a defense mechanism. Too cool to feel. Deep inside, though, his soul had longed to praise his Father, but he'd been tied down by peer pressure.

Then one day he'd been set free. He'd realized these emotions were a gift. That he'd been created to worship, and music was his vehicle. The same was probably true of Charlee. She just needed to be unbound. *Set her free, Father. Please set her free.*

~*~

Somehow Charlee managed to climb back up the path from the lake without slipping this time. As she stood at the top wiping the mud from her shoes onto the grass, frustration and disappointment filled her heart. Nothing was going the way she'd planned. She'd hoped to create the perfect moment for her and Noah, but, of course, Chance had ruined everything. She pushed back the tears that threatened.

Heading up the path to the inn, she stopped at the small fountain across from the chapel and plopped onto one of the benches facing it. Chance always showed up at the wrong times.

And that whole business of hearing music in nature? His words had sounded crazy at first, but then…she'd heard it. She hadn't wanted to, but she'd actually heard it. The tears came. If he was crazy, she was, too.

Just like that Sunday last month when he'd led worship at church, the music had started to chip away at her defenses. When she was around him, her resolve to keep her promise to never let music into her life again had begun to weaken, and she couldn't have that. No matter what the cost, she needed to maintain control of her life. Never again would she be hurt by a man.

As tears trickled down her face, she lifted the burnt orange sweatshirt to dry her cheeks. It smelled like Chance. She threw it onto the ground.

"Tsk-tsk. Angry are we?" The tone in Noah's voice was teasing.

She turned and peeked over her shoulder. Wearing a suede jacket over an argyle sweater and a pair of jeans, he looked like a mannequin that had stepped out of a Dallas men's store window. Red-nosed and teary-eyed was not how she'd planned for him to see her.

The smile vanished from his face as his eyes opened wide. "My goodness, Charity." He sat beside her on the bench and placed his arm around her. "What is it, my dear? You look horrible." He drew her close and offered his shoulder as a pillow.

The tears came harder now. She leaned in but stopped. Tears and suede were not a good combination. "Noah, your jacket."

He placed his hand on her cheek and gently guided her head down to his shoulder. "You, my dear, are worth far more than any piece of clothing." He began to rock her back and forth. "Now, what in the world has happened? It can't be that bad."

She took a deep breath. "I'm just disappointed, that's all. I had something planned that didn't work out."

He kissed the top of her head as her father would have done. "I was on my way down to the lake. Would you like to accompany me?"

Noah's embrace had calmed her. "No, we can't go now. Chance

is down there."

"Really?" He removed his arm from around her and held her hand. "Since I know you're a member of the SDS, I'm sure you've read the correspondence between the Bride and Bridegroom."

"Yes, I have." Her heart began to race. He'd opened the door.

"Are you certain you don't want to go down to the lake? It could be quite entertaining." He smiled and winked.

Entertaining was the last thing she'd wanted this time to be. Nothing was going as she'd planned it, but if she kept waiting for the perfect moment, they'd never have this conversation. "Can…may I ask you a question?"

"Anything." He squeezed her hand.

She took a deep breath and looked into his eyes. "Why aren't you married?"

He released her hand and focused his gaze on the ground. Then he looked back up and smiled. "I've never found the perfect woman. I thought I had once, but things didn't work out between us." He reached over and patted her knee. "And you? I'm assuming you've never been married before, either."

"No…never. I came pretty close once, though." She waited to see if he'd get the hint.

"Perhaps it was for the best. I know my breakup was." He grasped her hand again and stared into her eyes. "I take marriage extremely seriously, and my standards are very high. I refuse to settle for someone who is not my equal, who is beneath me, as so many people do. I'll not marry until the perfect woman comes into my life."

Maybe that's what he was always trying to do. Make her into the perfect woman. But he was a well-educated man. He had to know no one was perfect. He was simply using a figure of speech.

"Charity, now that you know my thoughts, I hope you'll take my next statement as a compliment. I find you very intriguing and would like for us to begin a serious dating relationship." He leaned over to kiss her, but she backed away.

For weeks, this is what she'd wanted to happen, but now uncertainty overcame her. "Noah, I'm very flattered, but I don't know how much time I would have to devote to a serious relationship right now. With Christmas a few weeks away, most of my spare time will be spent involved with my business. However, if you're willing to begin dating under those circumstances, we could give it a try." Her words sounded more like the response to a business proposal than the beginning of a romantic relationship.

He grinned. "I wouldn't dream of dating a woman who was not dedicated to her work. That's perfect." He leaned in to kiss her again.

His kiss was sweet, not passionate. The goose bumps that had covered her arms the first few times they'd kissed were missing. But wasn't that the way it was with relationships? As familiarity increased, the newness wore off and excitement decreased. Good grief, if they ever got married, she couldn't possibly feel excitement every time he kissed her.

"I have the week of Thanksgiving off, and I wondered if you could steal away a few days. My mum's going to be gone, and I thought we could go to Fredericksburg for Thanksgiving. They have some old-fashioned Christmas activities that weekend, and I know a charming little bed and breakfast there. It will give us an opportunity to become even better acquainted." He winked.

She couldn't go, but she wouldn't have, anyway. She knew what he was suggesting. "I can't, Noah. I've got plans. One of my family's traditions is to serve Thanksgiving dinner at a homeless shelter during the day and then have a big dinner at home in the evening and put up the Christmas tree. Earlier this year, my parents moved to California to be close to my brother and his wife, so I'm planning dinner at my house. Ally and Trey are coming, and I'd love it if you'd come spend the day with me. Please, say you will." She smiled.

He ran his fingers through his hair. "Maybe we could visit Fredericksburg for New Year's. I'll be happy to come for Thanksgiving dinner." He pulled her close in an embrace. "But you must know, I've never helped in a homeless shelter before. I've always thought that most of those people are in that condition due to their lack of a good work ethic. By continuing to give them hand-outs, we only prevent them from learning to become self-sufficient. You and I have both worked hard to be successful. They can, too."

His feelings couldn't be as harsh as his words. Certainly, he had the capacity for compassion just like anyone else. She'd give his argument some thought, though. Maybe a part of it was right. Maybe there was a better way to help the homeless.

"Plus, I'm concerned about catching some sort of horrible disease…" He grasped both of her hands. "But for you, I'll do it. What time shall I be at the shelter, and what shall I bring for dinner?"

They stood, and she hugged him. "How about ten o'clock, and bring only yourself."

She placed her arm around his waist and moved toward the path back to the inn.

Noah stopped. "Aren't you forgetting something?" He nodded his head toward the fountain.

She turned back. A white longhorn in the midst of a burnt orange puddle stared up at her from the ground. Chance's shirt…if only forgetting him was as easy.

13

Although unexpected, Monday night's call from Mom hadn't been a complete surprise. Charlee would be forever grateful to her parents for their servants' hearts. Not a Thanksgiving or Christmas had gone by that their dinner table hadn't included both close friends and also guests who were either new to the area or had no family in their city.

Today, she'd carry on the family tradition. Mom had called to tell her that Dad had invited Ashley, the daughter of an old college friend, to Charlee's house for Thanksgiving. He'd known she wouldn't mind having another guest. Sharing holidays was their family norm.

Not being with the rest of the Bennett clan this Thanksgiving would be hard. But she couldn't have left Ally alone at the shop this time of year. Tomorrow, the day after Thanksgiving, would be crazy-busy as the Christmas shopping season officially began.

She laid down her calligraphy pen after putting the finishing touches on the place-cards and walked into the dining room. The table looked lovely. Not as pretty as one of Mom's. She was an entertainment goddess. But Charlee's looked better than most. Setting it with some English stoneware and Irish linens had been the right decision. All that was missing were the place-cards.

Even though there'd be five of them for dinner, she'd set six places, an extra one, as Mom always did. Just in case. She put a tented card at the top of five of the plates: Ally, Trey, Noah, Charlee, and Ashley. The turkey was in the oven with the timer set to come on in a bit. The bare Christmas tree stood in the corner of the living room waiting to be decorated tonight. Everything was as ready as she could get it.

She turned off the light in the dining room and hurried into her bedroom to get dressed. In less than an hour, she needed to be at the shelter.

~*~

Charlee had way too much hair for one of these hairnets. Getting it all tucked under this thing was proving to be impossible. As she pushed one tendril in on the right side, another popped out on the left. If only she had pulled her hair back into a ponytail before she left home. One good thing, though, Noah wasn't here yet to see her like this. She was light years away from "perfect" at the moment.

His comments about the homeless and disadvantaged had been on her mind since he'd made them a couple of weeks ago. She understood the ideas behind his words, but she couldn't agree with them. A few years ago, she might have, but no longer. Not everything that happened in someone's life was a result of something he did or some decision he made.

Sure, being in control was important. And after Jake, she no longer liked surprises. But while the idea of living a planned life with minimal spontaneity now held more appeal for her than ever before, there were things out there way beyond her control. Some bad, some good.

She'd made a bad choice in not balancing her books that entire first year she'd been in business. If it hadn't been for her parents, she might have lost everything and ended up homeless. But it wouldn't have been because she hadn't worked hard or had been lazy as Noah suggested. It would have been caused by a poor decision and unfortunate circumstances. Not everyone had as loving and supportive a family as hers.

And then when Jake abandoned her, or Noah's fiancée failed to show up at the wedding, neither one of them had a choice about that. So as much as she'd tried to make herself believe she was in control of what happened in her life, she could only control how she reacted to whatever life brought her way.

Looking in the mirror, she sighed. Right now, she couldn't even control her hair, much less her future. But work waited, so this would have to do. She washed her hands, turned off the light, and walked into the kitchen.

Marty opened his arms anticipating a hug. "There's my favorite girl." His eyes had more laugh lines radiating from them than the sun had rays.

"Hi, Marty." She fell into his big bear hug.

"Hello, Charlee. It's good to see you. How's your family?" Her first memory of serving on Thanksgiving was when she was four, and Marty held her hand as they walked around among the diners handing out extra rolls and corn muffins.

"Good. This Thanksgiving will be strange without them here, though. What's my job today?" Marty and Joyce were in charge, as usual, even though they must have been in their mid-seventies by now. Over the years, people who volunteered at the shelter on Thanksgiving came and went, but they were constants.

"Today, you are the Queen of the Kingdom of Cranberry." He bowed. "We need two hundred individual cups for the diners. Joyce has everything laid out for you in the back."

"If that's the case, then you should have given me a tiara instead of this 'lovely' hairnet." As she grinned, she grabbed a pair of latex gloves and headed toward the stainless-steel counter along the far wall.

Although dinner was a while away, the large common room was already bustling with noise and activity as today's guests came early to visit with the volunteers from local churches, play board games, take showers, and just get in out of the cold November wind. Last Thanksgiving, the weather had been warm enough to play tennis, but not today. Today's brisk temperature felt like January.

The buzz of conversation and activity behind her was enhanced by the tinkling sound of the old upright piano in the far corner as an assortment of old hymns mixed with Christmas carols and songs warmed the room. The music provided a homey festiveness to this otherwise cold, cinder block room.

She put the last dollop of cranberry sauce into the last cup and began carrying the trays over to the serving line. A piano duet of "Chopsticks" filled the air. Her heart ached. This was her and Dad's song, their annual contribution to the Bennett family Christmas tree decorating ceremony. Every Thanksgiving evening since she was six...until this one. Funny how something like a simple song had become so ingrained within her heart. If she ever got married and had children, she'd make sure the "Chopsticks" Duet Tradition carried on.

Laughter rose up from the piano as the players started over. She glanced that direction to watch, but all she could see was the currently increasing group of onlookers gathered around the old, walnut upright, not the musicians. The one playing the melody was obviously a very inexperienced pianist. Maybe a child. The person playing the bass was accomplished. She could hear it in the touch and embellishment of the basic chords.

Charlee set the last tray of cranberry sauce on the counter behind the serving line when the "Chopsticks" duet started over. She pulled off the latex gloves and stepped toward the piano, but before she got there, they finished, and the crowd laughed and applauded.

The players jumped up and began a complicated pattern of hand movements, culminating with a fist bump. The first was an older elementary or middle school aged boy. The second was a man dressed in jeans and a plaid pearl snap western shirt. His hair was combed back in a relaxed style and light brown in the absence of gel. But his smile was as big as ever.

Chance clapped the young man on the back and then looked toward the kitchen—her direction. His gaze found her, and his eyes widened. For a second, the grin on his face disappeared. He nodded a greeting toward her, and the smile returned.

Her breathing quickened. Of all people...she would never have expected to see him today. Especially here. And worst of all, she was at her loveliest in this stylish hairnet. But this wasn't a beauty contest, so it shouldn't matter.

The phone in her pocket vibrated. She pulled it out and looked at the display. A voice mail from Noah. But it hadn't even rung. She turned her back and listened.

"Hello, Charity. It's Noah. I imagine the reason you were unable to answer your phone is because you are up to your elbows in greasy food by now. I've had something arise, and I have to cancel our plans. An old friend called unexpectedly, and she's in town today. It's been years since I've seen her, and we have a great deal of catching up to do. I feel dreadful canceling at this late date, but I simply cannot abandon her, and I know you have other guests coming to your house this evening. Thank you for being the sweet, understanding woman you are. I'll make it up to you. Happy Thanksgiving, my dear."

The excitement in his voice spoke volumes more than his words alone. The woman he was meeting was not just an old friend. More like an old girlfriend. So much for their new serious dating relationship. He'd stood her up. Him, of all people. And on Thanksgiving, of all days. Sweet and understanding did not describe her feelings at the moment.

Wanting to give him a piece of her mind, she pushed the button to call him back, but before the phone connected and began to ring, she ended the call. She needed to take a breath and give him the benefit of the doubt. Besides, whatever the circumstances, he'd made his choice, and she wouldn't beg. She jammed her phone into her pocket and turned back toward the piano.

"Hi."

She jumped. Chance was about a yard away. The same cologne that had been infused in his sweatshirt before she'd washed it floated toward her. "Hi. This is unexpected."

The corners of his mouth twitched as if he were trying not to smile. "Yeah. I didn't expect to see you here either."

She placed her hands on her hips. "Don't you dare laugh. This hairnet thing is horrible."

"Me? Laugh? Never." Gazing down at the floor, he cleared his throat. When he looked back up, his face was serious. His eyes held an emotion she couldn't quite read. Concern, tenderness, affection? "You doing OK?"

The last time she'd seen him was that day at the lake when she'd hurried away with his sweatshirt. Although she owed him an explanation, she wasn't ready. He probably thought she was some kind of nut, and maybe she was. "I'm great. If I'd known you were going to be here, I'd have brought your sweatshirt. It's all clean."

"Not a problem. You can bring it to church sometime." He raised his eyebrows and smiled. "Speaking of which, haven't seen you there recently."

She'd found reasons not to go to church at all since he'd become the worship pastor. She pulled her gaze away from his and focused down at her feet. "I've been extra busy at the shop. The Christmas season's started." She looked back into his gray eyes. Her words probably sounded as lame to him as they did to her. "And I, uh, likely won't make it this Sunday. Friday and Saturday are our biggest days of the year, so I'll be exhausted by Saturday night."

He opened his mouth to speak when the dinner bell sounded, and Marty began giving instructions to the diners and the volunteers. "Let us pray…"

Charlee slipped to her station behind the steam tables. In addition to handing out cranberry sauce, she'd be dishing sweet potatoes onto disposable plates. Normally she enjoyed this time of speaking with and serving the diners, but Noah's phone message completely occupied her thoughts.

Ever since she'd found his SDS letter, she believed they had a special emotional bond, and that if she could break through his exterior, they'd share a connection she couldn't share with anyone else she knew. So she'd tried to do and say the right things that would make her into the woman he wanted. But no more. The man who was on the quest for the perfect woman was far from perfect himself. Everything was all about him. Just like Jake had been all about Jake.

And, anyway, Noah wasn't nearly as charming as she'd first thought. Nor as handsome.

"Thank you for taking time away from your family to be here today." Before her sat an unfamiliar woman in a wheelchair. The boy who'd played the piano with Chance, presumably her son, pushed his tray and hers along the stainless-steel bars of the serving line. Behind them were three young girls. His sisters, for sure. All five members of the family were blond with bright blue eyes.

"It's my pleasure." Charlee smiled and spoke her stock greeting. "Happy Thanksgiving. God bless you."

"Oh, He has, and He is, and He will. Happy Thanksgiving, and may God bless you, too, my dear." Her eyes sparkled as she smiled.

"Let me give you a hand with that." Chance stepped behind the woman.

"Thanks, Chance. You're such a kind man." She smiled up at him as he reached down and picked up her tray.

So, this woman knew Chance, but Charlee had never seen her at church, or anyplace else for that matter. And he'd been in Crescent Bluff only a few weeks, not long enough to know many of the town's people.

"I guess some people would call me young. Not so sure about kind." He winked. "C'mon guys. I'll find you a place."

As Charlee placed a spoonful of potatoes on the last child's tray, Chance led the group across the room to a space at the end of one of the rectangular, paper-covered tables.

Like a robot, she spooned sweet potatoes and spoke holiday greetings, but her attention remained on Chance. He'd gotten the family seated, and now he had picked up a pitcher of water and was going from table to table refilling glasses.

He seemed to be in no hurry but looked each person in the face, smiled, and spoke briefly with them. Most often he would shake hands or rest an open hand on the shoulder or back of the men. A few of the women he hugged, but generally he just smiled and spoke with them.

He certainly wasn't afraid of catching some "horrible disease" like Dr. Perfect. A picture of Noah in hospital scrubs with gloved fingers raised and wearing a surgical mask as he poured iced tea flashed into her mind. At least the hairnet prevented her from pulling out her hair in frustration.

~*~

Charlee finished putting the last metal tray in the dishwasher. From the room next door, she heard Marty praying at the end of his Thanksgiving devotional. The gentle melody of "Silent Night" being played on an acoustic guitar drifted into the kitchen. The musician had to be Chance. Even though only a few short weeks had passed since she'd startled him on the patio at the inn, his skill had progressed beyond simple strumming to artistry. After removing the hairnet and gloves, she ran her fingers through her smashed style to bring it back to life.

As much as she tried to resist, the music beckoned her toward the small chapel. She tiptoed down the hall until she could peek around the edge of the doorway. Chance and the lady in the wheelchair were at the front. Charlee hadn't even asked her name.

Chance sat on a stool, the heel of one boot hooked on a rung, the guitar resting on his thigh. As the lady began to sing the old carol, he smiled and nodded, his fingers coaxing a beautiful accompaniment from the strings.

Charlee had heard this song sung hundreds of times in her lifetime—by children, by symphony chorales, by church choirs. But never sung as beautifully as this. The woman's voice was pure and sweet, untrained. And the light of joy in her eyes was like nothing Charlee had seen before. With the fiery brilliance of a lightning bolt, truth pierced deep into her heart. This woman was in a wheelchair, she and her family were spending Thanksgiving in a shelter, and yet she was peacefully joyous.

As the second verse began, Chance's rich, warm harmonies enhanced the woman's voice. Charlee turned to leave but couldn't. Quietly, she stepped through the doorway. She scooted into the back row of chairs, closed her eyes, and listened. As the rest of the group added their voices to the duet, she opened her eyes and looked at Chance. Joy covered his face, too.

The song ended, and the woman wheeled back toward the front row while Chance moved to the piano and started playing "Joy to the World." Attendees and volunteers all began to file out of the back door, but Charlee stayed seated as Chance continued to play.

She hadn't even considered his Thanksgiving plans. It was too late in the day for him to go home to Austin, and he hardly knew anyone here in town. Her breathing quickened. She had the extra place set—no, two extra places thanks to Dr. Imperfect. Thanksgiving would be a terrible time for Chance—for anyone—to be alone. Besides, she wouldn't really have to entertain him because Ally and Trey would be there, and then Ashley, too.

She'd do it. Mom and Dad would be proud.

The small chapel was empty, and Chance stopped playing. He pulled the black case out from the corner behind the piano and began to pack away his guitar.

Taking a deep breath, she stood. For some ridiculous reason, her knees began knocking.

Her movement must have caught his attention because he looked her way. "Hey."

"Hey, yourself." She weaved down the aisle toward him. "Wow! You've really mastered the guitar over the past few weeks. 'Silent Night' was beautiful."

He grinned. "Thanks. You're kind. I've spent many hours practicing, but I've got a long way to go."

By now she was close enough to see his individual eyelashes. She'd never before noticed how long and how thick they were. "I, uh." Maybe this was a mistake.

"Yes?" His grin softened. "Something on your mind?"

She couldn't do it. "Happy Thanksgiving, that's all. See you around." She turned and strode back up the aisle.

"Happy Thanksgiving." His words followed her toward the doorway.

She was being ridiculous. Mom and Dad had always taught her that a big part of Thanksgiving was sharing what you had with others. She stopped and turned back. "Actually, yes, there is something on my mind."

He jammed his hands into his front pockets. "OK. Shoot." He leaned his head to one side, and smiled patiently as if she were a tongue-tied child.

"I'd like to invite you to my house for dinner tonight at six." She blurted it out before she could change her mind again.

"Well, I..." He looked down at the floor.

Nervousness quivered her mouth as she tried to smile while she babbled on. "Trey and Ally are both coming. And another girl that you don't know. Noah was going to come too, but...something came up. So I have an extra place—well actually, two—and I thought, why should you spend the holiday alone when I have plenty of room? I mean, you don't know many people here and all." She stopped to take a breath, and he looked back up.

"Charlee, I appreciate the invitation. Thanks for thinking of me, but I won't be spending this evening alone. I have plans." He nodded his head and waited.

"Of course, you do. I mean I figured you probably did. But just on the slim chance that you didn't or something, I wanted to check. Happy Thanksgiving—again—Chance."

"Thanks, Charlee. Don't work too hard the next couple of days. See you around."

She rushed out the chapel door. For some ridiculous reason, her heart pounded, and her knees knocked even harder, but she'd done the right thing. She had asked him over so he wouldn't have to spend the holiday alone. That was all.

And he wouldn't be alone. One of the church families had been much more thoughtful than she had. A knot formed in her stomach as a foreign thought invaded her mind. Or maybe he was spending the evening with his girlfriend.

14

Charlee arranged the crackers and cheese on the tray.

"You can't be one hundred percent sure Noah's seeing an old love." Ally placed some grapes between the cheese and crackers.

"You're right. So, how about 99.999 percent?"

The announcer's voice from the television floated into the kitchen.

"Poor Trey. Nobody here to talk guy stuff with tonight."

"Don't worry about him. As long as he's got a remote in his hand and a football game on the TV, he'll be fine." Ally smiled. "Besides, Charlee, in all honesty, he and Noah don't have much in common, anyway."

"Yeah, I guess. Come on. Let's go have a seat in the living room and wait for Ashley." She picked up the cheese tray, and Ally followed with their water glasses. "I saw Chance at the shelter this morning."

Ally eased onto the sofa next to Trey. "Really? That's surprising."

Trey looked up from the TV, leaned over, and pecked Ally on the cheek. "What's surprising?"

"Charlee saw Ace working at the shelter this morning."

"Nah. That's not surprising. That's his thing. Just about every holiday and some weekends, too." As a cheer rose from the TV, Trey turned back toward the screen. "Touchdown!"

Every holiday and some weekends, too. Despite what Trey thought, that really was surprising. Charlee glanced at her watch. Ashley should have been here by now. Dad hadn't thought to get a phone number from Ashley's father so Charlee couldn't even call to see if she needed directions. Charlee's house wasn't that hard to find, though. Any GPS would lead someone right to it.

She hadn't had anything to eat since breakfast except a slice of pumpkin pie at the shelter. To placate her rolling stomach, she leaned over, piled some bleu cheese on a cracker, and crammed the whole thing into her mouth. If Ashley didn't show up soon, they'd have to start without her.

The doorbell chimed, and Charlee stood. She covered her mouth to keep any cracker bits from escaping. "She's here. I'll get it."

Managing to swallow most of the mouthful by the time she reached the foyer, she grasped the knob and pulled the door toward her.

~*~

Chance ran a hand through his hair as the black painted door swung open to reveal his host.

"Hello. You must be Ashley. I'm..." Charlee stopped mid-sentence, her eyes opened wide.

She was the last person he'd expected to open that door. She was supposed to be having dinner guests at her house, and yet she was here, and she was calling him that.

He stepped back and looked at the brushed nickel numbers on the door frame—3792. That's the number he'd put into his phone.

"Chance, what a surprise! What happened with your other plans? Did they fall through?" Her face was flushed, and she had a small speck of something white on the corner of her mouth. "Well, it doesn't really matter," she continued. "I'm glad you felt comfortable enough to come on."

"I'm confused. Is this your house? I'm supposed to be having dinner with the son of one of my dad's college buddies." Maybe Mom had sent him the wrong address. Too weird that it just happened to be hers.

"You must have the wrong house." As she tilted her head to one side and looked at him from the corners of those emerald eyes, she grinned. "You're welcome to join us, though."

She actually looked happy to see him.

"We're still waiting on the daughter of an old college friend of my father—Ashley. She should be here any minute. In fact, I thought you were her."

Oh…now he got it. He held out his hand. "Hi, I'm Ashley. Nice to meet you, Chuck." Despite the fact he'd become really cold standing in the windy, November twilight, perspiration prickled his upper lip and forehead. "My dad never was good with names."

"What?" Her brow wrinkled.

"I can explain, but could I do it out of the wind? That is, if you don't mind." His teeth began to chatter.

"I'm so sorry. Please, come on in."

He stepped into the warmth of her house, and holiday scents embraced him. The comforting, smoky odor of a fire in the fireplace, and the pungent clean of evergreen. The savory saltiness of turkey and dressing. The cinnamon-sweetness of pumpkin and apple pies. His stomach growled. If he'd closed his eyes, he could have been home. All that was missing was classical music in the background instead of the clamoring of a football game.

She closed the door behind him and then stepped around to face him. "Explain away…"

He wouldn't say anything about the little speck by her mouth. Things between them were awkward enough without embarrassing her, and he sure didn't want her to think he was staring at her lips. "Did your dad go to UT?"

She nodded.

"Mine, too."

She tilted her head to the side and narrowed her eyes again.

"His name is Ashley Travis Jackson. After my great grandfather. I'm not exactly a junior, but…" He smiled and waited.

Her eyes opened wide.

She got it.

"Really? You're kidding, right?"

"Nope. You think I'd make that up?" His stomach rumbled again from all the enticing aromas. The fact that all he'd had to eat today was two rolls at the shelter and his last ChocoCrumble bar probably contributed as well.

She shrugged her shoulders and grinned. "So where does 'Chance' come from?"

"My mother's maiden name. They substituted it for the Travis part."

"What a weird coincidence! Chuck and Ashley." As she tossed her head, her auburn ponytail bounced. "So, let's see. You're Ashley, Ace, and Chance. How many other aliases do you have, Mr. Jackson?" Playfulness blanketed her tone.

"Only one. My family calls me 'AC.' That's where the Ace came from. But now I prefer 'Chance.' A new name for a new time in my life."

She smiled. "Out of all those names, that one certainly suits you the best." Her face suddenly reddened. "Can I, I mean, may I take your coat?"

He'd forgotten the gift bag in his hand. "Sure. And this is for you." He held it out. One thing Mom had taught him was never to go empty-handed as a dinner guest. Plus, this was something he could drink besides water. "It's nothing big, just a couple of bottles of sparkling cider."

"How thoughtful! That's one thing my family always has on holidays, and I forgot to get some at the store." Her eyes twinkled. "Thank you so much."

As she took the bag, he slipped off his jacket and handed it to her. "You bet."

"Come on." She hung his jacket on the oak hall tree and then turned and walked through the doorway into the living room. "Trey, Ally, meet our dinner guest—Ashley."

~*~

Charlee sat on one end of the sofa, and Ally leaned her head back on the other. "That was nice of Ace to volunteer for the guys to do the dishes." Ally giggled. "His offer certainly took Trey by surprise."

Trey wasn't the only one who'd been surprised by Chance's offer. Jake would have never done dishes. And Noah? Well, that was totally inconceivable. "Yeah. Trey looked at Chance as if he was speaking Greek." Charlee chuckled.

"Well, I must say, there's nothing more attractive than a man in the kitchen with bubbles up to his elbows."

Charlee would have to give that statement some future thought.

Ally pulled a fleece blanket from the arm of the sofa and covered herself with it. "Is it cold in here?"

"This old house can be really drafty." Charlee rose and put another log on the fire. "That should help." As she turned back toward the sofa, the guys came into the living room.

"Mission accomplished. The dishwasher's running, and the pots and pans are in the drainer." Chance grinned at Ally. "I did the best I could with what I had." He punched Trey in the arm. "But our guy here may still not be up to speed by the big day. You really need to make him practice some more."

"Funny, dude. I'm just a paper plate kind of guy." Trey dropped down onto the sofa by Ally. "You OK?"

"Sure. A little cool but Charlee just put more wood on the fire."

Chance pulled his phone out of his pocket and looked at the screen. "I gotta take this. Excuse me a minute." He stepped into the foyer and turned his back. When he returned, his brow was wrinkled.

"Everything OK, man?" Trey pulled Ally close.

Chance looked at Ally and then back at Charlee. "Don't suppose you ladies know of any female singers at church other than the four regulars. That was Anna. She was the only one available this Sunday, and now she's sick and has to cancel. Any suggestions?"

Ally drew away from Trey. "There was this one other girl that used to sing all the time. But she hasn't in quite a while."

Charlee's stomach churned.

"Do you remember her name, Charlee?"

"I'm not sure who you're referring to." She shot Ally a don't-you-dare-or-I'll-kill-you look as she fought to keep her dinner down.

Ally's eyes twinkled. "Let's see. I think her name started with a C."

This wasn't a game.

Ally continued, "Yes, C for Charlee."

Chance turned and flashed his magnetic grin. "I didn't know you were a vocalist."

Charlee stared at Ally. "That's because I'm not." Ally was in big trouble.

"Did your nose just grow?" Ally grinned.

She was enjoying this way too much.

Charlee looked back at Chance. "Let me rephrase that. I'm not anymore."

"Uh-oh," Trey said. "Look's like my baby's got herself in trouble." He kissed Ally on the forehead. He pulled away, his smile gone. "You're burning up. I don't know much about doing dishes, but I have four younger brothers and sisters. I know a fever when I feel it. I need to get you home."

Charlee made her way over to Ally and placed her hand on her friend's forehead. "Ally, Trey's right. You should go home and get in bed."

"I'll be fine. Just give me a few minutes. I'm not leaving until we get your tree decorated."

Ally's face had been flushed throughout dinner, but Charlee assumed excitement had reddened her cheeks. She might have figured it out earlier if she hadn't been so distracted playing hostess. "The tree can wait."

"I know how much you like getting your tree decorated before the Christmas craziness hits at work. Last year you didn't get it done by Thanksgiving, and you never put one up. If we leave now, you won't have a tree again this year."

"You go on. I promise I'll get it done." Charlee looked over at Trey. "Let me get your jackets."

As Charlee stepped into the foyer, Chance spoke. "I've hung many strings of lights in my day. I'll stay and help her."

"You promise, Ace?" Ally croaked.

"Promise. Go home, and get some rest."

The other three joined her in the foyer, and Charlee handed Trey their two coats. "Feel better soon, Ally. Call me if you need anything, OK?" An icy blast pushed its way inside as she opened the door, and Trey ushered Ally down the walkway. He certainly was kind and attentive toward her. Maybe Charlee's initial judgment of him had been wrong.

She closed the door, turned around, and leaned against it. The friend part of her was concerned for Ally and wanted her to get better soon. The businesswoman portion, however, whispered that handling tomorrow, the busiest day of the year, alone would be a nightmare. If only she hadn't put off hiring a part-time person for the Christmas season. But it was too late to worry about that now.

"You ready?" Chance broke into her thoughts. He'd stepped into the foyer.

"Chance, you really don't need to stay and help me with the tree." As much as getting the tree decorated would be good, resting up for tomorrow might be even better.

He raised his eyebrows and spoke with exaggerated seriousness. "Oh, yes I do. I promised Ally, and I'm a man of my word. Now, point me toward the decorations."

He smiled, and she couldn't help smiling back. "In the corner at the end of the piano. The lights are in the box with the green lid, and the ornaments are in the one with the red lid."

He carried back the two large plastic boxes and set them on the floor in front of the tree. "Here you go. What do you think about a little music?"

He didn't really want to know what she thought about music. Her family always played Christmas carols or *Messiah* while putting up the tree, but that was no longer her personal tradition. He waited, the only sound in the room the hissing and crackling of the fire. If she declined, she'd have to offer an explanation, and this was not the time for that. She barely knew him.

"Of course, quiet is good, too. Kind of relaxing." He lifted off the green lid and began pulling out the strings of lights. "Let's start at the top."

His height gave him an advantage, and he expertly placed the lights in record time. No words were spoken, the popping and hissing of the logs in the fireplace occasionally breaking the awkward silence. Maybe he didn't want to be here. She'd give in. "I guess some music might be OK, after all."

He turned and looked at her. "Sorry I've been so quiet. I was just rethinking the set list for Sunday's service." He pulled his phone out of his pocket. "I've got the perfect tree-decorating accompaniment.

Would you mind?"

As she shook her head, he placed the phone on the coffee table. Strains of *Messiah* warmed the room. Her breath caught. It was the perfect thing. "Thanks, Chance."

She lifted off the red lid and looked into the box that symbolized her life. Her parents had collected a Christmas ornament for her every year since she'd been born. Some were souvenirs of vacations, some reflections of milestones in her life, and some handmade artwork from her childhood. Their beauty far surpassed that of today's perfectly coordinated Christmas decor. Each piece was a treasure, a part of who she was.

As she knelt down beside the box, Chance looked over her shoulder. "Now that's what Christmas decorations should be about…memories."

She glanced up at him and smiled.

For unto us a child is born… Sweet strains filled the room as they hung her life on the pungent evergreen tree.

When the ornament box was empty, they both stepped back. "OK, Chance, the true test." She reached over and turned off the lamp next to the sofa, and the tree burst to life, its gentle glow warming the room. The "Hallelujah" chorus rang out, and they both broke into laughter.

"A perfect commentary on our handiwork, if I must say so, Ms. Bennett."

"It's absolutely lovely, Chance. Thanks so much for your help."

Hallelujah, hallelujah…

Only one tradition remained, but her father wasn't here to help her play the duet. She glanced over at the piano and then back at Chance. No, the tradition was too personal for her—something she'd shared only with her father.

Hallelujah!

The music over, they both stood in silence. He'd helped her, and she should return the favor. Maybe that was his whole reason for doing this.

"Chance, I know you need help on Sunday, but I just can't do it. It's not that I don't want to. I can't." She looked up into his face, golden in the glow of the Christmas tree lights. "I don't really want to go into detail, but a few years ago, I had a life-shattering experience that would have never happened if I hadn't been involved in music. So I promised myself music would not be a part of my life after that. And I've kept that promise until the last few weeks. I let my guard down. But no more. I refuse to let myself get hurt again."

"Charlee." He spoke barely above a whisper. "I'm just trying to be a friend, here. That's all. No ulterior motives. Sunday will work out fine."

Turning toward her, he dropped his gaze toward the floor. His brow wrinkled, and he tapped the toe of his boot against the floor. There was obviously more he wanted to say, but instead, he looked back up and smiled. "Thanks for having me over tonight…even though you didn't know it would be me. Dinner was great."

Surely, those weren't the words he'd so carefully considered speaking. "I'm glad you could come. And thanks for your help with the dishes…and the tree." Her stomach churned. She couldn't get sick, too.

"Sure. Hey, how about another glass of that cider before I hit the road?"

She glanced over his shoulder at the clock. Eleven. As she looked back into his eyes, a chill covered her arms. "Chance, I'd like to, but I really need to get a good night's sleep. Tomorrow will be a bear."

"Oh, yeah, sure. I need to get back to the inn and redo Sunday's music anyway. You should come for the service."

She followed him as he stepped into the foyer and removed his leather jacket from the coat hook on the hall tree. He slipped it on and flashed a grin, one that was the perfect size for his face.

"See you Sunday?" He zipped the jacket and pulled up the collar.

She reached over and opened the door. "I'll try. No promises, though."

"That'll work." He stepped out onto the porch and then turned back and held out his hand. "Thanks, again, for this evening."

She grasped his hand and squeezed it. Once again, her stomach fluttered and goose bumps tingled her arms, but it wasn't from illness. This couldn't be happening. "Good night, Chance." She eased her hand free, watched him turn and step into the freezing Texas wind, and closed the door. No matter how kind he seemed, or how generous his heart appeared, one truth remained. He was still a musician. A musician. Nothing could change that.

And she wouldn't allow herself to be hurt again. Nothing could change that, either.

15

Leaving the music store, Chance slipped the guitar strings into his front pocket. Now he was ready for Sunday. Well, not quite. He'd still like to have someone to sing harmony, but whoever showed, he'd make it work.

The next thing on his agenda…ChocoCrumbles. He glanced down Main Street toward Charlee's shop. Every parking place between here and there was full. Something must be going on down there. Oh, yeah, Black Friday. Better to leave his truck parked and walk. He needed the exercise anyway. He'd eaten way too much last night. Charlee was a great cook. If he ate like that very often, he'd have to buy bigger jeans.

What a weird coincidence that their fathers were old college friends and had arranged yesterday's dinner "date." Dad wouldn't believe it when he told him on Monday.

He climbed the steps, walked across the porch, and opened the door. The bell sounded, but no one paid any attention. The small shop buzzed from wall to wall with customers. Charlee stood behind the counter ringing up a sale, and two more people waited in line to pay. No Ally in sight.

"Hello, Chance." Mrs. Williams smiled. "What a nice surprise to see our new worship leader today."

"Hi, Mrs. Williams. Thanks. It's good to see you, too." With her white curly hair and eyes the cool blue of a January sky, she reminded him of Grandma Jackson. "Wow, it's crammed in here."

"Yes, poor Charlee. She really has her hands full. I hear Ally's sick." She cleared her throat and then raised her eyebrows. "She sure could use some help."

"You're right about that. Maybe I should come back later when she's less busy." The ChocoCrumbles could wait. "See you Sunday."

"I'll be there."

She moved toward a display of teapots on a shelf next to the fireplace, and he turned and headed back out the door. The last thing Charlee needed right now was one more person to wait on. Especially one who wanted only candy bars.

When he reached the first step, he stopped. He didn't have any other plans today, and he couldn't leave her alone like this. He turned around and walked back into the shop. No one noticed the bell jingling this time either.

He made his way to the counter. Charlee tied some curling ribbon on the handles of a bag and handed it to the last person in line. It was only noon, and she already looked exhausted. "Hi, there." He leaned on the counter.

"Hi." Her forced smile fell short of her eyes, and her gaze drifted over his shoulder to the sea of shoppers flooding her store. She looked back into his face. "Can I, I mean, may I help you with something?"

"I think a better question is, 'Can I help you?'"

"What?"

"I've worked a lot of retail and waited many a table. If there's one thing I can do, it's run a register." She'd lost her summer tan, and her freckles dotted, more than dusted, her nose today. "How about we tag-team? You start out on the floor, and I'll work the register."

"Chance, thank you, but I'm sure you have plans today." Her refusal sounded unconvincing at best.

"Only to buy some more ChocoCrumbles." He smiled. "Plus, it's the least I can do to help pay you back for yesterday's dinner. Which was, by the way, awesome. What do you say?"

"Well…" Her face relaxed.

He had her.

"That would be wonderful."

He stepped around the counter. Gift bags, tissue paper, and bright colored curling ribbon filled the shelves beneath the register. "I'm not too good at this wrapping thing, but I'll see what I can do." He glanced at the register and the credit card scanner. Yep, he was familiar with them both. "I'm good here."

He leaned close. Her perfume reminded him of the scent of the

Hill Country after a spring rain—fresh and clean. As she headed out from behind the counter, he held up his fist. "And now, stepping into the ring…Chuck."

She grinned and bumped her fist against his. Her eyes sparkled like the sun dancing across the green-blue waves off Padre Island.

Mrs. Williams called out from the front corner. "Oh, Charlee, dear…could you please come and get this teapot down for me?"

"Certainly." She turned back toward Chance and mouthed, *Thank you*.

The afternoon flew by, and in what seemed like no time, Charlee flipped the OPEN sign around, closed the door, and locked it. Her phone vibrated against the oak counter top. Chance stole a look at the display. Walsh. For like the millionth time today.

"Chance, thank you so much. I don't know how I would have made it without your help." She reached the counter. "Do you have time to put up your feet for a second? And maybe have a cup of tea or coffee?"

"Sure, but don't forget your final sale."

Her forehead wrinkled.

"My ChocoCrumble bars."

She grabbed a box from the shelf and set it on the counter. "On the house. That's the least I can do. Seriously, I'd really like to pay you."

"Not necessary. 'Will work for food.' Actually, it was kind of fun to revive the old cash register skills. In fact, I'll come back tomorrow if you'll give me another box."

Her phone vibrated. Walsh—again. She reached behind the counter, checked the display, and then dropped the phone into her pocket. Surprising.

"He's called a bunch today."

"I'll call him back later. I need a cup of tea right now."

They walked to the buffet in the back corner, made their teas, and sat down in the chairs facing the fireplace. Charlee kicked off her shoes and propped up her feet on a little footstool. She took a sip, leaned her head back, and closed her eyes. Her hair shimmered copper in the soft firelight.

"Chance, thanks again so much. I can't believe you gave up your day off."

"Glad I could help a friend. Good I came along when I did."

"I, uh…" She lifted her head and stared at the fire.

He waited for her to finish her statement.

She gazed at him out of the corner of her eyes. "Do you have lyrics and chord charts for Sunday?" She bit her bottom lip.

He tried in vain to read her eyes. "Not on me." He winked.

She took a deep breath, just as he'd done to calm his nerves before he went on stage. "I can't make any promises, but I'll try to sing Sunday."

He didn't want her to do it out of obligation. "Only if you really want to. You don't owe me anything."

She smiled. "Would you be able to go over the songs with me? I'm sure you're tired, but if you have time tonight, we could meet at my house. I've got leftovers from yesterday. Say about seven thirty?"

He checked the antique pendulum clock on the mantel. Six thirty. "As I said, 'Will work for food.'" He'd call John and let him know he couldn't make the meeting tonight. He stood. "What about the fire?"

"We just leave the flue open. It'll burn itself out." She pulled her phone out of her pocket and read the display. Then she shook her head and turned it off. "Give me a few minutes to lock up, and I'll meet you there."

~*~

Charlee pushed out a breath as Chance placed the song sheets on the piano and settled onto the bench.

"I think the reruns were just as good as opening night. Nothing like Thanksgiving leftovers." He smiled up at her. "Thanks, again."

"Sure." Her mouth was Saharan, and she was as jittery as she'd been during finals week at college when she'd made it through only because of coffee and chocolate. In a moment of weakness, she'd really offered to do this. The fear of the recurrence of the painful memories of Jake she'd had that first night she and Chance had dinner together and that first Sunday he'd led worship only compounded her nerves. But after his help today she had to do something to pay him back.

"OK." Excitement underscored Chance's tone. "There are five songs. The ones that really need harmonies or BGV's, uh, that is, background vocals…"

"I know what BGV's are." Her voice shook, but if he noticed, his face didn't reflect it.

"Great. OK, the songs that really need them are the two traditional hymns and the heart attack song. The others are optional. You're more than welcome to sing along with any of them if you'd like."

"The heart attack song?"

"Yeah, you know when you tried to do me in on the patio at the inn a few weeks ago?" A playful smile crept across his face as he looked at her out of the corner of his eyes.

"Ha, ha. Funny." Any other time the memory of his expression that morning would have made her giggle. But not now.

As he began the intro for "This is My Father's World," she was sitting on the root-bench by the lake the day she first heard it—the music of the spheres. He sang, but when she opened her mouth to join him, nothing came out. Instead, her heart raced, and her stomach felt as though she'd eaten rocks for dinner.

"Join in any time." He began the chorus.

"I can't, Chance. I can't." She'd made a mistake. As she walked to the sofa and sat down, the music stopped.

He came over and sat on the other end. "Hey, what's up?"

The room blurred as she fought to keep the tears from streaming down her cheeks. "I'm sorry. I was wrong. I don't think I can do this."

He clasped his hands together and rested them behind his neck. A tattoo she'd never noticed on his upper arm peeked out from the sleeve of his T-shirt. "Charlee," his tone was gentle. "The Bible says God rejoices over us with singing. Over you and over me. You heard the symphony of creation that day by the lake. God created music. It's good. Music didn't hurt you."

She'd been betrayed. Ally must have told Trey about Jake, and he, in turn, told Chance. She widened her eyes, but a tear escaped anyway.

"Look, I don't want you to do anything you're uncomfortable with. Sunday'll be fine either way. God's got this." A gentle smile warmed his face. "But there is one other thing I'd like to say. Something for you to think about."

"What?" She sniffed.

He rested his arms on the back of the sofa and angled toward her. "You know how when you first go to bed at night and turn off the light, it's so dark you can't see anything? You just rely on your memory to 'see' the furniture in the room. But then slowly your eyes become accustomed to the lack of light, and you can make out the shapes."

She nodded. Everybody knew that.

"The longer you stare into the dark, the more comfortable your eyes become until you think you can see things really clear. But then when the sun rises and pushes the darkness away, you discover how wrong you were, how distorted your perception was." He paused and looked straight into her eyes. "Charlee, you've been living in darkness these last few years, and the blackness has distorted your perception."

His words stole her breath away, their truth resonating within her soul. They warranted no fact-checking. She'd been living in a self-imposed fortress of blackness since Jake left. A fortress built for her protection.

He stood. "Thanks for dinner…again. I'll see you tomorrow morning about ten." He walked into the foyer and took his jacket from the hall tree.

While the fortress walls had protected her from pain, they'd also cut her off from life. Because pain was a part of life. But so was joy, and that was the portion she'd been missing. Music had always brought her joy.

He slipped on his jacket and opened the door.

"Chance, wait." She caught up with him. "You're so right. Thank you for speaking truth to me." More than anything she wanted to throw her arms around him and pull him close in a hug of gratitude. But she couldn't. She barely knew him.

His grin brightened his face.

"Can we try again, Chance? Please?"

"Absolutely." He closed the door and hung his jacket on the hall tree.

She led him into the living room.

Sitting down on the bench, he started where he'd stopped a few minutes earlier. The arrangement was not the same as the traditional hymn. Some of the chords were different. Standing behind him, she read the words over his shoulder. On the second verse she joined him and sang through 'til the end, matching her harmonies to the variations in the arrangement. The music made her soul soar.

At the end of the song, he put his palms on his thighs and looked straight ahead. His silence overwhelmed her, and his gaze avoided hers.

"I'm afraid I'm a little rusty. Maybe we could run through it again."

He scooted over and patted the bench beside him. "Have a seat."

She sat and then continued, "Before you say anything, I'll certainly understand if you think it would be better if I don't sing."

He looked straight into her eyes. "Charlee, those harmonies were sick."

"Sick?" That one word confirmed she'd made a huge mistake when she offered to help him. "I'm sorry."

"Sick." He grasped her shoulders. "So tight. Lots of tension. Most people can't even hear harmonies like that. You have a real gift."

"So, then, 'sick' is good?"

"Good?" He released her and jumped up. "Are you kidding me? It's way beyond good. I'd love to have you sing every Sunday."

Her stomach fluttered, but this time not from fear or nerves. "Thank you."

"Ready for the heart attack song?" He sat back down and began playing.

~*~

Charlee glanced at the grandfather clock in the dining room as it struck eleven times. Three hours had passed like three minutes. Chance grasped his hands together and lifted them high over his head. More of the tattoo on his upper arm showed this time.

"What's that tattoo mean?"

"This?" He pulled up the sleeve of his shirt. His arms were more muscled than she'd realized.

She forced herself to concentrate on the knotted triangle symbol. She'd seen something similar in some of the books at the shop.

"It's a symbol for the Trinity. I sneaked out and got it after I was baptized when I turned seventeen. I wanted a permanent visual symbol of that day." He yawned. "Guess I better head back to the inn and rest up for tomorrow."

He was right. Today had been a long day. She was physically tired. But mentally, the music had energized her. There was no way she could sleep right now.

"How about that glass of cider before you leave?" She stood.

"That'd be great." He followed her into the kitchen. "You're gonna do just fine on Sunday." He leaned against the counter, his ankles crossed and his thumbs hooked in his front pockets.

So attractive. Her heart raced. She turned her gaze and mind away from him and filled the glasses. She couldn't allow herself to go there. "Thanks. I was nervous earlier, but now, I'm just excited." She handed him a glass, and they walked back to the living room. "Have a seat."

He eased onto the sofa, and she turned on the tree lights. "Flip off that lamp next to you, please."

"Sure."

The warm glow of Christmas lights filled the room.

"We did a pretty good job last night." He grinned.

"Yes, we did." She willed her heart to slow as she snuggled down on the far end of the sofa. "Thanks for your help."

"You bet." He sipped some of the cider. "Hey, I have a question for you. How are you at covert ops?" He raised his eyebrows.

She could have never guessed that question. "I can honestly say I've never done any."

"Well, I've got a mission planned, and I could use some help…if you're willing." He turned to face her. "There's this family I know. The parents were in a car wreck a couple of years ago. The father was killed, and the mother ended up in a wheelchair." He paused, his eyes opening wide as he grinned. "You know her. It's Beth, the lady that sang at the shelter."

Beth…that was her name. Charlee nodded.

"They lost their house and until recently were homeless. A few weeks ago they moved into a little rental house around the corner from the church. Christmas for them will be pretty bleak this year, to say the least. Beth would never complain, but I want to get them some stuff and deliver it in secret—you know, covert." His eyes danced. "I could sure use some help picking out stuff for the girls and then delivering it. Marty gave me a list, but a lot of it's Greek to me. So? What do you say?"

He looked like a puppy begging for a treat. "Sounds like fun. I'd love to." She finished her cider and set the empty glass on the table. A yawn escaped before she could control it.

He stood. "It's getting late. I better hit the road. We both need some sleep if we're gonna take on the shopping hoards again tomorrow."

She looked at the tree. Despite its beauty, her spirit lacked the normal Christmas excitement. And she knew why. "Chance, before you go, I have a favor to ask." Her cheeks warmed. Hopefully, he couldn't see it in the soft light of the tree. "It's really kind of silly, but my dad and I have this tradition. We always play a 'Chopsticks' duet after we decorate the tree. And since he's not here this year, I was wondering, I mean, if you're not too tired…"

"I'd be honored. Treble or bass?" He headed back over to the piano.

"Doesn't matter to me. You choose."

He grinned over his shoulder as she followed him. "I have an idea." He slid the bench away from the piano. "I'll start on bass, and then we'll switch."

"OK." She stood at the right-hand end of the keyboard.

Chance reached both hands out in front of him and wiggled his fingers. "Just loosening up." He looked at her out of the corner of his eyes and grinned. "When I say 'switch,' you move in front of me and take the bass." He stooped to reach the keys. "Ready, Chuck?"

"Ready, Ashley."

The calliope of the bass chords began. Charlee let him run through them twice before beginning the discordant pounding of the treble. They played the song one time, and Chance picked up the pace. About halfway through the second time, he said, "Switch!"

She slid down to the left as he jumped up to the treble, and they only missed one beat. Then he began showing off by playing some fancy rendition of the melody. Whatever. She'd get him back by increasing the tempo of the bass line.

His voice sounded over the duet. "So, that's how it is, huh?" He laughed. "Switch!"

"Chance!" She giggled like a middle school girl. She'd never had this much fun playing the piano.

"Switch, I said!"

As they traded places this time, their hands brushed, and electricity surged through her body. They finished the verse and then as if preplanned, they both stopped. Silence filled the room. She glanced over at him to see if he had felt it, too. His face was red, but it could have been from the frantic playing. "Thanks, Chance. Now the Christmas season has officially begun."

He cleared his throat. "You're welcome. Haven't had that much fun at the piano in a long time. Maybe never." He stuck his hands in the front pockets of his jeans. "Well, I better get back to the inn."

They stepped into the foyer, and she handed him his jacket. "Thanks, again, for everything today." More thoughts begged to be spoken, but she couldn't. Not right now. His earlier words had broken away some of the prison bars. She'd taken the first steps on her journey from darkness into light. But obtaining complete freedom required time. More than one evening.

A soft smile painted his face. He knew what she meant. "Sure. Maybe this is a new line in your poema." He slipped on his jacket and opened the door. "See ya."

"Bye." In the porch light, she watched him walk across the yard and to the street. Poema. So appropriate. In senior English, she'd learned not to take poetry at face value. Reading poems was like customers opening a Bits of Britain shopping bag. At first, they couldn't tell what was inside. The showy strands of curled ribbon had to be untied and multiple sheets of tissue paper had to be withdrawn before the beautiful porcelain tea cup was revealed.

Chance. The more she was around him, the more intriguing he became. She hadn't seen it at the first glance. Just like poetry, just like the gift bag. The true beauty was not displayed on the surface. She'd looked only at his outer appearance and had misjudged him. Many layers had to be gone through before she could reach the best part. His heart.

As his truck pulled away, she waved and closed the door.

Reaching into her pocket, she pulled out her phone and turned it back on. Twelve missed calls. One from Ally and eleven from Noah. Chance was right. He had called a lot today. The message tone sounded. Two new ones. She'd listen to Ally's in a minute, but not Noah's. She couldn't deal with him right now.

She walked into the living room and picked up the empty cider glasses. She looked first at the glowing Christmas tree and then at the piano, its bench still pulled out. She smiled, and she felt them…

Goose bumps.

16

The last thing Charlee needed…wanted…right now, at five fifty-five on Saturday evening was another customer. She'd slipped into the office just to sit for a second and have a sip of water.

Chance offered to finish up with Mrs. Williams. She'd finally decided on an antique teapot for her daughter's Christmas present.

And now, the bell on the door had jingled.

Charlee was grateful for all the business she'd had the past two days and especially for Chance's help handling it. But her feet screamed to stay seated. She took a deep breath, plastered her salesperson's smile on her face, and stepped out into the area behind the counter. "May I…Noah!" Definitely the last person she expected or wanted to see. She walked out onto the sales floor while Chance wrapped the teapot.

Noah's smile was straight out of a college yearbook. "Well, well, hello, Charity. I'm glad to see that you're still alive and in good health. Is your phone broken? Did you not get my messages?" His eyes were cool, his tone sarcastic. He was angry, but that was OK.

She was too. He'd cancelled Thanksgiving to be with another woman. "Yes, I got them. The past couple of days have been so busy I haven't had a moment to spare. Ally's got the flu, and I don't know what I would have done had Chance not stopped by and offered to help."

Mrs. Williams bustled by. "Thank you again for your help and patience, Charlee."

"My pleasure. Thanks for the purchase."

"By the way, you should consider keeping Chance on." Mrs. Williams leaned close and whispered. "He's quite a cutie, don't you think?"

"I appreciate the suggestion, Mrs. Williams." Charlee followed her to the door, opened it, and closed it behind her. She flipped over the OPEN sign and locked the door.

By the time she turned around, Chance had made his way to Noah and they were shaking hands. "Good to see you, Noah."

"The same, Chance." Noah gestured her direction as she made her way toward the two. "I hear you've been helping my lady. Quite chivalrous of you."

Chance's jaw tightened. Only slightly. Noah probably didn't even notice it, and last week, Charlee wouldn't have either. But she'd spent enough time around him the last few days to have become more familiar with his mannerisms and expressions.

Noah slid next to her.

"Just happened to be in the right place at the right time," Chance replied. "I'm sure you would have done the same if you'd been around." Chance smiled in her direction.

Noah reached over and put his arm around her and pulled her close.

Chance's jaw tightened again, and then he glanced at his phone. "Well, I better be going. Gotta be someplace by seven."

She pulled free from Noah. "Thanks again, Chance. Don't forget your ChocoCrumble bars." She walked toward the candy shelf by the counter.

He took his jacket from the hall tree by the door. "You just keep them for me, OK?" He unlocked the door and opened it. "Besides, if you'll show up at church tomorrow, we'll be more than even. Good night, Noah." He looked back over his shoulder and grinned. "Good night, Chuck."

"Good night, Ashley." As Chance closed the door, she giggled.

"Chuck? Ashley? What does that mean?" Wrinkles creased Noah's forehead.

If he had come on Thursday, he'd know. "Nothing. Just a misunderstanding."

"Whatever you say." He shrugged his shoulders and smiled. "I'd like to atone for missing Thanksgiving. I came to take you to dinner at the inn."

The pain in her feet had crept up into her legs and was on its way to her back. She really wanted to go home and soak forever in a bubble bath up to her neck. "I'm not sure I'd be good company, Noah. I'm pretty tired."

"I feel dreadful that I had to cancel Thanksgiving on such short notice. Please let me make it up to you." He grasped both her hands.

"Noah, you really don't have to. Everything worked out fine. Chance ended up coming in your place."

He raised his eyebrows. "Really? He took my place?"

"Yes. Well, not exactly. He took Ashley's place. I mean he was Ashley." She was making no sense.

As Noah wrinkled his brow in confusion again, she stifled another giggle. "Sorry. I think I'm brain dead." She pulled her hands free. "So, how was your Thanksgiving with your…old friend?" She shouldn't have said it like that, but she couldn't help herself.

"The proper emphasis would be on the word *old*. Sara and Harry were our next-door neighbors when I was a child in Swindon. They had no children of their own, so they adopted me. The summer I turned ten, Mum fell and broke her wrist. Sara stepped in and helped care for me."

Ally was right. She'd jumped to the wrong conclusion.

"We'd bike to the library several times a week. I guess that's where my love affair with literature truly began." His face reddened, and his gaze left hers. And for a brief moment, she glimpsed the vulnerable heart hidden behind all his posturing.

He grasped her hands again. "She was passing through on her way out west when she got stranded at the airport. I simply could not leave her out there alone on Thanksgiving. As much as I hated to cancel on you, I knew at least you had other guests coming. Thank you for being such an understanding woman."

She'd been a self-centered brat. "Noah, that was a kind thing to do. She would have been welcome to come with you, though."

"There wouldn't have been enough time." He slowly drew her toward him. "Am I forgiven? You've not accepted my dinner penance."

He'd driven all this way to make everything right. "I could meet you there about seven thirty. I'd like to go home and freshen up first, if that's OK."

"Certainly. I can see where that might be a good idea." His arms encircled her, and as he bent down to kiss her, his nearness smothered her. "I've missed you, Charity."

She gave him a quick peck and then placed her palms on his chest and gently pushed back. "If I'm going to make it to dinner on time, I'd better get moving. I've got to close out the register and straighten up before I can leave to go home."

He grasped her hands. "Why don't you bring an overnight bag and stay at the inn the next two evenings?"

"I can't. I've already spent my weekend there this month. My budget won't allow it, and besides, I don't have a reservation."

He smiled. "Well, I do." He pulled her close and kissed her. When he drew away, his eyes were dreamy.

Not this again. She should have been more direct with him that day by the fountain. "Noah, I can't do that. I…won't do that. I'm an old-fashioned girl. I hope you'll understand."

He grasped her right hand, brought it up to his lips, and brushed a kiss against the back of it. "I've known all along you were different from other women I've dated. Your innocence is really quite charming." He drew her into an embrace.

She broke free before he could kiss her. "If I'm to make it to the inn on time, I really must get going."

He released her hand and reached for the doorknob, "I'll see you about seven thirty."

She locked the door behind him and walked back to the register. Sometimes his persnickety behavior really infuriated her. He "could see" where her freshening up might be a good idea? She'd been on her feet for over eight hours with no break. It was only normal that she should be a bit wilted.

But maybe all this behavior was just a matter of self-preservation—a wall that he'd built for protection after he'd been abandoned by his fiancée. Like the dark fortress she'd placed herself in after Jake left. If she could just break through into his heart, surely, she'd find the caring man that had expressed himself in the letters at the inn.

Tonight. Maybe tonight would be the time to free him just as Chance had freed her.

17

The tapping on the car window startled Charlee. As Chance waved through the glass, she hit the unlock button, and he opened her car door.

"Morning, Charlee. What in the world are you doing here so early? The sun's not even up."

He wore jeans and a blue and brown plaid pearl snap shirt. Not his signature black. He seemed even taller this morning. She glanced down at his feet. No wonder. Cowboy boots. But the hair was still PR, unnaturally natural looking.

She smiled. "Memorizing lyrics. I couldn't sleep so I went to The Perks, got a large latte, and came on over here to study." After he'd left Friday night, she'd been excited about today. But now as she sat in the church parking lot, the excitement had transformed into fear.

"Nerves, huh?" His smile was kind. "You're gonna do great. And don't worry about words. You'll have a monitor on the back wall and someone will be feeding you lyrics."

"That's different from how it was when I sang with the worship team years ago. We used to have to memorize everything." Her stomach was in knots. "Any other advice?"

He reached in and squeezed her shoulder. "Just worship. That's it. God will take care of everything else."

Chance waved as another car parked a few spaces down. "Soundman's here. Ready?" He offered his hand, and she took it. As she stood, her knees wobbled.

"Pray for me, Chance," she whispered.

He picked up his guitar case in his right hand and then put his left arm around her like a brother. "Already have, Charlee. Already have."

They walked together toward the church. The rising sun crept up behind them and painted the shadowed image of their embrace on the sidewalk in front of them. Chance cleared his throat and dropped his arm. As they each moved away from the other, the goose bumps returned in the morning dawn.

Charlee made her way to the front row while the soundman got the microphones set up and Chance tuned his guitar. The other musicians trickled in and found their places on the platform. Charlee didn't know any of them. Things sure had changed in the past few years since she'd dropped off the worship team, since Jake had been one of the worship leaders. But all that was in her past. Today was a new line in her poema.

"OK, guys, let's talk through the service before we rehearse. But first, I want you to meet Charlee Bennett. She'll be doing vocals this morning." He motioned for her to join them on stage and the other musicians waved and spoke their welcome. "She used to be a part of the worship team a few years ago, and I'm really stoked to have her back today."

She moved to the mic stand to the right of Chance. He led them in a prayer and then discussed the order of service and the arrangement for the first song. "Everybody got it? Let's go."

The drummer counted down the song, and then the electric guitar began the fast-paced intro for the first song. This was one she hadn't heard until they'd practiced the other night, but she liked it a lot. The drums hammered in her chest, yet when they and the bass joined on the next line, she realized what she'd felt was not drums but the racing of her heart. She looked at the monitor on the wall in the back of the auditorium and breathed out. There were the words for the first lines, just as Chance had said.

She joined him on the chorus, and he smiled at her and nodded his head. Still strumming his guitar, he walked over to her and spoke into her ear above the music. "Sick, really sick. Love it."

~*~

Recorded music played as the congregation exited the sanctuary, and Chance packed up his guitar. Charlee sat on the front row staring straight ahead. The lights were still low, so he couldn't see her face clearly, but he knew what was going on. She was soaking it all in. She turned her head slightly, and her eyes glistened. Tears.

After the last few days, he understood a part of her. All that prickliness from a couple of months ago was a smokescreen to hide her feelings. Her spirit was sensitive, just as his was. One part he didn't understand was her attraction to Walsh. From the little he knew of Noah, something about that didn't make sense. But no one would ever call Chance an expert in understanding relationships.

He closed the latches on the case and walked down to the front row. As he sat down beside her, he looked straight ahead to avoid embarrassing her. "Thanks so much, Charlee. I'd really like you to consider becoming a regular part of the team."

She sniffed. "I don't know. I..."

"Just think and pray about it, OK?"

"OK."

As she turned toward him, he looked into her eyes.

"Thanks, Chance."

He understood her emotion. He wanted to place his arms around her, draw her close, and brush her tears away.

But he couldn't. They were barely friends, and she was in a relationship with another man. So he reached over and squeezed her hand. "You bet."

"Hey, I was thinking if you don't have any plans, maybe we could grab a sandwich at The Perks." The lights had come up in the sanctuary. Her nose was red—dotted by those freckles.

If he only could. "I can't. I have to go someplace."

"Sure. OK." She stood and dropped her gaze away from his.

She didn't believe him. "Really, Charlee. Tomorrow's my dad's birthday, and I have to drive to Austin this afternoon for a surprise party tonight." Standing, he again fought the impulse to hug her.

"You have to eat, don't you?" She bit her bottom lip.

"I have some ChocoCrumbles in the truck. What about Noah? I'll bet he'd like to have lunch with you."

She shook her head and rolled her eyes. "I don't know. Men!" She opened her eyes wide. "Sorry."

He chuckled. "Maybe you should say man. We're not all the same, you know."

He looked at his phone. He should have already been on the road. "Hey, I have an idea. I'll be back in town Thursday afternoon. Remember our covert op? Wanna go shopping for the stuff Thursday night after you get off work?"

"Well, I don't have any plans." She sniffed again.

"OK, then. I'll pick you up at the shop about six thirty. We can do dinner and covert ops. Deal?" He offered his hand.

She smiled and shook it. "Deal."

Thursday night couldn't come soon enough.

18

The envelope lay by the cash register begging Charlee to open it. The postmark was from Crescent Bluff, but no return address marked the back or front. She drummed her fingers against the countertop. She knew the handwriting. She'd seen it before, but she refused to remove the note until she remembered the writer's identity.

As the bell jingled, she looked up. "How was lunch?"

"Good." Ally hung her coat on the hall tree. "I'm just about back to normal." She made her way over to the counter. Looking down at the unopened envelope, she grinned. "Can't figure out who it's from, huh?"

"Not yet, but I will." Some rounds took longer than others, but she always won the "Guess Who" game.

The phone rang. *Unknown Caller.* "Bits of Britain. This is Charlee."

"Hey. It's Chance." Static interrupted his words. "How's everything going?"

"Good. Are we still on for tonight?" Please say yes. Until now, she hadn't realized how much she'd been looking forward to their plans. Holding her breath, she awaited his answer.

"Hope so."

She exhaled.

"I'm running late. Just getting on the road. So, I have a favor to ask."

"Sure."

"I won't be there 'til after dinnertime. What if I drive straight to your house and then we go shopping and maybe get a coffee or dessert after? I can give you a rain check for dinner."

"That'd be fine." Goose bumps tingled her arms.

"Now the favor. I left Marty's list of stuff to buy for Beth and the kids on the desk in my room. Would you mind going by and picking it up? I'll call the colonel and let him know you're coming."

"Glad to. Be careful, and I'll see you about eight." She hung up the phone.

Charlee had just purchased an antique copy of *Alice in Wonderland* for the shop, and Ally's grin mirrored that of the Cheshire Cat on the book's frontispiece. "Didn't mean to eavesdrop, but that sounded like a date. Noah?"

"No. Chance. And it's not a date. It's a mission project."

"Really? So is Chance in need of mission work?" Ally's eyes danced. "If I were in your spot and didn't have Trey, I'd certainly consider making him my mission."

"We're only friends." Her tone sounded defensive, even to her own ears. "You know I'm dating—"

"Noah. I know. Good old Noah." Ally's tone grew philosophical. "Charlee, I love you like a sister, but I have to be honest. I don't get your fascination with him."

"We have a lot more in common than you might think. It's just...complicated." Yes, it was certainly that.

~*~

"Hello, Charlee. I've been expecting you." The colonel smiled and held up a key. "Is this what you came for?"

"That's it. Thanks, Colonel Clark. I'll bring it right back."

Starting down the hall, she glanced at the key. He was staying in the Nairobi Room. As she reached the door, she inserted the key in the lock and followed the instructions Noah had given her the night they first met.

The grayness of the early winter dusk blanketed the room. She reached to turn on the light. Everything looked the same as the last time she'd stayed there. Except for the desk. Papers of different sizes and hues cluttered the desktop. She walked over and began to look for the list. Song sheets and chord charts covered the top of the pile. She flipped through them. Underneath was paperwork that looked like a legal document. A contract, perhaps. She pulled her gaze away. She wouldn't invade his privacy by reading it.

The shopping list lay on the very bottom. She picked it up and put it in her pocket.

One final thing remained on her agenda. She opened the secret drawer and found the envelope with her letters in it. She peeked in. No additions. But why would she think there would be? Chance had been staying in this room since he moved to Crescent Bluff, and neither she nor Noah had been able to leave any messages.

She eased onto the chaise by the fireplace, propped up her feet, and reread the letters between Noah and her. Her heart jumped. That was it. She bolted up. She grabbed her purse and pulled out the notecard. The writing on the envelope matched that of the bridegroom. She'd won the Guess Who game, once again. The note was from Noah.

She slid her finger under the envelope flap, lifted it, and pulled out the card.

Dear Charlee,

Noah never called her that.

Thank you so much for Thanksgiving dinner and letting me be a part of your family traditions. Thanks also for singing with us on Sunday. I hope you'll pray about that becoming a regular happening. Can't wait until we can do it again.

Your friend,

Chance

Her throat constricted as if she'd swallowed a handful of cotton balls. She picked up the SDS letter again and held it beside the note. The shaking of her hands rustled the papers. The block printing was identical.

Impossible. She couldn't have been so wrong. Chance was not the bridegroom. Maybe he was playing a cruel joke on the SDS.

No. She'd gotten to know him fairly well over the past couple of weeks. He would never do that. He had a kind and thoughtful heart.

She pushed her head back against the chaise and closed her eyes. Thank goodness, she'd never had the opportunity to reveal her identity to Noah.

So, all these weeks, she'd been wrong about him, just as she'd been wrong about Chance. Noah wasn't the person she'd thought he was, either. She'd spent weeks trying to force him into a mold that he would never fit. In the same way, he was trying to shape her into something she would never be...could never be. Deep inside she'd known it was wrong, but she wouldn't allow herself to admit it. The letters had clouded her judgment.

But Chance...Chance had never tried to make her into anything she wasn't or criticized her, even when she'd been rude to him.

As she stood and put his notecard and their letters into her purse, the truth exploded within her. Chance's heart was the one she cared for.

Confusion smothered her. She should call him and cancel tonight. She needed time alone to process all this—to think and, most of all, to pray.

Something she'd never done about Jake or Noah.

19

Charlee stared at her front door. When the bell chimed, her first impulse had been to hide, but as good as it sounded right now, avoidance only prolonged the inevitable. She'd made her decision this afternoon at the inn. Tonight, she and Chance would talk about the letters. Stomach churning, she forced her hand to turn the doorknob.

"Agent Jackson reporting for duty." Chance stood in his shirt sleeves saluting her and grinning in the early winter cold.

"Chance, it's freezing. Get in here." As he stepped into the foyer, she closed the door behind him. "Where's your jacket?"

"Austin. I've got another one at the inn, but I'm late and didn't want to waste time stopping to get it."

She opened the hall closet and pulled out the orange sweatshirt. "How about this? Guess it turned out to be a good thing I kept forgetting to give this back."

"Guess so. Thanks." He pulled the shirt over his head, and suddenly, she was at the lake standing with him and hoping the Bridegroom would come. Yet he'd been beside her all the time. She just hadn't seen it, because her perception had been clouded by the darkness.

"Hello?" He grinned and snapped his fingers. "Anybody home?"

"Sorry." Maybe she should cancel. "I'm, uh, just a little tired tonight."

"We can reschedule. Would tomorrow be better?"

She drew in a slow, deep breath. Prolonging this wouldn't make it any easier. "No. Tonight's fine. Let me grab my coat." She reached into the closet again and pulled out her jacket.

"Yeah, it's freezing out there. I don't remember it ever being so cold this early." He eased the coat from her hands. "Let me help you with that."

She turned her back to him, and he guided the sleeves onto her arms. If only she could lean back against him and let his strength uphold her. He had the capacity to understand her on a level no one else she knew could.

"Ready, Agent Bennett? Got the list?"

She turned to face him and smiled. She pulled the list from her jeans pocket and held it out to him. "Ready, sir."

They walked in silence to the truck. A strange mixture of fear and excitement swirled within her.

Chance held the passenger door open and offered her a hand up. "Careful. It's a big step." She grasped his hand and climbed into the passenger seat. Then he jogged around the truck and jumped into the driver's seat. "You get a chance to look over the list?"

"Yes."

He backed the truck out of the driveway and headed toward the department store. "If I remember right, there's nothing on there for Jonathan except clothes. Every kid should have something fun for Christmas. So, I figured we can check out the electronics department and see what we can find."

Charlee looked at her watch. "It's getting kind of late. We could divide and conquer."

He grinned. "Great idea, Agent Bennett."

She loved his smile.

~*~

Standing in the main aisle, Charlee held up the shopping list so Chance could read it over her shoulder.

"You keep the list," Chance suggested. "I'll go find something fun for Jonathan, and then we can meet up in the kids' clothing section."

"Sounds good. I'll get the toys for the girls and then meet you there."

Chance headed to the back of the store.

Charlee pushed the cart toward the pink and purple toy aisle. She located the items for the two older girls but had trouble finding a particular doll for the youngest daughter. She would not surrender to defeat. She rifled through the inventory of princess dolls until she finally found the requested one and dropped it into the cart.

"Charlee? Is that you?"

She'd focused all her attention on her doll dilemma and hadn't noticed anyone else enter the aisle. Probably a customer of hers. She painted a smile on her face and turned around. "Yes, it's—" Her voice caught. It couldn't be. Her knees wobbled. She gripped the shopping cart to keep from dropping to the floor. "Jake. Hi."

His face was fuller, but other than that he looked the same. A skinny blonde who had to have been at least ten years his junior stood beside him. A groupie, just as she'd been once.

"Hi." Jake looked down at the floor and then back up. "How've you been? You look...good." He glanced at her left hand and then into her eyes. His face glowed crimson.

She stared straight into his eyes, willing her voice not to shake. "I'm doing good. Really good. You know what they say. Everything works out for the best."

Rolling her eyes, the blonde looped her arm through his. "C'mon, Jakie. Let's go."

"Give me a minute, Isabella." He looked again at Charlee. "I just moved back, and I'm off the road for the next couple of months." His eyes held a strange mixture of sadness and warmth. "We should get together and rehash old times."

He must be insane. "I don't think that would be a good idea." She squeezed the cart handle until her knuckles blanched.

A strong hand grasped her shoulder. Chance drew her close and dropped something into the cart. "I got what we needed."

He must have sensed what was going on. She put her arm around his waist and leaned into his protection.

Jake's eyes widened.

"Jake, this is—"

"Ace." Chance cut her introduction short. "Ace Jackson." He offered his right hand while his left arm still held her close.

Jake's eyes grew even larger. He grabbed Chance's hand. "Jake Woods. A pleasure, man."

"Thanks." Chance nodded his head and then looked down at Charlee. "I guess we better get moving if we're going to get the rest of the stuff before the store closes."

"Yeah, us, too," Jake replied. "We were headed to the bicycle section when I saw Charlee down here." Jake held his hand out to Charlee, but she didn't take it. "Good to see you. Let me know if you change your mind about getting together. Number's still the same. Oh, and so unbelievably awesome to meet you, Ace."

Jake and Isabella walked down the aisle, turned left, and disappeared.

"I think we've shopped enough for tonight." Chance squeezed her shoulder. "We've got a good start. We can finish up later."

He loosened his grasp, but she couldn't let him go. Her eyes burned, and a mixture of anger and embarrassment squeezed her chest. She wanted to bury her face in his shoulder and sob.

He hugged her close for a few seconds and then let her go. "Hey, how about coffee and dessert at The Perks?"

Although she wasn't ready, she released him. "No. Let's get everything done. I'm OK." But she wasn't.

~*~

Chance was pretty sure Jake recognized him. He knew the look of surprised wonderment on people's faces. But he'd used his stage name to leave no room for doubt. He'd promised himself and his Father he'd never do that again—never use his God-given talent or accomplishments for selfish reasons. But he hadn't exactly done it for himself. He'd done it for Charlee. Over the past several days—since Thanksgiving, since helping her in the shop—he'd really come to care for her. Still, whatever his motive, his pride had taken over. *Forgive me, Father.*

The barista handed him their two coffees, and he headed back to the booth next to the fireplace. Charlee was facing his direction, her eyes trained on the empty spot that he was getting ready to fill. In them, he saw the same pain he'd felt the first time he'd run into Will and Amanda after their wedding day. He'd understood Charlee's hurt in the store and wanted to do anything that would soften it.

He set the cups on the table and slid into the booth across from her. She still resided in the same silent world she'd occupied during the ride over here. "Hey." He whispered to avoid startling her.

Her gaze rose to meet his.

"Thanks again for coming with me tonight. I appreciate your help."

A slight smile brightened her face. "You're welcome." Then as quickly as it had come, it disappeared.

A soothing harp rendition of "Greensleeves" filled the silence between them. "I ordered a grilled cheese and tomato soup. Comfort food for a cold night. Hope you'll share."

She ignored his comment, her eyes glistening. "Chance, that guy, Jake…he used to be my fiancé."

"Kind of figured it was something like that." Figured? No, he'd known exactly what was up.

"I'm so thankful you were there with me." A single tear tracked down her cheek. "That was the first time I'd seen him since… I don't know what I would have done if I'd been alone."

He wanted to rescue her from the pain, but he couldn't. Only time and God could do that. Instead, he took a napkin from the dispenser on the table, leaned forward, and gently dabbed away the tear. Tonight, he didn't feel as if he were invading her personal space. Now they were friends. "I'm glad I was there, too."

The server set a platter on the table. "Y'all need anything else?"

Chance shook his head. "No, thanks." As the server left, Chance set half of the sandwich on a napkin and pushed it toward her. "Have some."

Then he took a bite of his portion. "So did you and Noah have a good dinner the other night?" Her relationship with Walsh seemed improbable, at best.

"The food was great." She raised her eyebrows as if she thought he could read her mind.

"Speaking of great food." He hadn't realized how hungry he was. Breakfast had been hours earlier. "Man, this sandwich is awesome. You should try it."

She shook her head. "No, thanks."

"Sorry. Got distracted. So, the food was good?" He set the sandwich down and looked straight into her eyes. "You don't have to answer this, if you don't want. But what's with you and Noah? I got the impression from what he said at the shop the other day that you guys are pretty serious, but you keep ignoring his calls and texts."

"There are things other than Noah I'd rather talk about right now."

She'd slammed that door shut. "Didn't mean to overstep the boundaries. Y'alls' relationship is really none of my business." He smiled at her, but she didn't smile back. "So what do you want to talk about, then?"

She pulled something from her purse and then held it out. "This." His thank you note.

"Oh, good. You got it." As far as he could remember, he hadn't written anything that needed discussing. Unless…maybe she'd decided to become a regular on the worship team.

"Thank you, but you didn't need to send a note." She set it on the tabletop and stared down at it while her fingers traced its outline.

He waited.

When she looked up, her face was flushed. "I have this game I play when I get a handwritten card or letter. I see if I can recognize the writing. You know, try to figure out who it's from before I open it."

"Yeah, I do that with gifts. Try to figure out what's inside before I unwrap them."

She held up the envelope. "This handwriting was very familiar. I knew I'd seen it before, but it took me a while to figure out where."

So, she'd seen his handwriting somewhere. Maybe some comments on the lyric sheets from last Sunday, or maybe he'd jotted down some notes when he'd helped her at the shop. It didn't really matter. "Your detective skills are pretty impressive, Agent Bennett."

The smile he'd expected to see in response never appeared. For some reason, his little thank you note was more than just a folded piece of paper. It was some sort of big deal.

Her face reddened even more. "I didn't really figure out who it was from," her voice began to quiver, "until I went by your room this afternoon to get the shopping list." She reached back into her purse and pulled out another envelope and set it on the table, too. The SDS letters. His heart thumped. So now she knew.

"The handwriting… Chance, all along I thought it was Noah. Everything seemed to point to him. But I was wrong. It's you, isn't it?"

He pushed the plate of food aside. "Why do you think I was at the lake that day? I'd come to meet you like your letter suggested. Only I didn't know who to expect until you showed up."

"So, you've known all that time?" She covered her face with her hands and shook her head. When she looked back at him, her eyes glistened. "I was so sure it was Noah. I knew you went for walks by the lake, so I thought it was just a poorly timed coincidence that you were there. That's why I was so impatient."

Now the fascination with Walsh made some sense. Maybe she didn't really care for Noah, but for the man she thought he was, the man in the letter. The man sitting across from her. "So, now you know."

"Yes, now I know. It's not Noah. It's you." As another tear followed the path of the first, she opened her mouth to speak but then stopped. Whatever she wanted to say wouldn't be voiced right now.

Years ago, Dad had told him God would heal him and use the wound of Amanda's rejection to minister to others…if Chance would let Him. But Chance hadn't believed it. For years, he'd looked everywhere else for peace but never found it until he'd finally returned to God. And when the Lord healed him, he promised to use his pain to help others. Even though he'd meant it, Chance had never really thought about how he'd have to fulfill his part of the agreement. At least, not until he ran into Charlee that day at the lake. He glanced down at his forearm. *Poema.* Show time.

~*~

Charlee closed the front door while Chance dropped the last two shopping bags on her sofa and then walked back into the foyer.

"That's it." He smiled.

The ride from The Perks had been quiet, but not uncomfortable. He must have understood her need to absorb the truth. He'd had weeks—since that day beside the lake—to do so. But she'd had only a few hours.

"You sure you don't mind wrapping all this? I'll be glad to help."

"No, thanks. Contributing the wrapping's the least I can do. After all, you wouldn't let me help pay for anything." She returned his smile and placed her hands on her hips. "Besides, I've seen your handiwork at the shop."

"Whoa, there. I warned you up front that I was wrapping-challenged, didn't I? You gotta admit my register skills were perfect, though." His grin lit his entire face. "But still, it's my op, not yours."

"I think we're in this together."

"I think we are." He nodded. "So, let's initiate final maneuvers tomorrow night. That is, if you can have everything wrapped by then. And if you and Noah don't have anything else planned that night, of course."

"Final maneuvers?"

"Yeah, delivering the stuff. I still owe you a dinner, so what if I pick you up about seven? We could eat and then deliver the gifts." He raised his eyebrows and nodded his head, willing her to agree.

"That sounds like fun." She grinned at him.

"Great! Oh, and be sure to wear dark colors. This is covert, remember." He hooked his thumbs into his front pockets. "Thanks again for helping me tonight. Charlee, I…" He looked down at his feet and then up into her eyes. "Just…thanks. I'll see you tomorrow." He reached back and grasped the doorknob.

Whatever he'd wanted to say, wouldn't be said tonight. "Good night, Chance."

He stepped out onto the porch and turned toward the street. The weatherman had predicted rain, but the click of the drops hitting the pavement told her it was sleet. "Wait."

He turned back toward her and grinned. "Yes?"

"I don't know. I mean, the weather is bad, and—" She was babbling. "I don't have your cell number in case we need to reschedule." Blaming the weather. Really? She should have been able to come up with a better excuse than that. Why couldn't she just come right out and ask him for his number?

Because he'd never asked for hers, that's why, and she hated to be first. He'd always called her on the shop phone. Even in the icy wind her face burned.

As he stepped back onto the porch, he pulled his phone out of his pocket and held it out to her. "Here. Call yourself."

She took his phone and punched in her number. Her pocket sang.

"There you go. You got it." He took the phone back and jogged over to his truck.

"Drive carefully."

He waved and then jumped into the pickup.

She shut the door, leaned against it, and closed her eyes. That was totally embarrassing. He hadn't even asked for her number in return. Maybe he'd thought she was too forward.

The goose bumps tingled. He hadn't had to ask. That's why he'd made her call herself. She'd put her own number in his phone. How cute was that!

Very cute. She really liked him, and now she was pretty sure he liked her, as well. After all, he'd known she was the Bride for weeks, and he was still around. Uneasiness gnawed at her heart. But he was a musician. Different from Jake, all right, but still a musician.

This afternoon when she'd come home after picking up the list at the inn, she'd prayed God would give her wisdom about her relationship, if she could even call it one, with Chance. And buried deep inside her heart a tiny seed of peace had begun to sprout up through the blackness of distrust that had occupied her spirit since Jake left.

She headed to the bedroom, pulled on pajamas, and grabbed her laptop. Then she slipped into bed and checked her e-mail. Nothing pressing. After setting the computer beside her on the bed, she turned off the lamp and snuggled back into the pillows.

She closed her eyes to sleep, but her mind swam with images of this evening. Thank goodness, Chance had been with her when she ran into Jake and Isabella. In the few seconds Chance had put his arm around her, nothing Jake might have said or done could have hurt her.

And Jake had sure looked surprised. He must have decided she was such a bad catch that she'd never have a relationship with another man after him. And maybe he was right. But until now, that had been OK. She hadn't wanted any kind of relationship since him.

Then the look on his face had gone beyond surprise or even shock to something else. Recognition, almost as if he'd met Chance before, but he couldn't have. Chance hadn't acted as if he knew Jake.

She grabbed the computer and opened it. Nerves made her pulse race. She'd never done this before. It was like spying on her neighbor through a crack in the fence. She typed "Chance Jackson" into the search field, took a deep breath, and then hit enter.

A whole list of entries including those words came up, but none matched him. The breath she'd involuntarily held rushed out. Reaching to close the computer, she stopped, recalling the image of Jake and Chance shaking hands. Placing the cursor in the search field again, she changed "Chance" to "Ace."

As pages of entries came up, her heart sank. Most of them referred to a musician. "Talented musician…brilliant keyboardist…accomplished singer-songwriter." As she clicked on *Images*, her gasp knifed through the darkness. Multiple pictures of Chance covered her computer screen. The hairstyles varied, the amount of facial hair changed, even his weight fluctuated from one image to another. He looked rough in some and more polished in others, but the man in the photos was definitely him. The most recent images and entries were from about three years ago. After that time…nothing.

She closed the computer again and snuggled under the down comforter. As the *tick-tick* of sleet sounded against her bedroom window, her eyes filled. So, who exactly was Ashley Chance Jackson? The devastated man in the SDS letters or the talented worship leader? The compassionate servant at the shelter, the caring friend who had taken Ally's place at the shop, or the wild musician in the pictures?

Probably none of them was the true Chance Jackson. Many of the images reflected nothing of the man she'd begun to know. Maybe he, like Jake, had fooled her by pretending to be someone he wasn't. The fingers of the old darkness reached in to steal away any new born light.

As much as she tried to run away from the old darkness, she could never outpace it. It always won the race. She wanted the blackness gone.

Father, please speak to my heart, and show me Your truth. Remove the darkness and replace it with Your light.

In her heart, a flicker of truth shone. Chance was not Jake.

20

Charlee should have stayed home today. A little bit of ice on the ground and central Texans holed themselves up in front of their TVs and fireplaces—surrounded by milk and bread, if the empty shelves at the grocery store meant anything. And she'd be snuggled up at home right now if she hadn't needed to wrap the gifts for tonight's "op." Charlee had put all the gifts in her car to wrap at the store. She also took a small toiletry bag and her "covert" clothes so she could change there.

Ally went home at lunch. The cost of operating the store had far surpassed the profit from the three small sales they'd had.

After tying the last red bow on the final package, Charlee glanced at the mantel clock. Six forty. She'd texted Chance this morning—for some reason calling the first time she'd used his cell number seemed forward—and asked him to pick her up at the store. Wrapping took much longer than she figured, so she had barely enough time to slip into her office bathroom to change clothes, brush her teeth, and comb her hair before he came.

As she pulled into her jeans and a black sweater, last night's images from the Internet assailed her for what had to be at least the hundredth time today. She could have read some of those articles, but that wouldn't have been fair. When she learned about his past, she wanted it to come from him, not the unreliable Internet.

Maybe she could swing tonight's conversation that direction. Maybe he'd explain the photos, because the pictures on the web sure didn't match the man she knew—or barely knew—and that was the issue.

She cared for the man in the SDS letters, especially when she'd been so sure it was Noah. But now that she knew the letters' author wasn't Noah but Chance, she could only describe her feelings as fearful confusion.

Yet last night's flicker of truth had grown into a gentle whisper in her heart.

Trust Me.

She wanted to trust her Father. She really did. But the thought of getting involved with another musician and opening herself to being hurt again scared her. Yet God was asking her to trust Him. Not another person. Him.

But she didn't know if she could. She had trusted once before and only ended up betrayed and in agony. All she could do was follow her heart.

She ran her fingers through her hair, and then grabbed her makeup pouch.

She removed her compact, and the memory of Chance's comment about her freckles that day he'd embarrassed them both replayed in her mind. She smiled and placed the powder back into the pouch. Maybe only a little blush and lip gloss instead. She applied them and made one final check in the mirror. Not too bad for the end of a work week.

The shop doorbell sounded. Chance was early. She turned off the bathroom and office lights and walked out onto the floor.

Noah smiled through the glass pane in the front door. Oh, no. If only he had called her ahead of time. She could have told him about her plans tonight and saved him a trip. She shouldn't feel disappointed by a surprise visit from the man she'd agreed to date seriously. But she did, because he wasn't who she'd thought he was. Waving, she walked across the wooden floors to the door and opened it.

"Surprise, sweet Charity! I was afraid you weren't here. Where's your car?" He stepped into the shop and closed the door behind him.

"Ally and Trey took it home for me earlier. But, why are you…what are you doing here? I thought you weren't coming to the inn until next week."

He removed the driving cap he'd worn the first time they'd gone to The Barn for dinner. "My classes for tomorrow have been cancelled. So I've come to rescue you from the doldrums of this frigid weather."

She glanced at the mantel clock. Chance should be here any minute. "I wish you'd called first."

He laughed. "Don't be concerned. I've allowed enough time in our schedule for you to freshen up before dinner."

Isn't that what she'd just done? Freshen up? "It's not that. It's just that I have plans tonight."

"Plans? I must say, I didn't anticipate that." He pulled her close and looked deep into her eyes. "I'll bet you could rearrange them." Desire radiated from him.

As the doorbell sounded, she pushed free. "Not tonight."

Dressed in signature black, Chance waved through the window, a stiff smile covering his face.

She opened the door, and he stepped inside. "Hi, Charlee. Noah." He removed a black stocking cap to reveal a new haircut. Shorter on the sides and back, but spiked on the top. The ever-present stubble was gone, too. He looked younger, like some of the pictures she'd seen last night.

"Chance." As the men shook hands, she pictured those two rams fighting a territorial battle in that ad for a wildlife magazine's article about Yellowstone. It didn't make sense. She and Chance were only friends. But whatever the reason, the room was definitely full of tension.

And Noah wasn't happy.

"Hi, Chance. Noah surprised me with a visit. I was just beginning to explain to him about our plans tonight." Although she'd done nothing wrong, an irrational feeling of guilt gnawed at her stomach.

Chance grinned and leaned forward as if sharing a secret. "You mean our covert op, Agent Bennett?"

"Yes." She stifled a nervous giggle.

Noah stood in silence, staring at her with his eyebrows raised and arms folded across his chest, obviously awaiting an explanation.

"Noah, Chance asked me to help him deliver some Christmas presents for an underprivileged family. See the stack of gifts on the counter?"

Noah nodded in silence.

"Yeah," Chance continued. "We're going to grab some Tex-Mex and then go deliver them—undercover, like a covert op." Chance grinned and leaned his head to one side. "Hey, come with us, Noah. We could use a third pair of hands."

Please say no.

"Had I known, I would have brought appropriate clothing." He reached out and grasped her hand.

"Had I known you were coming, I would have told you so you could have." She tried to sound more teasing than frustrated.

Noah pulled her into a hug and laughed. "I'll just go on to the inn. I need to spend some time grading, anyway, so I may as well do it tonight. We can have dinner together tomorrow."

Before she could pull away, he leaned down and kissed her. Right in front of Chance.

Noah loosened his hold on her and turned toward Chance. "I hope your mission is a success. Take care of my lady. It's slippery out there."

~*~

Chance struggled to keep his eyes on the road. Her hair flashed copper every time they passed under a streetlight, stealing his attention away from driving.

"Chance, those were the best enchiladas I've ever had. How is it that I've lived here most of my life, and I've never been there?" She leaned her head back against the headrest and closed her eyes. "I think I'm going to pop."

She'd eaten more than he had. Awesome. Other women he'd dated would have munched on three chips and half an enchilada and then pretended they were full. No pretense with her. But after that "no croutons" comment the first night they met, he knew she watched her weight. Yeah, well he liked watching it, too.

He jerked his attention back to the highway. He'd let his thoughts get way off track. As long as she was another guy's girl, or in Noah's case, "lady," he could never pursue her. He'd lost his bride to his best man, and he wouldn't put anyone else through that pain.

Relationships were precious, and every serious one had taken a part of his heart. In the end, he prayed joy would outweigh the pain. He needed to save what heart he had left for the woman God would bring into his life. If there was to be one.

"Hellooo? Are you in a Tex-Mex coma?" She was staring at him, her tone demanding. "I said, 'How are the roads?'"

He liked that spunk. "Not too bad. A little slippery." He kept both hands on the wheel. "I figured most of the ice would have melted by now, but there're still a lot of slick spots."

He slowed and turned off the highway onto a side road and headed south. A block past the church, he turned right. Clouds swirled across the crescent moon, and the streetlights were sparse. Perfect conditions for their covert op.

He eased off the gas and crept down the street. "That's it on the left. The rock house with the porch swing. We'll park down a ways and wait."

"Hey, a house like that would be perfect for you. You could even walk to the church if you wanted. I mean, it's none of my business, but staying at the inn can't be cheap. Wouldn't you be better off purchasing or leasing a house?"

Ever the business woman.

"That is my house. Well, at least my name's on the lease." He stopped in the next block, pulled over, and parked. "When I met Beth and the kids at the shelter and learned they didn't have any place to live, I offered them this house until they could find something. Staying in a shelter's sure a lot better than living on the streets, but it's still no place for kids."

From the dashboard lights, he could make out the confusion on her face. Either she didn't believe him, or she didn't understand. "Anyway, I worked out a deal with the colonel. He's letting me stay at the inn for free. And as payback, I'm going to perform some piano concerts in the chapel over the next few months."

He cut the lights and the engine. She undid her seatbelt and turned to face him. Her eyes glistened. Tears. She whispered something he couldn't understand.

"What?" he asked.

"Are you for real?" Her voice cracked. "I've never known anyone who would do something like that." She turned her face away and looked out the passenger window.

"Why wouldn't I?" As the porch light on Beth's—his—house went out, he reached over and squeezed her shoulder. "You ready?"

~*~

She was ready, all right. Ready to throw her arms around him and pull him close. She hadn't felt this attracted to a man in years. No, never. He was perfect, almost too perfect. "Ready for what?"

He raised his eyebrows and grinned his perfect smile. "You're joking with me, right? It's zero hour, Agent Bennett. The whole reason we're here. Operation Christmas Gifts."

"Oh, that. Of course, I'm ready." She zipped up her jacket.

Chance pulled the knit cap over his head. "You bring a hat?"

"No. The only one I have is white, and I didn't think that would work." She hated hats. They were one step up from hairnets.

He pulled off his cap. "You can use mine. That is, if you don't mind. My hair's dark enough, but even with little moonlight, yours shines too much."

She twisted her hair into a bun, took the cap, and pulled it over her head. It smelled like the cologne on his sweatshirt. Warmth spread throughout her. As she pushed the tendrils around her face under the cap, others escaped. "Will this work?"

"Let me help." He leaned forward and pulled the right side of the cap away from her face and then gently pushed the stray strands under the cap. He repeated the process on the left side. Even in the frigid weather, his hands were warm against her face, and she wanted to let them cradle her head.

As the dim lights of the dashboard illuminated his smile, he rested his arm on the back of the seat and stared at her without moving. "Perfect."

Condensation had begun to accumulate on the windows. "What about zero hour, Agent Jackson? Shouldn't we get going?"

"Uh...yeah. I'll get the tree and decorations out of the bed of the truck and carry them up to the porch. You get the gifts out of the back seat and set them on the ground. Then we'll make one final trip together. That's all it should take."

Despite the slick ground, he had delivered the tree and was back at the truck by the time she finished unloading the black garbage bags full of gifts. His eyes sparkled in the slight moonlight. "What a rush! Made me feel like a kid again. See those bushes near the sidewalk? I think we can hide there and watch them without being seen."

As they grabbed their bags, he looked down at her. "Ready, Chuck? Stay low."

"Ready, Ashley." She tiptoed behind him down the street to Beth's yard. Twice she almost lost her footing. He hadn't been kidding when he'd said it was slick. As she took tiny, sliding steps, her heart raced, and she suppressed the urge to giggle. He was right. What a rush!

After Chance set his bags on the porch, he turned to help her up the steps with her bag. They crept over and set it beside the swing. Then he leaned over and whispered, "Why don't you go hide behind the bushes? I'll ring the doorbell and then join you."

She nodded. She turned to tiptoe down the stairs, but her leg brushed a flower pot hidden in the shadow. The ensuing crash exploded through the silence. Her klutziness would ruin everything. Frozen, she looked back up at Chance.

His eyes were huge as he leapt down the steps, grasped her hand, and began trying to pull her to their hiding place. Like cartoon characters with churning legs, they made no progress.

The porch light flashed on and the deadbolt on the door shot back. No way would they make it to the bushes near the street.

Chance grabbed her and dove for the end of the house. He fell on his back, pulling her on top of him, cushioning her fall. As the porch light cast a glow on the front yard, he rolled them into the shadow at the side of the house.

She'd almost ruined his op. She looked into his eyes and mouthed, Sorry.

He winked in reply. His body shook, not from the cold, but from silent laughter.

As excited voices sounded from the front porch, he pulled her head close and whispered, "I think we're OK here. Just lay really still until they get everything inside. Oh, and Chuck, you're fired."

"No way. I quit," she whispered back. "And you owe me combat pay for hazardous duty."

He shook with silent laughter again, and she raised up to look into his face. All was silent. The joyous clamoring of Beth and the kids faded away, and she heard nothing except her pulse pounding in her ears. He was the most attractive man she'd ever met. Physically, for sure, but his heart.... His heart was beautiful.

His eyes searched her soul, and his body stilled, the laughter gone. She tried and failed to slow her breathing. More than anything she wanted him to kiss her right now. And she saw it in his eyes...the same longing. But he just stared.

She'd never done this before. Never initiated a first kiss. Never even wanted to until now. Slowly she leaned forward and gently placed her lips on his. His response was tentative, unsure. He pulled up onto his side and slowly drew away. Then he rolled onto his back again, grasped her head, and drew it to his chest. His heart pounded like a bass drum. But now she knew, certainly not from passion.

Embarrassment nauseated her. He hadn't even kissed her back.

She raised her head and whispered, "I'm sorry. I shouldn't have done that."

~*~

Charlee stared out the passenger window. The second after he'd started the truck, Chance had reached over and turned the radio on to the local Christian station. He'd been completely silent thus far. And she had no more to say. She'd already apologized. He probably thought she was some loose woman throwing herself at a man she hardly knew...while she had another boyfriend. She couldn't wait until his truck pulled into her driveway and she could jump out and run into her house.

Chance turned onto her street. "Thanks again for coming tonight. I really appreciated your help with the shopping, wrapping, and the delivery." Formality shrouded his words.

"Thanks for including me in your mission. Christmas this year won't be the same as in the past." That was for sure. Nothing would be the same. Not only had she ruined their friendship. She'd ruined the prospect for it to grow into something more.

He pulled the truck into her driveway, and when she reached to open the door, he hit the lock button. "Can we talk a minute?"

"I was wrong. I already apologized. I'm not sure what else I can say."

He turned off the truck, undid his seatbelt, and leaned back against the driver-side door. "You can answer a question you avoided earlier."

She couldn't remember any question she'd failed to answer. "What? When?"

"Last night at The Perks. What exactly's up with you and Noah? I got the impression you guys were pretty serious." His forehead wrinkled.

"He wants to be serious, and I did too…because I thought he was the man who'd written the SDS letters. That's the part of him I liked the most. The person I thought he was," that Chance was, "but he's not." She rested her hand on the door handle again. "Anyway, it won't work out. I'll talk to him tomorrow."

He just stared at her and nodded slowly. His thumbs drummed a syncopated rhythm against the steering wheel.

"Anything else you want to know?"

He shook his head and hit the unlock button. "Thanks again for your help the past couple of days."

She opened the door and stepped out. "Sure. Anytime, Ashley."

No response. She closed the door and made herself walk, not run, to the porch. At least he was in the truck and couldn't see her face. It had to be purple by now.

His pickup just sat there. He hadn't even started the engine. Of course—he was waiting for her to get into the house. She dug around the bottom of her purse but couldn't find her keys in the dark. She waved for him to go on, but the engine never started. She rummaged through the main compartment with no luck. Then she stuck her hand into the side pocket.

Her fingers met cold metal. She grasped the keys and held them up toward him. Now he could go. She turned to insert the house key into the lock.

"Wait." The truck door slammed. Chance jogged over to the porch and bounded up the steps.

She backed against the door. If only she'd made it into the house quicker.

He faced her and placed one hand on each side of the doorframe. "I'm not," he whispered.

"Not? Not what?"

"Sorry." He smiled and leaned in until only their lips met. Electricity coursed through her body from the tiny area where skin touched skin. She wanted to pull him close, but the intensity froze her in place. Her breathing labored. He drew away, but her lips wanted more. He rested his forehead against hers. "I'm not sorry you kissed me," he whispered. "I'm just sorry I didn't kiss you back."

He moved his hands from the doorframe and closed the gap between them so their bodies touched. He placed his lips against her ear. "And, are you trying to steal my hat? First my sweatshirt, and now my hat?"

She couldn't speak. She'd never felt this level of attraction to a man before. Even Jake.

He reached up and gently lifted the knit cap off her head. "Your hair's beautiful. Don't hide it."

She rested her head against his shoulder as his fingertips caressed her hair.

"Rich auburn silk."

Her arms encircled his waist as she tried to melt into him.

"Good night, Chuck."

Goosebumps covered her entire body. He couldn't leave now.

She tightened her embrace. "It's still early. Can you come in for a little while?"

His lips and then his whisper kissed the hair above her ear. "Don't think that's wise, Charlee." He turned the keys in the lock and then opened the door. "I'll call you tomorrow."

He bounded down the steps and jogged over to his truck.

"Chance."

He turned back.

"I'm not sorry, either."

He gave her a thumbs up and smiled.

Perfect, just perfect.

~*~

The sweet melody of Christmas carols floated up the path from the chapel toward the inn. The deed was done. Charlee imagined she'd be happy, but she was sad. For Noah. To say he'd been surprised was an understatement. He hadn't seen it coming at all. Yet prolonging the breakup would have only made it harder.

And now, all she wanted to do was see Chance. He'd texted her this morning and said he'd be in the chapel tonight practicing, waiting. As the hours of the day crept passed, doubt had pushed its way into her soul. Last night's passion might not have been real but only a result of shared emotions after their "mission." And if so, Chance might have had time to realize that and change his mind.

Of course, there was always the possibility he could have just been playing her. No, if he'd been toying with her, he would have come inside last night. And old-fashioned girl or not, she would have had a hard time controlling herself.

She'd done the right thing, whether her relationship with Chance worked out or not. She was wrong for Noah. And he was wrong for her.

She opened the chapel door and looked at the man whose heart she loved. The man she'd loved before she knew it was him. The man in the SDS letters.

She'd never seen him like this. His non-PR hair was softly tousled. He wore plaid flannel pajama pants and suede moccasins with shearling lining. A red, white, and blue Lone Star flag splashed across the front of his gray sweatshirt. As she closed the door behind her, he looked up and then stood and smiled. "Hi."

"Hi, yourself." She willed herself to walk rather than run as he stepped out from behind the piano and moved toward her. "It's done. I'm no longer Noah's 'lady.' Not that I ever really was."

"No, I'd pretty much say you're your own woman."

But she'd love to be his girl.

He reached down and grasped both of her hands and then brought them up to his lips and kissed them.

Her hands tingled as he drew her down to sit in one of the pews. "Practicing for church tomorrow?"

"Yep, and for the Christmas concert next Saturday." His thumbs caressed the back of her hands.

She'd seen the poster in the parlor of the inn. "Payment for your room and board?"

He grinned. "Yeah." He looked down at the floor and then back up, his smile gone. He stroked her cheek with the back of his hand and then placed one hand on each of her shoulders. He stared into her eyes. "Where do you see this going, Charlee? What do you want to happen?"

The earthy scent of his cologne swirled around them. "Chance, I..." Warmth covered her cheeks.

"Charlee, what do you want?" He placed his forehead against hers.

"Want?" Goose bumps covered her body. She couldn't. Not here. Not in the chapel.

"Yes. What exactly do you want?"

She wanted the feelings of inadequacy and treachery to go away. She wanted someone to love her unconditionally, to put her first. She wanted to be rid of the constant running away without making any progress. She wanted off the treadmill. Her tears blurred his image. "I want," she whispered, "I want to be free of the past. To stop running away from something and run toward something."

"Yes. And I can't do that for you. I can try, but I'll fail. Only God can set you free."

She leaned her head against his shoulder. Tears dampened her cheeks. He was right. These last few years she'd been running away from the One she should have been running toward. Her perception was wrong, obscured by the darkness just as Chance had said the other day.

She glanced up at his face. His eyes were closed. He was praying. Exactly how she knew, she wasn't sure. But she did.

He opened his eyes, and his gaze found hers. "Charlee, I really care for you. A lot. And I don't want to do anything that could possibly hurt you. But you need to know…I'm damaged goods. It's only by the grace of God I'm still alive."

"Chance, we're all damaged goods. Only the degree and the type of damage differ from person to person." She covered his hands with hers. "Remember that darkness you told me about the other day? Don't surrender to it."

He stood, drawing her up with him. "I'm in, if you're in."

"I'm in."

"It won't be easy."

"Chance, I'm in."

He leaned forward and brushed a kiss on her forehead. Then her nose. Then her lips. Electricity from last night returned as she leaned into him. He drew away and placed his cheek against her head. They stood in silence as he slowly swayed her to some melody only he heard. "Hey. I almost forgot. I need a vocalist for next Sunday. What do you say?"

"Oh, now I get it. Put a girl in a weakened state and then take advantage of her."

"If that had been my goal, I'd have come into your house last night." His eyes sparkled as he grinned.

She smiled back in spite of herself. "I'll do it on one condition."

His eyebrows raised in question.

"That I can run my fingers through your hair."

His face turned bright red, and he shrugged his shoulders. "Whatever beats your drum."

As he leaned toward her, she buried her fingers in the soft, brown silk. She could do this forever.

21

Charlee should be understanding, but instead selfishness was winning the battle. She jammed her phone into her pocket and dropped onto the overstuffed chair in the Victorian Garden Room. First Thanksgiving, and now Christmas. Her sister-in-law was pregnant and sick, so Mom and Dad had changed their minds and weren't able to come to Charlee's for Christmas. She was almost thirty. Surely, she should be old enough to spend Christmas without her parents, but she wanted them here. Tears of frustration threatened.

Plus, she hadn't seen Chance since last Sunday. He'd been busy preparing for the concert tonight, and she'd been slammed at work. They'd called and texted, and she was singing with the worship team tomorrow. But she hadn't seen him or felt his touch for a week.

Some appointment of his had prevented them from sharing dinner last night. An "obligation." That was all his text had said. Her mind raced in all directions. Maybe he'd changed his mind. Maybe he was having second thoughts. Or maybe she'd read more into last weekend than he intended. The mystery of romantic relationships.

Neither one of them had mentioned the "D" word. Yet, they were dating, seriously dating, even if he'd never officially asked her out. Last weekend's conversations and kisses had been anything but casual.

Every morning this week she'd prayed about their relationship, and the same gentle words from earlier repeated themselves. *Trust Me.* She had committed to do that, and she really was trying.

Knowing only a wall separated her room at the inn from his had made finishing this month's work harder than usual, but she'd spent last night and all today with her head in the books, and it was done. He was great motivation. Now she was free, and she couldn't wait to see him.

She took one last look in the mirror, closed the door to the Victorian Garden Room, and headed down the hall to the front desk. The concert would start in a few minutes.

"Colonel Clark, could you put a ticket for the concert tonight on my room tab, please?"

"Sorry, young lady. Can't do that." He smiled.

"Oh, I can pay cash, then." She opened her purse.

"Can't do that, either, Charlee. It's sold out." His smile widened.

"Sold out?" Good for him, terrible for her. Now she really did want to cry. "I had no idea I wouldn't be able to get a ticket."

"Yes, that's why your young man reserved you a seat on the front row." He winked.

Her breathing quickened. "Chance?"

"How many young men do you have?" His eyes sparkled.

"Only one." She really wanted him to be hers and her to be his.

The colonel looked at the old pendulum clock on the wall behind the desk. "Almost time for things to start. Guess you better get going. I'll be there as soon as I can."

Charlee hurried down the path from the inn to the chapel. Candlelight, recorded carols, and a good portion of the population of Crescent Bluff filled Travelers' Rest. The colonel should be thrilled with the turnout.

The grand piano had been moved out from the alcove into the center of the stage area. The seats on the right front row had reserved signs on them. Charlee took the one that gave her the best view of the piano bench so she'd be able to see Chance's face.

Two older couples slipped into the other end of the row. One was Dr. and Mrs. Lewis. Charlee leaned forward and waved to the pastor and his wife. The couple with them seemed familiar, but she couldn't put names with their faces. Probably from the church, too. It had gotten so big that she no longer knew everyone.

Before she could go speak to them, the music stopped, and the small chapel grew quiet as Colonel Clark stepped up to welcome them. Her heart pounded with nervousness for Chance, although he'd never looked anything but comfortable in front of the church leading worship.

As the colonel left the stage, the lights dimmed, and Chance walked out from the side room. Her breath caught. He was dressed in white tie and black tails.

Memories of the day she'd made that comment about men and tuxedoes after she'd stumbled upon him playing Mussorgsky ebbed back over her. And she'd been so right about him in a tux. He looked even more handsome than she'd imagined. He was saying something in welcome to the audience, but all she could do was soak in the sight of him.

He moved to the bench, flipped out the tails of his coat just as she'd seen professional pianists do, and sat down. The room was silent as he placed his fingers on the keys. He looked straight up at her and smiled. As her heart raced, she smiled back. Then he closed his eyes and began playing.

~*~

Charlee watched as members of the audience went forward to compliment and congratulate him. The concert had been a beautiful combination of traditional carols and classical pieces culminating with an artistic medley of Pachelbel's *Canon in D* and "O Holy Night."

Her heart was soaring. As much as she wished he were there beside her, she had to share him right now. Much of the audience was church members. In the few weeks since he'd come to the church, he'd become well-loved by the membership and by one member in particular.

Later. Her time would come later. She'd take him in her arms and tell him what a beautiful job he'd done and how handsome he looked and how wonderful he was. And how she would never hurt him as he'd been hurt before.

Small groups of people lingered in the warm setting. Dr. and Mrs. Lewis and the other couple went up to him. Chance and the pastor shook hands, Mrs. Lewis hugged him, and then the other man grabbed Chance in a bear-hug just as she'd seen her father and brother do many times. Then Chance turned to the lady, hugged her, and kissed her on the cheek. Whoever they were, they knew Chance well.

They moved toward her, Chance leading the lady by her hand, the man following behind. As Chance spoke, she saw the resemblance. "Charlee, I want you to meet my parents, Ashley and Rebecca Jackson. Mom and Dad, this is Charlee Bennett."

Chance's father took her hand. "So you're Chuck." When he smiled, she saw Chance in thirty years. "Sorry about that mix-up, Charlee."

Charlee wasn't. Thanksgiving was the best mistake she'd ever experienced. "Please don't apologize. It turned out quite well."

Rebecca stepped forward. "Yes, that's what AC told us, too. Thanks for feeding my boy. Hello, Charlee." She grasped her hand. Her hairstyle was short and contemporary. And even though her hair was silver, she looked closer to thirty than sixty. Too young to have a son Chance's age.

AC...Ashley Chance. "No problem. Any time."

Ashley and Rebecca shot each other sideways glances and smiled. They reminded her of her parents—reading each other's thoughts.

"We've heard so much about you. We're very glad to finally meet you." Rebecca smiled.

"Thank you. I'm honored to meet you both."

Ashley and Rebecca both stood there staring and grinning. If they'd pulled out magnifying glasses, Charlee wouldn't have felt any more scrutinized.

An awkward silence invaded the space between them. They obviously had more to say, but before they could, a rattling to Charlee's right broke the silence as Chance cleared his throat.

His parents snapped out of their trance.

"Well, we really must get back up to the inn," his mother said. "We hope you'll come visit us in Austin soon, Charlee." Still grinning, Chance's parents hooked arms and walked up the center aisle to the back door.

The chapel was empty, and she and Chance were alone together for the first time in a week. She wanted to melt into him.

"Well." His eyes sparkled as he shook his head. "That was awkward. Sorry if you felt uncomfortable. It's just been a really long time since I've thought about dating anyone, or even had a close female friend like you. So they are uber-excited, to say the least."

Friend…they were just friends. Her heart ached. "Sure, I understand." But she didn't. She'd read much more than friendship into that kiss the other night. Yet men and women often viewed relationships through different lenses. And she really didn't know him that well. It was so unfair that the man she wanted to date wanted to be just friends, and the man she wanted to be friends with wanted to date.

Trust Me.

She hid the tears that threatened behind an insincere smile. "Your friendship means a lot to me, too." The words stuck in her throat.

Chance leaned his head to one side, looked at her out of the corners of his eyes, and smiled. He reached down and grasped her hands, "Charlee, you're definitely the best friend I have here in Crescent Bluff."

As he spoke that word again, she stared down at her feet.

"Hey." He placed his fingers under her chin and gently lifted her head until he gazed directly into her eyes.

She held her breath.

"Maybe I didn't define the boundaries of our relationship clearly the other night. And, I'm sorry. I can see how you might have misinterpreted my intentions. After all, I go around kissing every woman I meet." His whisper tickled her ear. "But just so you'll know, I only let women I date touch my hair. So, Charlee Bennett, will you let me date you?" He drew her close.

Relief giggled through her. "I'd like nothing more." She reached up and fingered his smoothed back hair. "The concert was lovely, and the chapel was packed. The colonel should be pleased."

"Thanks. Like my tux?" He posed.

"Love it. I can't believe you remembered. You look so…" unbelievably handsome "so professional. You know, like a real musician."

"As opposed to a fake one?" His eyes sparkled with laughter.

With pretended gravity, she pushed back. "You know what I meant. Were you nervous?"

"Maybe a little...mostly before the concert started. It's been a long time since I've performed like that. You know, alone on the stage with all the attention on me."

"What about Sundays at church?"

He smiled. "That's totally different. It's not a performance, and all the attention is directed toward worshipping God."

"I prayed for you."

"I can't tell you how much that means to me." As he encircled her with his arms, she turned her face up to his. He bent closer.

"You kids about done in here?" the colonel boomed from the back door.

Chance released her and replied, "Yes, sir. Even if we're not, we need to be."

~*~

Chance unplugged his guitar and packed it into the case. This morning's service had been amazing. Charlee and his parents stood in the aisle talking as the congregation slowly filed out while a Christmas song played over the sound system.

Charlee's vocals were unbelievable. She had no idea how talented she was, what a gift she had. And that made her even more appealing. Good thing the colonel spoke up when he did last night.

Chance hadn't felt this way about a woman in a long time. Rewind...never. And that scared him. He understood exactly what she'd been through with Jake, because he'd been through it with Amanda. Charlee deserved someone without baggage, someone she could commit to without reservation. And as much as he wanted to be that someone, he wasn't. And never could be. She deserved so much more than him.

Yet, they'd come together, and not by their own design or plan, but by that of the Master Designer. God had kept everything under control for an eternity, so He certainly didn't need Chance's help now. Maybe Chance just needed to chill and step out of the way.

Charlee's hair shone as she nodded at something Mom said, and for a second, he held his breath.

He flipped closed the latches, picked up the guitar case, and walked down the steps into the aisle. Last night's awkward silence between his parents and Charlee was gone. Mom was animated and smiling.

"Hi, guys. Thanks for coming."

"Great service, son," Dad said. "We're so proud of you."

"Thanks." He set his guitar case on the chairs.

Mom hugged him and kissed him on the cheek. "And I was just telling Charlee how good the two of you sound singing together. Your voices really complement one another."

He looked over at Charlee and grinned. "Yeah, I'd love it if she'd sing with me every Sunday."

Her face turned bright red.

"But she's being difficult. Seems she has commitment issues." The words were out of his mouth before he realized their possible impact, but relief filled him when Charlee grinned.

"Well, we got a commitment out of her." Mom grasped his hand. "Charlee's spending Christmas with us in Austin."

Charlee looked at him with raised eyebrows and a tentative smile.

"Really? Awesome." Christmas together at his house, with his family. More than awesome.

Charlee's smile widened.

As he grinned and put his arm around her, his tattoo showed. Poema. He couldn't wait to read the next line.

22

In a church where every seat was occupied, Charlee sat alone amid a sea of Christmas Eve worshippers. Darkness cloaked the sanctuary except for the small circle of light on the stage and the golden glow in the corners cast by flickering white pillar candles in black iron candelabras. Christmas was family time, and she had none. Her parents and brother were in California, and Ally was spending the holidays with Trey's family in Dallas.

Rebecca's invitation was a blessing. Being alone on Christmas Day would have been more than Charlee could have handled. Mom had called day before yesterday and tried to talk her into flying out to California for the holidays, but she couldn't leave the shop this time of year. And Mom knew that. She just didn't want her only daughter to spend Christmas alone.

For two seconds, Mom had sounded relieved when Charlee told her she was going to Austin, but then the barrage of questions poured out of the phone. Why haven't you told us you were dating someone? Who? What does he do? What do you mean you haven't gone out on a real date?

Charlee had already dealt with this last question but failed to explain it to Mom's satisfaction. After all, dating was about getting to know someone and sharing your heart and mind, not about where you went or what you did. So a couple could date without going to dinner or a movie. Lots of people did long-distance or virtual dating.

Chance had asked her to date, and as far as she was concerned, they were. Besides, official or not, their covert op was the best first date she'd ever had.

Anyway, going out on a date currently ranked low on their priority lists. Between her working late on Friday nights and him preparing for church on Saturday nights, their jobs consumed them both. At least she figured that's what he was doing. Although…he'd never come right out and said, and she'd never asked. But he was always busy on Saturday nights, so the assumption was only logical.

When Mom hadn't bought her explanation, Charlee invented a reason to get off the phone. She loved Mom, but after Jake left, Mom wouldn't accept the idea that Charlee might never want to get married. The next time she saw her folks, they'd give her the third degree.

Dr. Lewis finished praying. He walked down the steps, leaving the platform empty except for Chance, a violinist, and a cello player. No drums or electric guitars tonight, only gentle acoustic tones. Even in its simplicity, Chance's music awoke something in her heart that had been dormant far too long. Worship.

Chance was gifted, his music artistry. But beyond the beauty, he moved people from being observers to participants. Jake had never been able to do that. Never really wanted to. Everything had been all about him.

The flicker of tiny flames passed from one worshiper to another as they lit their candles for the final song. Chance transitioned into "Silent Night." As the light grew from the one initial flame, the darkness disappeared. Just as it had in her life. She'd been living in the darkness of deception until Chance's words had kindled a tiny flame in her heart. Peace blanketed her while the velvet tones of the cello enhanced the richness of his voice.

Music had always been her pathway to worship, and after Jake left, she'd slammed the gate across that route shut. She'd allowed his behavior to influence her belief about music and musicians. And she'd been so wrong. The difference between these two men was like night and day…darkness and light.

Forgive me, Father.

As they sang the final verse and the congregation filed out, she sat and waited for Chance to pack up.

They had a four-hour drive to Austin tonight. Good, quality time to talk with no interruptions. The perfect opportunity to get some answers to her questions.

~*~

Charlee opened her eyes. The aroma of cinnamon and mocha accompanied by the rich tones of a piano playing Christmas carols squeezed its way under the door into the guest room. The best alarm clock ever.

So much for last night's quality time. She'd fallen asleep before they made it to the highway as last week's twelve-hour-plus days took their toll. A foggy memory of Chance helping her out of the truck and showing her into the guest room was more like a dream than reality. Except, here she was.

She stretched and then picked up her phone. Ten o'clock! She'd never slept this late on Christmas. She might be holding up breakfast. She jumped out of bed and exchanged yesterday's clothes for some clean jeans and a sweater. After brushing her teeth, she ran her fingers through her hair. No time for makeup. She looked in the mirror and smiled. Besides, covering up the freckles Chance liked so much would be a crime.

She opened the door and followed her nose and ears down the hall. Rebecca sat on a barstool at the kitchen island, her open Bible and a Santa mug before her. Charlee glanced into the family room. No one else. The guys must still be asleep.

A Christmas wreath plate filled with what were obviously homemade muffins called to Charlee from the middle of the granite slab. Her stomach growled in response. "Good morning. Merry Christmas."

Rebecca looked up, smiled, and closed her Bible. "Merry Christmas, Charlee." She lifted her mug. "Coffee? Tea? I also have some hot chocolate on the stove." A rich, musical tone filled her voice. Chance probably got his vocal talent from her.

"Chocolate sounds great, please." Charlee scooted onto the stool next to Rebecca's.

"Help yourself to some muffins. Applesauce, AC's favorite. I always fix them for his birthday and other special occasions." Rebecca placed a steaming reindeer mug and Christmas plate before her.

Charlee sipped the rich, velvety liquid. "Mmmm, made from

scratch. And the muffins smell amazing, but I can wait until the guys get up."

Rebecca laughed. "Oh, honey, those two men left about six. AC said to let you sleep and to join them after you woke up…if you wanted."

"Join them? Where?" If she'd been able to stay awake last night, she might have known what the plans were.

"The Hope House. A homeless shelter downtown. Would you like to go?" As she held out the plate of muffins, Rebecca smiled. "We wouldn't need to be there until eleven-thirty."

"Sounds great!" Charlee loved the similarities between their families, but she'd never thought about serving the homeless on Christmas as well as Thanksgiving. She bit into a muffin. A cinnamon-sweetness filled her senses. "These are heavenly."

Rebecca smiled and rested her hand on Charlee's arm. "I'll give you the recipe. AC would love that."

"Chance…AC never mentioned that your Christmas tradition was to serve at a shelter." The rich chocolate tasted just like Grammy Bennett's.

"We've only done it a couple of years. Since AC came back home. After all that…you know…stuff." Rebecca raised her eyebrows, inviting Charlee to agree.

"Oh…sure." But she didn't know what Rebecca was referring to. Apparently, something she thought Charlee knew. Or should know. But something she didn't know. Images of Ace Jackson from the computer invaded her thoughts. She pushed them away as she had weeks ago. Any explanation needed to come from him, not from the Internet.

Rebecca patted her hand again. "Anyway, that's water under the bridge, and Ashley and I are so happy AC has found you. We've prayed for this…for you…for many years."

Goose bumps tingled her arms. Chance obviously had revealed more about his desires to his parents than he had to her. The kisses they'd shared had spoken volumes from his heart, but she still waited to hear his feelings voiced aloud. She'd never felt this depth of physical attraction toward a man before. Even Jake. But more than just hormones drew her to him. She loved the beauty of his heart.

They'd not yet discussed their pasts with Amanda and Jake much beyond what they'd written anonymously in the SDS letters. For their relationship to move forward that discussion needed to happen.

And it would.

23

Charlee eased back into the redwood loveseat. Chance's eyes were closed. His fingers moved in time with the melody of the Christmas carol floating across the patio. Flames in the stone fire pit took the edge off the winter cold. Charlee could have stayed here forever.

When she and Rebecca had arrived at the shelter, she'd found Chance sitting at a table talking with a group of men. His posture was one of openness. As they spoke, he leaned forward, intent on their comments, occasionally placing his hand on a shoulder or patting a back, just as he'd done at Thanksgiving.

He'd looked up and grinned when he saw her. As he stood and moved toward her, she clasped her hands together to keep from drawing him into her arms. He was all in black, unshaven, with bed-head-gelled hair. Mr. PR. Mr. Handsome.

Now, she looped her arm through his. As she leaned her head back, a relaxed sigh escaped.

Chance opened his eyes and grinned. He covered her hand with his. "You OK?"

"Yes. Sorry I didn't get up in time to go along with you to the shelter."

"You've had a busy few weeks at work. Although, I have to say, it doesn't do much for a guy's ego when his date's so bored she falls asleep as soon as they hit the road."

"I wasn't bored last night. Just exhausted. I didn't mean to—"

"Kidding, just kidding." His tone was sing-song as he chuckled and laced his fingers with hers. "You've had several full weeks. You deserve the rest. Just relax and enjoy the next couple days."

The patio door creaked open as Rebecca walked out, plastic container in hand. "Sugar cookies, anyone?" If Charlee spent much time around here she'd be the size of a small blimp. "Sounds wonderful, Rebecca." OK, a large blimp, but Christmas came only once a year.

"Thanks, Mom." Chance took the cookies and offered them to Charlee. "Have some."

Rebecca pulled her sweater around her and settled into the chair next to Chance. "Your sister just called. Looks like the weather in Denver's lifting, and they'll be in about noon tomorrow."

"That's great news. I'm glad we decided to wait to celebrate. Wouldn't be the same without Maggie here."

As the piano began the "Coventry Carol," Charlee closed her eyes and leaned her head back against the chair, the music flowing over her. This arrangement enhanced the beauty of the piece without destroying its graceful simplicity. "I love this song. It's one of my favorite carols."

"Mine, too." Rebecca laughed. "Performed by my favorite artist, as well."

"Mom."

"Well, it is, and you are." She reached over and patted Chance's knee.

Charlee raised up and looked at him. "This is you?" Even in the dim glow of the firelight, she could see the blush coloring his face. "I should have known. It's lovely."

"AC gave this to us for Christmas his first year at Juilliard. You do know he studied there." Rebecca's comment bubbled out.

"Mom. Yes, she knows. Thanks, Charlee." His embarrassment made him boyishly cute. "Can we change the subject, please?"

Rebecca laughed. "I'll bet I could get you a copy, Charlee. I'm well-connected with the artist."

"You are? Well, I'd absolutely love one."

He actually squirmed.

Chance held the cookies out to his mother. "Here, have one…or some. However many it takes to fill your mouth. Please."

Charlee giggled, leaned back against the loveseat, and looked up. Millions of tiny diamonds sparkled in the clear winter sky. One of them moved. "Look, a shooting star!" She pointed.

Chance sat up. "Naw. A jet, probably headed into Houston. There's too much light to see any shooting stars from here."

"Oh. Well, how would I know? I've never seen one." She was too young for a "bucket list," but if she hadn't seen a shooting star by the time she started one, it would definitely be one of the top entries. "Seeing my first one on Christmas would've been amazing, wouldn't it?"

Chance stood and held out his hand. "Your Christmas wish is about to be granted. Come on."

"You two better bundle up good. I'll get you some blankets to take." Rebecca obviously knew where they were going. She winked at Charlee. "Chance's dad took me there to see my first shooting star when we were dating, too."

~*~

Chance turned the truck onto a narrow, rutted road overgrown with brush. Obviously, no one had been this way for quite a while. His last time had been a couple of years ago when he'd moved back. The farther they drove, the darker it became, and the slower he crept.

One good thing, at least Mom wouldn't interrupt. She meant well, but he and Charlee needed to talk. Last night on the road would have been the perfect time if she hadn't slept the whole trip. He'd planned to share with her tonight until Mom showed up with the cookies. Well, nothing would bother them here.

Charlee had agreed to date him, but before they went any further, they had to talk. She needed to know exactly what she was getting into. Whether confession truly was good for the soul, or honesty really was the best policy, both were the right things to do. Relationships should be founded on truth. Although he'd prayed about this for weeks, tonight's discussion still wouldn't be easy.

"Do you even know where you're going?" she poked.

He barely made out her pursed lips in the dim light of the dashboard. But the attitude rang in her voice. "No. Are you kidding?" He suppressed a grin. "It's more fun this way. Who knows what we'll run into?"

"Chance, don't. Really." The spunk had disappeared. "I doubt there's even cell service out here."

"Probably not, but don't worry. I know exactly where we are. Been here many times." He reached over and squeezed her knee. "We just have to get as far away as possible from the lights of the city."

"Yeah, that's what's scary. What about coyotes or wildcats?" Her eyes were huge.

"Don't worry, I said. It's probably too cold for them, anyway. I promise, we'll be fine."

"You can't know that." The feistiness returned.

"Yes, I can."

"No, you can't."

"Look, I've got my dad's pistol in the back of the truck. Satisfied?" She was right about the animals, but he hadn't wanted to scare her. She should be more scared about being hurt by him, anyway.

That first kiss in Beth's yard—or his yard, actually—during the Christmas covert op, had revealed her feelings. And he'd tried hard not to kiss her back when he took her home. But he'd failed.

"OK." Her voice calm, she turned away from him and faced forward.

The pickup broke through the brush onto an expansive open plain. "We're here."

He put the truck into park and unfastened his seatbelt. "Better wrap up good. It's windy out there." He pulled his knit cap over his head.

She wrapped her scarf tight around her neck.

"Got a hat?" he asked.

"No." She shook her head and pulled her gloves out of her pocket.

He turned on the dome light so he could see her face better. "I was hoping you'd say that." He reached behind the seat and pulled out the small gift bag. "Merry Christmas, Charlee."

"Chance?" Frustration filled her voice. "I thought we'd agreed to give donations to the shelter instead of exchanging gifts."

He shrugged his shoulders. "Just open it."

She withdrew the card acknowledging his donation in her honor, looked at him, and smiled. Then she pulled out the black stocking cap.

"I figured you could use that for any future covert ops we might have."

She grinned and pulled it over her silken hair.

Gorgeous. "Looks awesome. There's one more small thing."

She reached back in and removed the Christmas ornament.

"Two hearts joined by music notes." He couldn't believe he'd found something so perfect.

Her eyes glistened when she looked back up at him.

"I remembered how you have so many milestones of your life hung on your Christmas tree." Pausing, he brushed the back of his hand against her cheek. Soft as velvet. "I want to be one of them."

"It's lovely," she whispered. "Perfect. Thank you." She leaned forward for him to kiss her, but he couldn't. Not yet. He pecked her on her forehead.

She frowned and then reached down into her purse. "Your turn." She handed him a gift bag. "Merry Christmas, Chance."

"I thought we'd agreed to give donations to the shelter instead of exchanging gifts," he parroted her.

She grinned and parroted back, "Just open it."

He untied the Bits of Britain curling ribbon and reached into the bag. He removed the donation card. "Thanks, Charlee. That means more than you'll ever know." Wrong. She'd know soon enough.

"You're welcome. Keep digging." She smiled.

He pulled out a box. "Croutons!" He laughed. The bag was still heavy. He reached in again and withdrew a bottle of his favorite cologne. Maybe Mom told her. "How did you know?"

"Yes!" She threw both hands up in victory. "I sniffed so many bottles of men's cologne at the store. The salesman probably thought I was trying to get high or something. But when I came to this one, I knew. It smelled like you."

He put the items in the bag and set it behind the seat. Fighting to keep from kissing her, he grasped her hands and looked deep into her eyes. "Thank you so much, Charlee." He ached with desire, and giving in would be so easy. But, no. He turned off the dome light and the engine. *Father, guide my words. Prepare her heart.* "Ready for the stars?"

~*~

Charlee carried the blankets Rebecca had given them while Chance carried the tarp…and the gun. She'd never dated a guy who had a gun, or at least, one she knew had one. In some weird way, it made her feel safe and nervous all at the same time.

The flashlight from his phone provided just enough light to be able to make out the narrow trail as he led the way.

She'd longed so badly for him to kiss her a few minutes ago, and his eyes had told her he felt the same. Yet, for some reason, he hadn't. After she'd initiated their disastrous first kiss, she'd promised herself she'd only follow his lead, but she was tired of waiting. Something was up, and she had to find out what. No more guessing and assumptions.

"Here we go." He stopped beyond a small rise and spread the tarp on the ground. "This'll give us some shelter from the wind." He reached out his hand. "Blanket please, Chuck."

After he spread one of the blankets, he took her hand, helped her sit, and then dropped down beside her. "OK, lay down, and look up."

She did as he said. "I don't see any shooting stars."

He chuckled. "All righty, Miss Impatient. You gotta give your eyes time to adjust. You'll see some. I promise." He covered her with the second blanket and then scooted in next to her.

"Where's the gun?"

"Over here on the ground."

"Can you reach it if we need it?"

"Yes." He grasped her hand and entwined his fingers with hers. "Would you just forget about it?"

"I'll try." She stared upward, scanning the sky. Nothing.

He drew her hand inside his jacket to his chest. His heart was racing. "I need to talk with you."

Her heartbeat matched the rhythm of his. "Me, too. But you go first." Hopefully he'd explain what had been going on so she wouldn't have to ask. She breathed in deeply and steeled herself in case his words were not what she hoped to hear. But the ornament. No, he cared for her just as she did for him.

"OK." For what seemed like forever, the only sound besides the winter wind rustling the tall dried grass behind them was his rhythmic breathing. Then he took one deep breath and spoke. "Charlee, before we get any more involved, there's some stuff you need to know about me…about my past." He exhaled with force.

As he struggled, she squeezed his hand and scooted closer.

"I had no clue, no hint, until the chapel doors never opened that day that there was a problem between Amanda and me," he continued. "I'd put all my hope and future in her, and the shock rocked the foundations of my soul."

She understood exactly how he'd felt. Confused, betrayed, foolish. Worthless.

"I turned away from God and toward the only other thing I really knew. My music. I moved to Nashville, hooked up with some other musicians, began writing, and made a successful career. But it wasn't enough to erase the hurt, so I began drinking, and when that no longer dulled the pain, I turned to stronger stuff."

Oh, please, no. She'd been right about him from the moment he'd sat down at her dinner table that first night.

"One day I was scheduled to play keys for a recording session. That's how I met Trey and the guys. They were getting ready to go on tour, and they'd just lost their keyboard player, so they offered me the job, and I took it."

As he paused, the pounding of her heart pulsed through her entire being. Tears burned her eyes.

"I loved touring. The new places and people. The audiences' enthusiasm. Everything was so exciting. But the best thing? Nothing reminded me of Amanda. When the tour was over and the guys returned home to Texas, I moved back to Nashville. Got a job as a studio musician. Wrote some more songs. I thought I had everything under control until the cost of my habit became more than my income."

The darkness of the last few years tried to push its way back into her heart.

Trust Me.

She jumped. The syllables carried on the wind were as audible as if Chance had whispered them. She remembered his words about the darkness the evening after he'd helped her in the shop that first time. No, she wouldn't let those old lies distort the new truth she'd discovered.

He was a musician, yes. A Jake? No.

She withdrew her hand from his and snuggled closer. She picked up his arm and draped it around her shoulders. She laid her head on his chest. His heart pounded with such force she was afraid she might not be able to hear his words.

He brushed a kiss against the top of her head. "I sold the rights to my songs to get drug money, and when the money ran out, I got kicked out of my apartment. I was homeless."

"But what about your parents?"

"I wanted to come home, so I hitchhiked back to Austin. And then I couldn't do it. I couldn't move back in. I'd be too much of a disappointment."

She knew his parents. "I can't imagine your folks ever thinking of you as a disappointment." She tightened her embrace.

"Of course, you're right. But I was in too much of a fog to understand. To ask for their help. That's when I met Josh—Dr. Lewis. One Christmas, he was serving at the shelter I went to. He really looked at me, talked to me. Shook my hand, touched my shoulder. After being ignored and stepped over for all those months, I can't tell you how good the touch of another human being felt. Josh saw me not as a thing but as a person. A creation. Made in the image of God."

Memories of Chance on Thanksgiving and again this morning filled her mind. Now she understood the hands on the shoulders, the claps on the backs, the attentiveness.

"Anyway, he got me into rehab and hooked up with a twelve-step group. Helped me find my way back to God. It took me months to work up the courage to contact my folks. I'd disappointed and hurt them bad. But they've been great." He paused and then whispered,

"Charlee, I'm in recovery, but I'm an addict, and I'll always be an addict."

As the frigid blast of the December cold blew over them, she eased up onto one elbow and felt in the darkness for his face. Then she scooted nearer and gently kissed his forehead, his right cheek, the tip of his nose, his chin, his left cheek. It tasted salty. Tears.

"Chance, remember a few weeks ago when you told me my perception was wrong and that I'd been deceived by darkness? Well, since then, God's been teaching me something. We're not defined by what's happened in our lives or who other people say we are, but by what God's done in our lives and who He says we are." She laid her head back on his chest. "And He says you're His workmanship. A masterpiece. A poema."

His arms wrapped her in a tight embrace. "Charlee," he whispered. His first kiss was gentle, tender. His hands caressed her face, her shoulders. He drew away as if waiting for her permission. Her approval.

"I'm all in, Chance," she whispered. "I'm not going anywhere."

He rolled over until she lay on the ground with him above her. Grasping his soft, wool cap, she guided his head down to hers in invitation.

The next kiss was anything but gentle. Fire raged through her. She'd never felt passion, longing, like this. His hands pulled his gift off her head as he ran his fingers through her hair. Her arms hugged him to her body as hard as she could. She no longer wanted to be an old-fashioned girl.

He drew away. Their labored breathing mixed with the Texas wind. She lifted her face up toward his. But he grasped her hand and flopped down onto his back. "Whoa. Danger zone."

No arguing with that statement. She looked up and saw them. Streaks of fire striped the sky from horizon to horizon. "Chance, look! The stars!"

"Where? I don't see anything."

"Really?" The sky was ablaze. Maybe this was some sort of oxygen-deprivation hallucination. "But they look so real."

He drew her hand to his lips and kissed it, and she felt his laugh.

"Yes, baby, I see them. And as much as I'd like to take the credit, I can't. They're real. I told you we'd see some tonight."

~*~

Chance drew her close as they walked arm in arm back toward the truck. She now knew his secrets. Tonight, another line of his poema had been written. *Father, thank You for bringing Charlee into my life. Please lead us.*

"Did you get the gun?"

Charlee and the gun. "In my waistband."

"In your waistband? Like in the movies? What if it goes off?"

"It won't."

"How can you be so sure?"

Attitude again. "The safety's on. Besides, it's not loaded."

"What? What do you mean, it's not loaded?"

"I never said I had a loaded gun." She didn't need to know the ammo was in his coat pocket.

"So how would you protect us from the coyotes and wildcats? Throw it at them?"

"I would have thought of something." He drew her close. "Besides, there was a lot more to be concerned about out there tonight than wildlife."

She laughed and leaned her head on his shoulder. "You can say that again."

24

Chance stood at the front of the chapel, palms sweating, heart racing. As the *Wedding March* began, the doors at the back opened, and there she stood. The most beautiful woman he'd ever seen. If he didn't make himself breathe, he'd pass out.

Charlee made her way down the aisle, her gaze locked onto his, and he saw a mixture of fear and affection. She'd never said the word "love," but then again, neither had he. Yet, love was what he felt.

He'd only said that word to one other woman, and that hadn't worked out so well.

He'd never imagined he could get to this point again, but he was really glad Amanda hadn't walked down that aisle six years ago. Those first few years had been painful, but God had used them to teach him something. His Father was taking the mess he'd made of his life and transforming it into something beautiful. And Charlee…she was worth everything he'd been through. He needed to tell her his feelings soon so she'd know his intentions. Maybe next year, she'd be the one in the white dress.

She stopped when she reached Chance's right. She smiled at him and then turned to face the back doors. He pulled his mind away from what might be to what was.

The doors opened again, and Ally started down the aisle. Chance reached over and placed a hand on Trey's shoulder. The groom was as white as a sheet.

~*~

The bell on the front door signaled the first customer of the day. Charlee could have probably handled the winter slump herself, but she wouldn't tell Chance that. He'd been kind to volunteer to help while Ally and Trey were on their honeymoon. Any excuse to spend time together. Saturday mornings were generally quiet, so he wasn't coming in until later.

She did a quick hair and makeup check in the mirror and headed out of the office to help the waiting patron.

Noah stood looking at some wool tartan scarves on the markdown table. Her heart sank. "Hello, Noah. How are you?"

He looked up. "Charity. How have you been?"

"Good, thank you." The last time she'd seen him was when she'd broken up with him. Then he'd been confused and angry. Today his face was expressionless. "And you?"

"I'm…fine." He placed his hands in his pockets and rocked up onto his toes. Something was on his mind. "My mum's a bit under the weather, so I thought I'd pick up some marmalade to cheer her. She quite enjoyed the brand you suggested last time."

"I'm glad." She walked to the shelf of jams and preserves, grabbed a jar of the same marmalade, and then headed to the register. "Are you staying at the inn this weekend?"

"Yes. Working on my manuscript. I'd hoped this was your weekend to stay at the inn as well." He walked toward the counter, a tartan scarf in one hand, credit card in the other. "I'll take this, too."

"My reservation's in two weeks." She swiped his card and handed it back.

"Oh, perhaps we could have dinner together tonight then." Raising his eyebrows slightly, he waited for her response.

That was what he was up to. "I'm sorry. I can't, Noah. I, uh, have other plans." Chance had his weekly twelve step meeting tonight—not planning for Sunday's service as she'd always assumed. But after that, he was coming to her house for dessert. "Here are some samples of orange flavored shortbread for your mom. Since she likes the marmalade, I'm sure she'll like these, too." She dropped the cookies into the bag and tied some strands of ribbon onto the handles.

"That's kind of you." As she handed him the bag, he grasped her hand and smiled tentatively, his eyes searching. "Couldn't you rearrange your plans? I'd really like to see you again."

His tone was quiet, less blustery than usual. He wasn't himself.

"Really, I can't."

The bell sounded, and Chance walked through the door. She pulled her hand from Noah's. "Good morning, Chance. Look who's here."

Chance made his way to them and placed his left arm around her shoulders. "Noah. Good to see you again." The picture of the rams from a few weeks ago resurrected itself.

"The same, Chance." The two men shook hands. "Well, I best get back to the inn. Please consider my offer, Charity."

Noah left, and the bell jingled again. "Morning, babe." Chance leaned down and kissed her. She wanted to lock the door, close out the whole world, and snuggle by the fireplace…just the two of them. But as enticing as it sounded, that would be dangerous.

No one would have possibly guessed last night was the first time he'd performed a wedding. He did a great job. When those doors had opened, and she saw him standing there, she had wanted to be the one walking down the aisle to her future husband. If he'd proposed, she would have accepted and married him on the spot.

She placed her arms around his waist and leaned her head against his chest. "Good morning."

"So what was Noah up to?"

She pulled away and looked at him out of the corner of her eyes. "He asked me out on a date tonight."

Chance crossed his arms and raised his eyebrows. "He did, did he? And what did you say?"

"I told him I'd check my calendar." She pulled her phone out of her pocket and looked back up at him. "Hmm. Seems I do have this one minor obligation, but I'll just reschedule it."

He held up both hands, palms forward. "Far be it from me to stand in the way of true love." His eyes twinkled as he drew her close and kissed her. She could stay in his arms forever.

The bell on the door jingled as Mrs. Williams stepped inside. "I'm glad to see you took my advice about keeping Chance on, dear." She winked.

~*~

Before Chance could press the bell, her front door swung open. Charlee looked amazing. So fresh, so innocent. By now he should've been used to those freckles. "Hi." As he bent down and kissed her cheek, citrus filled his senses. She smelled as fresh as she looked. After Christmas night in the star-field, he promised himself not to let things get to that point again. Tonight, staying in control would be a challenge. But he had to. He had something to discuss.

"Hi, Chance." Her emerald eyes sparkled in the porch light.

He stepped into the foyer and hung his jacket on the hall tree. A fire crackled in the fireplace, and plates of applesauce muffins and mugs of hot chocolate waited on a tray on the coffee table. He slipped his arm around the woman he loved. "Wow."

"Not exactly a traditional dessert, but I wanted to make something I knew you'd like. Your mom gave me the recipe at Christmas." She perched on one end the sofa.

"Thanks. They smell wonderful." As he sat on the other end, she scooted close and snuggled against him. Could life get any better than this? Oh, yeah, it could. But not tonight. Not 'til after they were married. He'd better not go there.

She handed him a muffin. "Anything I should know about the service tomorrow?"

"No. It's pretty straightforward. Any questions about the music?" This was heaven.

"I think I've got everything down." She sipped her hot chocolate.

"These are awesome, Charlee." He set the plate down and grasped one of her hands. "You couldn't have made anything I would have liked better. Thank you."

She set down her mug and snuggled back against him.

Perspiration prickled his upper lip. He needed to stay on track here. "Hey, scoot down to the other end of the sofa, and give me your feet."

Her brow wrinkled, but she did as he asked. He removed her slippers and began rubbing her feet. Many evenings he'd watched Dad do this for Mom after a hard day of work, and Chance had always known he'd do the same for his wife. He'd never rubbed Amanda's feet.

"Mmmm. That feels wonderful." She leaned her head back and closed her eyes. "Work was a lot busier than I anticipated. Thanks again for helping."

"Sure." She was relaxed. Game time. "Hey, I wanted to tell you about a business opportunity that's come up."

~*~

Charlee jerked her feet away and sat straight up. He was leaving Crescent Bluff. She'd known all along he was too talented to stay in their little town, but she hadn't thought it would happen this quickly. After all, he'd been here less than six months. As her stomach twisted into a huge knot, she pushed back tears.

His eyes opened wide. He scooted toward her and drew her into his arms. "Hey, what is it?"

She forced out her words in a painful whisper. "Don't go. Not yet. Please, don't leave."

"What?" He kissed her forehead. "I'm not going anywhere. In fact, just the opposite."

Drawing far enough away to see his face, she breathed deeply to calm herself.

"Keep a secret?" His eyes sparkled. "The colonel wants to sell the inn and the adjacent property. And, I'm considering buying it. What do you think?"

The last thing she could see him doing was running an inn, but then maybe she didn't know him as well as she thought. Purchasing the Wayfarer would keep him in Crescent Bluff, though. "I never pictured you as the innkeeper type."

"You're so right about that." He laughed. "OK, here's my idea. For a while now, I've felt led to establish a music institute for kids. There'd be different tracks. You know, vocal, instrumental, song-writing, even worship-leading for teenagers thinking about going into the ministry. I've got the contacts to get some really solid guest instructors. I'd like to use it as a ministry, especially for underprivileged kids that have musical talent or interest but don't have the funds to get traditional training."

"But you couldn't do that full time. What about the rest of the time?"

He shrugged his shoulders. "I haven't worked out all the details. At first, I'd probably live in the innkeeper's apartment and hire staff to run the inn during off times."

"And what about the money? That's a lot of land. It can't be cheap." His financial state was none of her concern right now. But it might be one of these days. And it certainly was a reality they'd need to deal with. All she knew was he had no access to the royalties he'd sold years ago.

"I don't know. I did studio work in Austin and saved up some while I was living with my folks the last couple of years. It's not enough, but the colonel's willing to work with me."

The whole idea sounded too risky. Altruistic, but risky.

He put his arm back around her and leaned his head on top of hers. "Charlee, I don't have all the answers yet. I just figure if God put this desire in my heart, and I give it my best shot, it'll work out. And if it doesn't, well, then maybe it's not from God." He drew her even closer. "But your opinion's important to me because this is something that could—will, most likely—affect both of us. I hope."

Her heartbeat quickened. That was the first time he'd made reference to a long-term commitment. An unexpected peace settled over her. "I hope so, too."

25

"Here you go, young lady. You're in the Nairobi Room." Colonel Clark handed Charlee the key to room five.

He must have made a mistake. "But I thought that was Chance's room."

The colonel smiled and raised his eyebrows up and down. "He moved next door to room seven for the weekend. Wanted you to have the Nairobi Room."

That was crazy. "I could have stayed in the Victorian Garden Room."

He patted her hand. "I'm sure your young man had his reasons."

Her young man. Certainly today, hopefully forever. "I guess so."

As she pulled her suitcase to room five, Chance's vision of excited young people filling the hallways flooded her imagination. She could see it. Maybe she'd be a part of this dream.

She opened the door and flipped on the light. The room looked the same as it had when she'd stopped by to get the Christmas list for Beth and the kids, when she'd discovered the truth of who The Bridegroom was. The only difference was the desk. Then, it had been covered with paperwork.

Today a faceted crystal bud vase holding a single white rose was the desk's only adornment. Pink curling ribbon tied around the stem cascaded down to the desktop. Chasing away a smile, she bit her bottom lip. How cute! No florist had tied that bow. That was the workmanship of "her young man."

She placed her suitcase in the closet and walked over to set her computer case by the old desk. The corner of an envelope peeked out from under the blotter. Their letters. She'd given them back to Chance after she confronted him in The Perks weeks earlier, and he'd obviously put them back in the desk.

She picked up the vase, pulled out the envelope she'd addressed to The Bridegroom months ago, and walked over to the bed. She could have never predicted the change these letters would bring to her life.

Her first night in this room when her regular one was reserved, meeting Noah in the hallway and his mentioning the SDS, Trey and Ally reconnecting, Chance playing with Trey's band at The Barn that night, his becoming their worship leader, and then the whole Ashley-Chuck thing. A few months ago, she would have called these interesting coincidences, but now?

No. Too many pieces of the puzzle fit together. They were all part of a wonderful plan for her life. Chance loved her. Even though he'd never said the words, she could tell. And she loved him. Since their night at the star-field, she'd prayed about him, his past, her past, their future. Her Father had asked her to trust, and she was doing just that. She relaxed back against the pillow, her heart at peace.

After slipping the three pieces of stationery out of the envelope, she read Chance's first letter. The anguish she'd once felt, the tears she'd once shed, were gone. She read her response and then his reply. The third sheet was her invitation to meet at the lake that day. She shook her head. How could she have been so clueless not to realize Chance's reason for being there? He was right. She'd been blinded by the darkness.

She began to refold the letters when she saw the writing on the back of her invitation. Her heart quickened as she turned the paper over and saw the familiar block printing.

Dear Bride, Friend, Love,

I have so much I want to say to you, but I will not do it in a letter. The words must be spoken in person, where I can see your face, touch your hands, hear your voice. Meet me tonight at Travelers' Rest at seven o'clock.

Forever yours,

The Bridegroom

~*~

Chance paced back and forth, straightening the bow tie from his tux. Until tonight, he'd only worn this thing for performances, and no woman could have motivated him to put it on for any other reason. Except Charlee. For her, he'd done it. For her, he'd do just about anything.

His feelings toward her were different from those he'd had for Amanda. He'd prayed about this for weeks and knew with as much certainty as he could that Charlee was his forever love. And tonight, he'd tell her.

She felt the same for him. Her actions showed it. But he wanted to be the one to say the words first. He understood just how hard it would be for her to commit to another man after everything Jake had put her through.

Plus, she needed time to really consider the consequences of marrying him. He'd never be cured. If she had any doubts about marriage, he wanted her to have the opportunity to work through them. Or…turn him down.

One last prayer wouldn't hurt. *Father, thank You for loving me and raising me from the wreckage of my mistakes. Please guide my words, our thoughts. Your will be done.*

He glanced at his phone. She should be here any time. He lit the candles on the piano and fluffed the bows on the three roses. Pretty awesome. He'd gotten as good as Charlee at making those bows.

He flexed his fingers and shook his hands as he did before a performance. Nerves. Maybe he should run through Charlee's song before she arrived. As he moved toward the piano, his pocket vibrated, and he pulled out the phone. A text from Charlee.

running late. had to go back to shop. b there soon.

Man, today had taken years to go by and now this. Who knew how long it would take? Change of plans. He'd meet her at the shop. He texted her back. *take your time. no hurry.* Riding back here together would be more fun than waiting around alone, anyway.

~*~

Charlee unlocked the door of the shop. She was in such a hurry, she'd forgotten the file of invoices. She loved the autonomy of running her own business, along with the opportunity to serve customers and bring joy into their lives. But she absolutely hated the paperwork. This past year had been her most profitable, so maybe she'd be able to hire a part-time bookkeeper in a couple of months.

When she read Chance's invitation this afternoon, her heart sensed something special was up. She could have stayed in one of the other rooms, but he moved so she could find his letter in the Nairobi Room. Then he left the single rose. Tonight promised to be a milestone in their relationship.

If she hurried, she wouldn't be too late. As she pulled the file out of the cabinet, the bell on the front door chimed. Oh, no, she'd forgotten to lock it.

"Yoo-hoo, Charlee? Ally? Anyone here?"

Mrs. Williams. Hopefully, she wasn't in the mood to chat. Charlee stepped out of the office and waved. "Back here, Mrs. Williams."

"Oh, my dear. I'm so glad I caught you. I hoped you might be working late tonight." Mrs. Williams bustled across the floor toward the counter. "I have a tea emergency. I'm having a group over to play dominoes in the morning, and I'm completely out of Black Currant. And I must say, that's one of our favorites. I'll only be a second, dear."

"Let me get that for you, Mrs. Williams." As the mantel clock began to strike seven, Charlee picked a box off the shelf. Now she really was late. "Here you go." Charlee dropped the tea into a shopping bag.

"You're a lifesaver, dear." Mrs. Williams pulled her purse open and began rummaging around. "Let's see. I'm sure my wallet's in here somewhere." She looked up and smiled. "I ran out so quickly, I think I left it at home. If I can use your phone, I'll call Harold and ask him to bring it to me."

Charlee just wanted to be able to leave. Chance was waiting. Even though he'd told her to take her time, any minutes she was late meant less time with him. She stepped out from behind the counter and handed Mrs. Williams the bag. "Now, don't think a thing about it. The cash register is all closed out anyway. We can settle up next time you're in." Charlee put her arm around the sweet grandmother and herded her toward the door. "Have a wonderful time playing dominoes tomorrow."

"You're such a darling, Charlee. I hope young Mr. Chance knows how special you are." Rays of sunshine radiated from her blue eyes.

Opening the door, Charlee couldn't help but smile back. In case he didn't, she was sure Mrs. Williams would let him know. "Thank you, but it's easy with customers as wonderful as you."

"By the way, dear, you are simply glowing tonight."

As the elderly woman toddled down the steps, Charlee closed the door. And, this time, locked it. She'd better text an update to Chance.

on my way

She walked back to the office and retrieved the forgotten file, the whole reason she was late for their date. Another knock sounded on the front door. Mrs. Williams was back. If she hadn't just left, Charlee would have hidden out in the office and not answered the door. But Mrs. Williams knew she was inside. Ignoring her would be rude. Pushing down her impatience, she took a deep breath, plastered a smile on her face, and walked out toward the door.

The face peering into the window didn't belong to Mrs. Williams. This was all she needed right now. Noah. His face somber, he lifted his hand in a slight greeting. She'd received several missed calls from him over the past few days, but he'd never left any messages. He just couldn't seem to accept the reality that they were through, that she loved Chance.

She unlocked the door. "Noah, this is unexpected."

He stepped inside and closed the door behind him. "I'm sorry to intrude, but I saw the lights were on, and I need to talk with you." His eyes welled up.

Their relationship was over. The last thing she wanted was to see him beg. "Noah, I'm, uh, just heading out."

"As I said, I'm terribly sorry, but I...my mum...she's got cancer, and the doctors say it's terminal." As his chin quivered, he looked down at his feet. "They've given her four to six weeks."

Regret seeped through every inch of Charlee's heart. She'd been so self-centered, assuming his feelings for her caused his tears. She placed a hand on his arm. "Oh, Noah, I'm so sorry. Here, come sit down." She motioned toward the chairs facing the fireplace. "How about a cup of tea?"

Shaking his head, he sat down and focused on the floor. She dropped onto the ottoman facing him.

He looked into her eyes. "There's nothing anyone can do. That's why I'm here." A coarse laugh followed his words. "I've never been a religious person, but Charity, I know you are. I didn't know whom else to ask. Would you…pray for my mum? Please?"

Her heart ached for him. "Of course, Noah. I'd be honored." She grasped his hands and then began to pray. "Dear Heavenly Father, I come to You tonight knowing that You love us and want only what's best for us. That You want us to ask good things of You. I ask now that You would please heal Noah's mother…"

As she continued praying aloud, compassion filled her. He'd recently lost his father, and now this. *Oh, Father, comfort him. Draw him near. Help him feel Your presence.* "I ask all this in Your Holy Son's name. Amen."

She opened her eyes to see tears trickling down his face. She wanted to know the details, but she couldn't inflict the additional pain asking would bring. If he wanted her to know more, he'd share. "Please let me know if there's anything I can do. Anything."

He nodded. "You can't know how much your concern means to me." He stood. "I'm certain you have something planned tonight, and I'm keeping you from it. I'd best get on to the inn."

As they walked toward the door, she squeezed his hand. "Noah, I always have time for friends." Chance would understand when she told him why she was late. He was such a kindhearted man.

"Hey, why don't you come to church Sunday morning? Chance is leading worship, and I'm singing with the band. There's a service at ten."

"I don't know. That's never been a part of my life." He shook his head. "But maybe it needs to be. I'll consider it."

"I'll save you a seat on the second row, just in case." She patted his arm.

He nodded, tears striping his cheeks.

She drew him close. "Noah, I'm so sorry. So, so sorry." His cheek pressed against hers as he returned the embrace.

"Thank you for your friendship," he whispered, "And your prayer."

~*~

Chance pulled into the parking lot. The MG was parked in front of Charlee's shop. Walsh. So he was the reason she was running late. He was sure persistent, but no wonder. Losing Charlee would be heartbreaking.

Movement in the front door window caught his eye. They were hugging. His heart pounded. They were kissing. The woman he loved was kissing another man. Anguish knotted his stomach. He put down the window to get some fresh air to keep from throwing up. Grabbing the end of the bow tie, he tugged until it unfurled and then dropped it onto the seat beside him. He pulled back out into the road.

He was nothing but a failure. A failure at love, at life. So much for being "in." She'd obviously thought about his past and decided it was too complicated. And he couldn't blame her. A life with him would only bring failure and pain.

Deep inside, a once familiar dark voice laughingly proclaimed his words were the truth. He wasn't good enough for anyone, especially her, and he'd been crazy to believe someone like Charlee might want him. He wished he'd never come to Crescent Bluff. Never met her.

Somewhere in the far corners of his mind, a gentle, quiet voice begged to be heard, to be listened to. He should go back and give her a chance to explain. But he couldn't. No quantity of words from her, from God, from anyone, could erase the picture indelibly burned in his mind. His love in the arms of another man.

Maybe it was for the best. She'd probably planned to break up with him tonight. And he wasn't putting himself, or her, through any more pain.

His heart cried out for comfort, and his body suggested he could find it in only one place. Only one thing could dull the agony.

His pocket vibrated. He didn't care who it was or what they had to say.

~*~

Charlee stepped into the candlelit chapel and tiptoed down the aisle toward the piano. Candles and roses—with Chance's bows. She'd never known a man, really anyone, with such a compassionate heart. Maybe his college professor was right. Maybe musicians did feel more deeply than non-artistic people. He was certainly evidence to support that theory.

She walked around to face the keyboard. Sheets of staff paper on the music stand waited to be played. Block printing across the top read *Heartsong – For Charlee.* Her heart fluttered. He'd written a song for her. She hungered for him to play it, to share with her something that was a part of him. A part of him that was hers only.

Tonight would be a special point in their relationship. Maybe he'd say the words she longed to hear, maybe not. But she didn't care. Forget Mom's old-fashioned idea about the man having to profess love first. She knew his heart. His actions showed it. Tonight, she'd tell him exactly how she felt. Exactly how much she loved him.

He hadn't responded to her last text, but that was OK. He'd be here soon. Maybe he'd forgotten something in his room—like a ring. She giggled. *Father, thank You for bringing Chance into my life.*

After Noah's visit and the anticipation of tonight, she was emotionally and physically exhausted. She lay down on the front pew to wait.

The odor of snuffed candles woke her. Her eyes searched the darkness for some frame of reference. Oh, yes, she was in the chapel. The tapers had burned completely out.

She jerked up. The hour had to be late, certainly well after midnight, and no Chance. Bile rose up into her throat. Something was wrong, terribly wrong. He should have been here hours ago. *Father, protect him. Please keep him safe.*

She ran up the aisle and out the chapel door. The moon provided enough light to see, but tears blurred the passing images as she stumbled up the path toward the inn. She trembled. The cold wind blew against her body, mirroring the iciness within her heart.

When the inn came into view, she stopped. His truck was in the parking lot. He must be here, but for some reason, he'd left the chapel and had not come back.

As the wind pushed a cloud across the moon, the darkness smothered her and began to creep back into her soul. She grasped a tree trunk to steady herself. Hot tears cascaded down her face. When commitment time came, he'd changed his mind and run out on her. Just like Jake. She shouldn't have expected anything different.

She was a fool for trusting, for letting this happen again. She should have never allowed herself to fall in love with him. But she hadn't been able to help it.

She'd lost part of her heart to Jake, and she'd wanted to give all that was left to Chance. But neither one of them wanted her. She loved Chance with a passion she'd never felt for Jake and would have given her everything to him. If he'd asked. But he hadn't. She'd thought it was because he was too much of a gentleman. But now she knew the truth. He hadn't really wanted her, loved her.

She was unlovable.

A quiet voice reminded her of the words she'd spoken to Chance that night in the star-field. *Who defines you? Not any man. Who do I say you are? My precious, beloved daughter.*

She wanted to believe those words, and she'd thought she did. She'd really thought she did, but life had proven otherwise.

26

A blinding light seared Chance's eyelids. His head was heavy. A block of cement. Every heartbeat...pounding agony. If only his skull would explode. Put him out of his misery. His clothes were wet. Clingy. He lay shivering on his stomach. Freezing. His right cheek pressed into damp grit. A brick dug into his ribcage. But the pain in his chest paled compared to that in his head. The throbbing. It needed to stop. He pressed his hands against his temples. No good. His tongue was thick. Dry. His mouth full of sour grit and stale vomit.

He rolled onto his side. Cracked open an eye. Grass. Dirt. Water. The lake. He was at the lake. He'd come down here last night. Right after he returned from the liquor store. That was all he remembered. The brick beneath him...an empty bottle. He'd bought two. He looked around. The second was gone.

The wind blew. His shivering intensified. He pulled his knees up until he was in a fetal position. It didn't work. No body heat. He had to get inside. He struggled to his knees. He grabbed a nearby tree to pull himself up the rest of the way. The throbbing in his head pulsed into his eye sockets. His stomach heaved, but nothing came out. It had been emptied hours ago. He picked up the bottle. Threw it out into the lake. Stumbling to the root-bench, he sat down.

The mental fog inched up to reveal the image of Charlee and Walsh last night at the shop. A squeezing pain in his chest took his breath away. He'd lost her. He should have waited to share his past with her.

No. Not telling her would have been wrong. Unfair. He couldn't blame her. Walsh was a better choice. She'd never have to worry about him staying clean. Chance loved her and wanted what was best for her. Even if it wasn't him. Or at least he should want that.

Low on the eastern horizon, the sun washed the surface of the lake in gold. He'd been sober two years. No…two years, three weeks, and six days. And now he'd blown it. Like everything else in his life.

Seeking warmth, he wrapped his arms around himself and rocked back and forth. He'd messed up so many times in his life, but God had always taken…welcomed…him back. For some ridiculous reason, God kept forgiving him over and over again.

But this time, it was too much. Surely, by now God would have had enough. Chance was on staff at a church. His job was to lead others in worship. He'd always known he was unworthy, and now he'd blown it. He was beyond use. His life was supposed to be an example. He couldn't get up there in front of the church and pretend to be something he wasn't. No. God would never honor that hypocrisy.

These last few months here in Crescent Bluff had been awesome. And now he'd ruined everything. He jerked up the wet sleeve of his tuxedo shirt and looked at his arm. The final stanza of his poem was written. Done.

God was through with him.

The wind skipped across the lake and swirled through the trees. Birds sang, greeting the new day. Music blanketed him. The music of the spheres. God was rejoicing, singing over him. But that couldn't be possible. He was so undeserving. Hot tears washed his cheeks.

He didn't get it. God should just let him go and suffer the consequences of his choices. But instead, He kept pursuing him. *Why, Father?* As the music continued, he closed his eyes and leaned against one of the tree trunks. As much as he wanted to run away, hiding would do no good. He could go no place where his Father couldn't find him, where He hadn't already been.

When his breathing evened, he pulled his phone out of his pocket and tapped in a number. "Josh?" His voice sounded weird, dull. "It's Chance. Sorry it's so early. I need to see you."

~*~

Charlee walked into the dining room, but she hadn't come to eat breakfast. She had no appetite. The anguish in her stomach left no room for the French toast on the buffet. She'd come, ridiculously hoping she'd see Chance.

When she'd returned from the chapel, she told herself she never wanted to see him again, but that was a lie. Having spent the night chasing after sleep that wouldn't be caught, her mind filled with unanswered and unanswerable questions, she knew one thing for certain. She still loved him. Nothing he could do would change that. With time, the intensity of her feelings might diminish, but she'd always love him.

When she'd tapped on his door both last night and then again this morning, he hadn't answered. She'd softly called his name, but no light had come from under the door. All was silent. If his truck hadn't been in the parking lot, she would have thought his room was vacant.

She'd gotten no response to her texts, and her phone calls had gone straight to voice mail. If she didn't hear something soon, she'd call the police.

As she poured some tea, heavy footsteps sounded from around the corner. The porcelain cup and saucer clinked as her hands shook. She sat down to steady herself and closed her eyes. *Please, Father, please…*

"Good morning, Charity."

Her heart sank, and she opened her eyes. "Oh, Noah." He looked as bad as she felt.

His eyes widened as he rushed around the table. "Charity, what is it?" He sat down beside her and placed his arm around her. Comforted by the nearness of another person, she leaned her head on his shoulder.

She tried to speak. Her mouth moved, but no words sounded.

"Sh-h-h-h. No need to respond." He slowly rocked her back and forth. "Let's move into the parlor, shall we?"

He led her out of the dining room to the window seat overlooking the front porch. They sat. Then he turned to face her and grasped both of her hands. "When you're ready to share whatever is going on, I'm here for you."

He was still hurting, but he was setting aside his personal

feelings for her.

A sad expression covered his face as he squeezed her hands. "Let's just sit here quietly, shall we?"

She scooted close and laid her head on his shoulder.

The sound of a car engine broke into the silence. She turned to look out the window. A shadowed silhouette was in the driver's seat of Chance's truck. He must have left through his patio door. She jumped up and raced out the front door and down the steps toward the truck. She had to see him. "Chance, stop. Wait!"

The truck jerked backward. He hadn't seen her.

Noah's arms slipped around her as the pickup moved forward and, once again, a man she loved deserted her.

~*~

New Age piano music filled The Perks. Chance pressed his head back against the booth while Josh just stared at him with unreadable eyes.

"What did Charlee say?"

Chance shrugged. "I haven't told her."

Josh nodded. "And that's because? I mean, I kind of got the impression y'all might be getting pretty serious."

"She deserves someone who won't fail her. Somebody she can depend on. Someone not like me."

Josh looked him straight in the eyes. "Don't you think you ought to let her decide?"

Chance shook his head. "It's just better this way."

Josh cupped his hands around his coffee mug and blew across the top. He took a slow drink.

"Not saying anything?"

Josh fingered his Bible, "I don't think you'll like what I have to say."

Chance would pack up his stuff and head home as soon as this meeting was over. No more ministry for him. "I'll write a letter of resignation to the elder board and get it to you later today."

Josh's eyes pierced deep into Chance's soul. "Son, it's not about you."

"What?" Wrong, it was all about him, all about his failures.

"It's not about you. None of us is worthy or deserving. I've been doing this a long time, and every Sunday when I get up to preach, I realize how inadequate I am and wonder how in the world God could have made such a mistake. And then I know. It's not about me."

Josh placed his elbows on the table and leaned closer. "We're all broken. But when we're at our weakest and feel completely inadequate, God does His best work. And there's only one way to learn that. So, Chance, that's exactly why you're gonna show up tomorrow morning and you're gonna get up there and let God use you."

"I can't." Josh had no clue what this was like.

"I know." Josh folded his arms behind his head and leaned against the back of the booth. "Did I ever tell you I used to play in a band? I've been into alcohol…and drugs."

But Josh was such a Godly man.

"Then I found the Lord, and everything changed. Chance, ministry isn't for cowards. God has called you, and it's not easy. Everyday is a battle, but He'll fight it for you if you'll let Him." Josh opened his Bible to Exodus and pointed to a verse that was underlined in red and highlighted in yellow.

The Lord will fight for you; you need only to be still.

"Take your Bible, get away from town, and spend the day with God. I'll see you in the morning." Josh stood and picked up his Bible. Stepping around the table, he placed a hand on Chance's shoulder and squeezed it. Then he walked toward the door.

Chance couldn't get up in front of the church and pretend to be something he wasn't. And he sure couldn't face God…or Charlee. Josh just didn't get it. He'd told Josh he couldn't lead worship tomorrow, and that was that. He'd fulfilled his obligation, and Josh had better find a substitute.

Chance was going home.

27

Charlee sat on the front row, her right knee bouncing up and down, her stomach churning. She didn't want to be here and sure didn't feel like singing this morning. But if she was here, Chance would have to see her, to speak with her, so that's why she'd come. She wasn't giving up without a fight.

The soundman was in the back reading some sort of audio-visual magazine, and the guitar players sat on stools working out the bridge in the second song. The rest of the band, except for her, sat in a circle on the stage and talked quietly.

Chance was now twenty minutes late.

Dr. Lewis walked through the side door and sat down next to her. "No Chance, huh?"

She shook her head. If she tried to speak, her voice would betray her pain.

"He'll be here." He patted her arm, stood, and then walked up the aisle toward the back of the auditorium.

Chance was never late for rehearsal. He wasn't coming no matter what Dr. Lewis said. She may as well leave.

She stood, and the door on the other side of the auditorium flew open. Chance rushed in, guitar case in hand. "Sorry I'm late, guys. Got stuck in traffic coming in from Austin." His explanation poured out. "There was an overturned semi on the freeway, and I left my phone at my parents' house, so I couldn't call. Give me two minutes, and we'll run through the front set."

She couldn't breathe. He had come. His hair was a mess, his face unshaven. To the casual observer, he might have looked normal. But not to her. This was not his PR look. Black circles underscored his bloodshot eyes. He looked rough. But he also looked wonderful.

He pulled the guitar strap over his shoulder and stepped up to the mic as he tuned his guitar. "Check, check, check."

She walked up onto the stage, her legs shaking and her insides quivering.

"Check…" He looked toward her and blinked slowly. His voice was low. "Charlee. Good of you to show up this morning." He turned away and spoke back into the mic. "We'll drop the back set today. I've decided to change it up and do an acoustic set. So, after the first songs you're free to sit in the congregation. OK, let's get started. Let's pray."

~*~

Charlee slipped into the seat next to Noah while the rest of the band exited the stage. Her invitation had been sincere, but she really hadn't expected he'd take her up on it. "I'm so glad you came."

"Me, too." He grasped her hand and squeezed it. "I had no idea you had such a lovely voice."

"Thank you." She'd been on autopilot up there. She'd sung the words and harmonies, but her heart had been far away. Far away from this place, far away from God. She hadn't worshipped. *Forgive me, Father.*

Dr. Lewis invited the congregation to turn to a particular scripture, but she couldn't concentrate on what he was saying. Her mind was on Chance.

Seated on the end of the front row, he leaned forward, elbows resting on his thighs, his gaze fixed on the floor. He was definitely a professional. His demeanor had been no different from any other Sunday. No one could have guessed everything wasn't perfect.

Gripping the seat, she closed her eyes and ignored the longing to move behind him and encircle him with her arms. The memory of his cologne filled her senses.

Noah pulled a Bible from the back of the seat in front of him and held it out to her. "Romans 8:38-39?" he whispered.

She flipped the pages to the scripture as Dr. Lewis read aloud. "For I am convinced that neither death nor life, neither angels nor demons, neither the present nor the future, nor any powers, neither height nor depth, nor anything else in all creation, will be able to separate us from the love of God that is in Christ Jesus our Lord."

~*~

While the lights dimmed and Dr. Lewis prayed, Charlee peeked out of one eye toward Chance's seat. He was gone. As gentle guitar music floated through the auditorium, a spotlight rose on the solitary musician seated on a stool center stage. No matter what had happened, she loved that man.

His voice was pure and rich as he led the congregation in an old hymn.

Holy, holy, holy! Though the darkness hide Thee,
Though the eye of sinful man, Thy glory may not see,
Only Thou art holy; there is none beside Thee,
Perfect in power, in love and purity.

Charlee had sung this song since childhood, and she'd never understood the darkness this verse spoke of until Chance's words had freed her from it that evening when she'd agreed to sing with him for the first time.

As Chance finished the last verse, the congregation stood. He then transitioned into a song she recognized from one of her worship CDs about surrendering our lives to God's will. She wasn't sure she could give all that she had and all that she was to God, as the words said. That she could let God have His way in her life, especially if it meant losing Chance. So badly she wanted to be able to say, "Yes." She should, but she couldn't.

Someone moved to her left. With his arms crossed over his chest Dr. Lewis leaned against the side wall, watching Chance and smiling like a proud father. Then he nodded his head and walked through the sea of worshippers toward the back door.

The last song was about how God's love is unfailing. Generally, an upbeat song, Chance's version was slower, more meditative…like a love song. The hour was approaching noon, and bright light made its way through the cracks between closed shutters, washing the auditorium in golden warmth. As he began the first chorus, Chance raised his eyes upward, closed them, and then smiled. Peace blanketed his face.

As the lyrics said, maybe this time was just a painful night and a morning filled with joy would come. If only she could believe that. An invisible, blinding light pierced her heart, its warmth filling every inch of her. Something was going on. Something powerful. She'd never before felt like this in church.

To her right Noah grabbed the back of the seat in front of him and sat down, his eyes closed, his head bowed in a posture of prayer. She closed her eyes. *Father, please comfort Noah with Your presence.*

~*~

Recorded music filled the sanctuary while Chance spoke with the last person who'd come up on the stage after the service. He hadn't expected any comments, at least not positive ones. Rehearsal with the band had been rushed, and they'd sounded pretty rough. Plus, he hadn't even been sure which three songs he would do for the back set until he'd walked on the stage after the sermon. But the platform had been flooded with church members after he'd spoken the final prayer. No one seemed to have noticed his shortcomings.

"Powerful service, young man."

Chance shook hands with the head of the elder board. "Thank you, sir. But it wasn't me. I didn't have anything to do with it."

"Yeah, you did. You just got yourself out of the way." Jim clapped him on the back, smiled, and turned to leave.

If his parents hadn't awakened him at three, he might still be asleep at home. What a mistake that would have been. God had fought for him today, just as Josh said He would, and Chance had almost surrendered before the battle even started.

His heart beat slowly and steadily. His body was relaxed, his soul at peace. If the auditorium had been empty, he would have dropped down onto the stool and soaked in the serenity of this moment. But it wasn't. Charlee, Noah, and Josh sat on the front row with their eyes closed, and Josh was praying.

Chance turned, unplugged his guitar, and hurriedly began to

pack it away. Maybe he could escape before Josh finished. He didn't want to speak to Charlee right now. Sure, his heart was peaceful, but the hurt was still there. In time, maybe he'd get over her, maybe he wouldn't. That was another battle God would have to fight for him.

"Chance." Josh's voice rang out.

Too late.

"Come here a minute."

Chance flipped the latches closed on the case and picked it up. "Sure." Taking a deep breath, he turned and headed down the steps. As long as there were other people around and he and Charlee weren't alone, he could do this.

Chance shook the hand Walsh offered. "Chance, I haven't been to church in probably twenty years. But today, here in this moment, your music was so powerful I felt something I've never felt before. Thank you."

"Bless you, Noah." Chance didn't know what else to say. Noah's worship experience hadn't been because of him, but in spite of him.

"Chance, why don't you keep Miss Charlee here company while Noah and I step into my office," Josh said. "I have a couple of books I want to give him." As Josh and Noah moved toward the right, the look on Josh's face was unreadable. "We'll only be a couple of minutes."

That was so low. Josh probably meant well, but after their conversation yesterday at The Perks, the preacher knew everything. Chance looked down at his feet and then back up over Charlee's shoulder. He couldn't make himself look into her eyes. "Thanks for coming this morning."

"When I make a commitment, I keep my word." Her voice trembled. "If I say, I'm in, I'm in."

He tugged his gaze over to find hers. Her eyes were full. Her chin trembled, and she bit her bottom lip. Not long ago, he would have gathered her into his arms to comfort both of them. But not now. This was not the time, and here was not the place for any kind of serious conversation. Besides, nothing Charlee could say would erase the picture of her and Noah at the shop. Absolutely nothing.

"Where were you Friday night, Chance?" Her words were barely more than a whisper.

"The question is, where were you?" His throat ached as he pushed out the reply. A part of him wanted her to confess.

"I was at the chapel. I was late, but I was there…for hours…waiting." Fire and water filled her eyes. "Where were you?"

"I was there, until I got your text and decided to surprise you at the shop." His breathing filled the momentary silence. "And I saw you and Noah. Kissing."

Her eyes opened wide. "What?"

"It's OK, Charlee. I understand."

"We weren't—"

"Noah's all ready to go." Josh's words knifed through the tension as the two men approached.

Chance looked down at his feet and then back up at Josh. "Good. I need to go, too. Josh, I'm headed to Austin for the week, but I'll be back for next Sunday."

An unseen force drew his gaze back to Charlee's. Her eyes mirrored the anguish in his heart. He needed to get out of here before he lost it. "Bye." Chance picked up his guitar case, and Walsh moved closer to Charlee. Chance had to go home and talk with Mom and Dad. And his Father.

Maybe he wouldn't be coming back next week after all.

~*~

The old chains groaned as Noah pushed the wooden porch swing slowly back and forth with his feet. Charlee had never seen him like this. All he'd talked about on the way back to the inn, during lunch, and since they'd moved out here to the porch was church. Dr. Proper-and-Cultured had become Dr. Exuberant. She couldn't join in his excitement because her heart was far away in a pickup heading toward Austin.

He placed his hand on hers. "Forgive me, dear Charity. I've been going on so. But I've never experienced anything like what I feel at this moment. My mother is still dying, and I'm still devastated. That hasn't changed. But deep inside, I feel an illogical calm that I can't begin to explain."

She sandwiched his hand between hers. "The Bible calls that 'the peace that passes all understanding.'"

"Yes, exactly!" He smiled and was off again talking about the music at church today and how talented Chance was.

Normally, she would have been able to concentrate on Noah's comments, but her mind was on Chance's words. So he'd come by the shop Friday night when Noah was there, yet he hadn't come in. Plus, he'd accused her of kissing Noah just because they'd been alone.

Friday night replayed in her mind. She'd held Noah's hands when he sat in the chair and they prayed. She would have done that for any friend who was in anguish.

She'd walked him to the door, and they'd hugged good-bye. Again, she would have done that for anyone hurting. Nothing.

That Chance could think she would betray him hurt more than if she'd been slapped across the face. Even though she'd never said "love" to him, he had to know exactly how she felt. She took a deep breath and replayed the scene again but this time from his perspective in the parking lot looking through the glass-paned window into the dimly lit store.

She saw the final hug. The image of the two shadowed figures inside the front door merged into one. Of course, this was all a huge misunderstanding!

A small flame of hope flickered in her heart, but then reality quickly snuffed it out.

Chance's accusation cut deep. He hadn't even given her an opportunity to explain before he'd jumped to conclusions—and false conclusions, at that. After what they'd been through with Jake and Amanda, he couldn't possibly think she would treat him like that.

Noah stopped the swing and squeezed her hand. "Would you care for some tea? I'll be happy to get a cup for you."

"No, thank you, Noah." She tried to smile as if nothing were wrong.

While the swing moved to and fro again, he resumed his one-sided conversation.

This whole mess could have been avoided if Chance had simply talked with her about it. After all, she'd gone looking for him, seeking an explanation. He should have done the same for her. But he hadn't.

Why? The unspoken answer pierced deep into her heart and hurt more than any words he could have said. Because he didn't trust her. And as much as she loved him, she could never have a forever relationship with someone who couldn't trust her.

Noah was quiet.

Charlee glanced toward him.

His eyes were warm, gentle. "I'm sorry I've gone on so, Charity. Whatever the issues between you and Chance may be, please know I'm here if you ever want to talk about anything."

"Thank you." But there was no need talking about Chance. She was done. Done with musicians, done with men. The time between Jake and Chance had been satisfying. Her friends and family, even her customers, loved her. She was a successful business woman, and that would be enough. At least her shop couldn't break her heart.

~*~

Chance had thought that by now he'd have definite feelings about the direction he should go. But the week at home was past, and still nothing—no answers about his job, his dream of the music institute, about Charlee.

The one thing he wanted above all was still beyond his grasp. Assurance. Life would be so much easier if God would just text people His will. But that would eliminate the whole matter of faith and trust.

Chance turned his pickup onto the rutted road they'd ridden down Christmas evening. When he got to the end, he shifted the truck into park and cut the lights and engine. He leaned his head back while his eyes adjusted to the dark. The moon was full, perfect for what he had planned. None of Charlee's shooting stars would be visible tonight.

When he'd moved to Crescent Bluff months ago, he'd been so sure he was where God wanted him. But now that certainty was gone. His feelings for Charlee clouded everything. In the beginning, he'd warned himself not to get involved with her. If only his heart had listened.

He glanced over at the small rise to his right where he and Charlee had lain, gazing upward, and she'd seen her first shooting stars. Where they'd shared that amazing kiss. His heart ached. Maybe things would have turned out different if he had let her get to know him better before he told her about his past. But he'd never know, because it was too late.

As the moon painted the field in silver, he could see with clarity. The time had come.

He pulled the bag from the liquor store out from behind the seat and then reached into the glove box for Dad's pistol. The safety was on like at Christmas, but tonight, it was loaded.

He slammed the door and walked out onto the field. Where was the best place to do this? About thirty yards away was another small rise. Perfect. He jogged over there and set out the five bottles of whiskey at about six-foot intervals from one another. Then he jogged back toward his pickup.

Slowly he pulled the pistol out of his waistband, flipped off the safety, and raised the gun. The first target was perfectly aligned. Gently he squeezed the trigger and the bottle exploded, then the second, and the third. Not too bad for target practice by moonlight. The fourth one took two tries, but when he got the last one with a single shot, invisible chains fell away, and he yelled, "Yes!" Triumph. This was better than any therapy.

He was done here. All he could do now was go back to the last place and time he'd felt he was in God's will and pick up from there. He'd pack up and head back to Crescent Bluff. Whatever happened with his job and his dreams was up to his Father. The rest of the battle belonged to Him.

28

Charlee awoke to the throaty hum of the MG engine. Unlike the first time she'd ridden in the convertible, the top was up tonight. She glanced at the clock on the dashboard. Midnight. Understandably, Noah had been emotional during the funeral today, but now he seemed calm.

Whether a blessing or a curse, his mother had died from a stroke rather than suffering for weeks or months with cancer. This coming Sunday would mark only two weeks since he'd come to church that first time—the morning Chance had been late for rehearsal, the last time Charlee had seen him.

Ally had told her Chance had led worship last Sunday. Charlee hadn't attended. The darkness of deception had been trying to inch its way back into her heart, but she was fighting to prevent it from taking over. So this Sunday she was going to church—Chance or no Chance.

She reached over and squeezed Noah's arm. "Sorry I fell asleep. Are you sure you don't want me to drive some?" He'd insisted that he come down early this morning and pick her up for the funeral and then bring her back home tonight.

"I'm quite fine. Please lean your head back and rest some more." Despite his sad expression, a glow blanketed his face. The peace he'd spoken of at lunch that day at the inn had changed him. "We're almost there, anyway." The kind heart that had been hidden by his airs and quest for perfection had begun to reveal itself.

She looked out the window to get her bearings. They were only a few miles away. "Noah, I wish you hadn't insisted on driving me today. Then you could be at home resting."

"There's nothing there for me now. I would simply mope about the house. Besides, I wouldn't want you driving back alone. And I want to go to church here this Sunday." He smiled and shrugged his shoulders. "So I'll be in Crescent Bluff a day early, that's all. I can work on my book about Elizabeth Graham." He paused. "And then maybe we could have dinner together tomorrow night. That is, of course, if you have no other plans."

"As friends?" He was still as handsome as ever. But they were only friends, and that was all they'd ever be.

"As friends." He grinned.

Music rose up from the car floor, and she reached down into her purse and pulled out her phone. Probably her parents. Mom always forgot about the time difference between California and Crescent Bluff.

Ally. Her heart jumped. She was calling in the middle of the night, and that couldn't be good. "Ally. Everything OK?"

"Charlee, where are you?" Ally's voice trembled. She hadn't sounded this upset since Jason's death.

Charlee's breathing quickened. Trey better not have hurt her. "We're about fifteen minutes away. What's wrong? Are you OK?"

Noah turned toward her, his eyebrows raised in silent question.

"It's the shop. Come to the shop. There's been a fire."

As Charlee's heart pounded, a knot rose up in her throat. "What happened? Is everyone OK? Hello, Ally? Ally?" She looked at her phone. No service bars. They were going through that dead zone.

"Charity?" Noah's eyes narrowed.

"Take me to the shop." Her stomach churned. "There's been a fire."

~*~

The caustic smell of wood smoke and melted plastic mixed with some sort of metallic odor she couldn't identify burned Charlee's eyes and lungs as the four stood huddled together, Noah and Trey on the ends, the two women in the middle. Floodlights illuminated the smoking mound of debris that had once been her shop. Even the chimney was destroyed, a pile of blackened limestone, bricks, and mortar were all that remained of the old fireplace.

As the firefighters packed up, any sense of urgency they might have had earlier was gone. Nothing was left to be urgent about. Everything she'd invested her life into these last five years was gone. Gone in a matter of moments. Her stomach heaved, and she breathed through her mouth to maintain control.

Ally leaned her head on Charlee's shoulder as tears washed her cheeks. "Oh, Charlee, I'm so sorry. I'm so sorry."

Charlee couldn't speak. The entire scene was surreal, like watching a movie in which she'd acted. Surely, this wasn't really happening. In a few minutes she'd walk out of the theater and her shop would be fine, just as it was when she'd locked up yesterday evening.

She released Ally as a fireman wearing a coat labeled "Callahan" approached them—Craig from church. "Hello, Charlee. I'm sorry about your shop. By the time we got here, the structure was completely involved."

For the first time since she and Noah had arrived, she spoke. "Thanks for trying, Craig." Her voice quivered. "I appreciate your effort and your service."

He reached out and touched her arm. "I'm really sorry. The department will contact you with the results once the official report's in. But if I had to guess, I'd say the fire started in the chimney."

She nodded as Ally shook with sobs. "OK. Thanks," Charlee whispered.

Craig turned and left.

Ally bawled. "It's my fault, all my fault. I should have never put that last log on the fire so near the end of the day."

Somehow, Charlee had to hold it together and be the comforter. She held Ally's hands and looked straight into her eyes. "Ally, if I'd been here, I could have just as easily been the one to put the log on. I did that all the time. It's not your fault."

Trey gently stroked Ally's hair. "Come here, baby." He wrapped her in his arms. Noah squeezed Charlee's shoulder. Not long ago that hand would have belonged to Chance, and she would have buried her head in his chest as his arms upheld her. But never again.

Bleakness pushed its way into her soul. She'd lost everything.

~*~

Chance hadn't been able to fall back asleep since the sirens had sounded. He'd prayed for the nameless victims of the unknown tragedy. Crescent Bluff was a fairly small town, and chances were he had run into the involved persons at some point since he'd been here.

Slipping out of bed, he wrapped the leopard throw around his bare shoulders and walked over to the French doors. The minute he stepped out onto the patio he could smell smoke. A fire. There had been a fire. All the people he loved in this town flashed through his mind.

A gentle, but persistent knock sounded on the hall door, and his heart began to race as he moved inside to open it.

The colonel stood in a blue plaid bathrobe, his face lined with concern. This couldn't be good.

"Chance, sorry to bother you, but I thought you'd want to know. The missus just got a call from the prayer chain at church. Charlee's shop burned down."

Chance prayed when the colonel left, prayed while he pulled on some clothes, and prayed as he sped across town to Charlee's house. He pulled into her driveway and parked behind the MG. Walsh was here.

In the middle of the night.

Coming over without calling first was a stupid thing to do, but she wouldn't have answered a call from him. His hands gripped the steering wheel while his mind argued with his heart. The porch light was on, and a glow from the lamp at the end of the couch shone through the living room curtains. He'd raced over here, but now he couldn't make himself get out of the truck and knock on the door. Because she and Walsh were alone in there.

In the middle of the night.

He should turn around and return to the inn. He reached to stick the key back into the ignition and stopped. No, he couldn't leave. He loved her and had to see her. He had to know she was OK. He closed the truck door, walked up onto the porch, and reached to press the doorbell. No, that would be too intrusive.

In the middle of the night.

He balled up his fist and gently rapped on the wooden door. His heart pounded in his head. The dead bolt shot back, and the door opened to reveal Walsh. His eyes narrowed. "Chance."

"Noah. I, uh, just heard about the fire and came to see if Charlee was OK. Is she awake?" The blood roared in his ears.

"She's awake. Understandably shaken. Come in."

He shook his head. "Better not. I'd appreciate it if you'd tell her I'm here.

Noah nodded. "One moment."

The door closed and Chance waited forever until it reopened.

"Charity thanks you for coming, and she hopes you'll understand if she's too tired to see anyone right now. She was just on her way to bed."

So, that's what he was to her now. Anyone. He deserved that. "I understand. Tell her to call me if she needs anything. Anything, OK?"

Noah nodded and placed a hand on Chance's shoulder. He lowered his voice. "Try again in a couple of days. She's overwhelmed right now. I'll try to get her to church on Sunday. You can see her then."

Chance nodded, but he wanted to push Walsh aside and force his way into the house. He wanted to gather her into his arms and hold her, never to let her go. But he wouldn't. She didn't want him. "Thanks." He put his hands into his pockets as the door closed, leaving the woman he loved alone with another man.

In the middle of the night.

~*~

"Thank you, Noah." Charlee couldn't make herself see Chance.

Noah sat on the edge of the chair facing her sofa. "You'll have to speak with him sometime, you know."

"Not tonight." She didn't mean that. Her heart ached for his nearness. Her arms longed to hold him close—forever. Suddenly, the pile of rubble that was her life crushed her heart. The things she loved most in this world were gone. The room blurred as tears filled her eyes.

Noah stood. "I should leave. You need your rest."

Clamminess covered her. She couldn't breathe. "No, please. Don't leave me alone. Stay." She stood and grabbed his hands. Her heart pounded as fear invaded her body.

He looked up to the ceiling and smiled. "How I would have loved to have heard those very words a few months ago!" His gaze found hers. "Honestly? I really don't want to be alone tonight, either."

"Oh, Noah, forgive me. I'm sorry." She should be comforting him. Earlier today, he had buried his mother. He'd suffered a much deeper loss than anything Charlee had experienced.

He drew her close. "If you have a blanket and an extra pillow, I'll make a bed here on your couch."

"Thank you," she whispered. "You're a good friend."

~*~

Chance wrapped his hands around a mug of strong, black coffee. He hadn't been able to go back to sleep last night after he'd left Charlee's, and this morning, tea wouldn't have cut it. The colonel sat down on the other end of the settee, the contract for the purchase of the inn spread out on the coffee table before them.

"I won't have the rest of the down payment together by the deadline." Chance's words were more bitter than the coffee. His life had been full of so much promise a few weeks ago. Then he'd been so sure about God's leading. But now nothing was working out. He didn't get it.

Everything was crumbling down around him—Charlee, the hope of the music institute. Two things he'd wanted so badly and had thought with certainty God had provided. "Beth wasn't able to take over the lease on the house until this month. I guess you should go ahead and list the inn. You've been more than patient in allowing me these months to try to raise the money."

The colonel leaned back, crossed his arms on his chest, and stroked his chin with one hand. "Why don't we wait until after the concert next weekend? I want you to have all the proceeds. I don't need any money for your room and board." The colonel's blue eyes twinkled. "I'm sure God wants to do something special with this old place."

Chance had thought so, too, but obviously God's plans were different from his. "Thank you, sir. That's a very generous offer, but I can't accept it."

And now the other reason he'd wanted to talk with the colonel this morning, why his mind had been racing last night. "You see, I want to put the money to better use. What if we turn the concert into a benefit for Charlee?"

The colonel grinned. "I like it!"

Excitement made Chance's heart pound. "I could get Trey to play, too. What do you think?"

"What do I think?" Colonel Clark placed his hand on Chance's shoulder. "I think you're a fine young man, and Charlee's a mighty blessed young woman."

Chance winced at the colonel's words. He must not know the situation. "We're no longer dating, sir. We've, uh, ended our relationship."

The colonel set his mug on the table and looked straight into Chance's eyes. "Just because a soldier's AWOL doesn't mean he's no longer in the army."

The front door opened, and in stepped Walsh, suitcase in hand. He obviously hadn't stayed here last night, and Chance didn't need an explanation of where he'd slept. The acid from the coffee rose from his stomach into his throat. Another man had spent the night with the woman he loved.

The colonel stood. "Hello, Noah. Thanks for your message. We would have wondered about you." He turned back to Chance. "Let me get Noah all checked in, and then we'll finish our conversation."

Chance stood. "I think that's all for now. I'll let you know when I have everything worked out for the benefit. Oh, and, go ahead and list the inn."

He looked over at Walsh. "Morning, Noah. How's Charlee?"

Walsh shook his head. "Not well. I imagine she slept about two hours after you left, if that."

That was two more hours of sleep than Chance had gotten, and he'd been alone.

"Charity's confused and upset right now. She needs support from her friends and some time to absorb everything that's happened." He set his bag down at the desk. "Be patient. I'm certain she'll come around."

Patience and time he could give her. Support, maybe. But he could never be only her friend. The pain would be too great.

29

Charlee sat on the front row of the small chapel next to Ally.

Noah stood at the back door, taking tickets from late-comers.

Charlee should be grateful for what she still had. But anger overshadowed any possible feeling of gratitude. She'd lost two of the things she loved most—her business and the man who made her heart sing. Over the past few days, she'd reminded herself of the many other things she'd been given, but right now, feeling blessed was a struggle.

Knowing her Father loved her enough to handle her anger, even if she wasn't ready to talk with Him about it, provided her sole comfort. Somehow, she'd make it, but getting through this would take time.

On the stage before her sat three men she loved. Her pastor, her best friend's husband, and the man who'd captured her heart. Trey picked his banjo while Josh and Chance both played guitars and sang the final song of the night—some bluegrass tune. Mom would have said their voices went together like salt and pepper. Opposites that apart were delicious, but together were amazing.

Earlier Chance played a combination of classical compositions, show tunes, and old standards on the piano, and Josh performed some classical guitar pieces and then played and sang some hymns.

The colonel sat on the other end of the row, all smiles. He looked thrilled that his idea had been so well-received. His initial offer to give her tonight's proceeds had surprised her. But when the benefit had grown from one to two and finally three performances, the support and generosity of her community had both overwhelmed and humbled her.

Yet even with that, tonight's income would provide only a drop toward the bucketful needed to cover the gap between her insurance coverage and the cost required to rebuild and reopen her shop.

Over the last week, she'd begun doubting whether she should reopen her business at all. If Chance stayed in Crescent Bluff, she didn't think she could. And a part of her felt guilty accepting the funds under false pretenses. At least they had a record of the concert attendees so she could return the money depending upon her final decision.

She hadn't seen Chance since the last morning she'd sang at church. Noah had tried to get her to go to church after the fire, and she'd planned to, but then she'd backed out at the last minute. She couldn't go with an unclean heart. Yet deep inside, she knew the only way to wash away the dirt was through worship.

Chance's hair had grown, and the soft bangs falling across his forehead gave him an innocent, boyish look. The memory of the first time she'd run her fingers through his hair, right here in this chapel, wrapped around her until she could hardly breathe. Living without him seemed an impossibility. And now she didn't even have her work for a distraction.

"How blessed you are to have so many people in your life who care for you," Ally said. "Tonight has been proof of the love the town has for you."

Tears welled up in her eyes. Her anger aside, she was deeply blessed. *Forgive me, Father.*

~*~

Tonight, Charlee had hugged half the town. Noah and Ally sat in the back corner talking with the colonel. Only a few people stood scattered around the chapel. Charlee took a deep breath and walked toward the stage.

Trey had switched to the guitar and the three guys were playing what appeared to be some sort of "Follow Me" game. One would start a chord progression and the other two would build on it. Trey and Josh laughed as the game progressed to "Watch This." Chance participated, but a blank look covered his face. His gaze was fixed on the floor. Apparently, his heart wasn't in it.

Maybe he was angry about giving up this money. And she couldn't blame him. The proceeds from this concert should have gone to pay for his room and board. Her heart caught. No, if he was angry, it wasn't about that. Chance was the most generous person she'd ever met. Something else must be on his mind.

The music stopped as the three men noticed her. They set down their guitars and stood.

"Thank you all so much for this." She refused to cry. "I can't begin to tell you how much it means to me…" In spite of her vow, her eyes filled, and her throat ached. Her voice quivered. "The proceeds from tonight will be a good start to raising the seventy-five thousand dollars not covered by insurance."

Josh and Trey stepped down onto the floor and each gave her a hug. Then Josh turned back toward the stage. "Chance, get over here and show the lady some love."

As Chance neared, her heart raced. She searched his face, but his eyes avoided hers. He placed an arm around her in a casual, polite embrace. The warmth of his cologne brought back memories of their passion in the star-field. His scent intoxicated her. She wove her fingers together to keep from wrapping her arms around him and drawing him close. She missed him, needed him, couldn't imagine a life without him. The tears broke loose and tracked down her cheeks. "Thank you," she whispered.

He drew away, picked up the box of tissues from the front pew, and held them out to her. "Charlee, I'm sorry…about your loss."

~*~

Chance pushed his head back into the shelter of the wingback chair and stared into the fireplace. The flames flickered shadows onto the walls. He'd almost surrendered to his heart and wrapped her in his arms to comfort her. How could something that felt so right and that she seemed to want so much possibly be wrong? But it was.

The shock of hearing how much money she needed had finally settled in. He'd saved every extra penny he had for about two years now, and even with that, he didn't have enough to close the deal with the colonel.

The front door opened and Colonel Clark walked in. His eyes danced. "Great idea, young man. The concerts raised over twelve thousand dollars." He hung his jacket on the hall tree and sat in the other chair.

The people here loved her. "That's awesome, Colonel, but it's not enough. The seventy-five thousand dollars she needs may as well be seventy-five million. How will she ever raise the rest?" The short-sighted decision he'd made years ago when he'd needed drug money had ruined any opportunity he might have had to help her, or anyone else for that matter.

Sure, he could give her a part of his savings, but it still wouldn't be enough to make up the balance of what she needed. Plus, Colonel Clark wanted him to have a few more months to get the rest of the money together. If he gave money to Charlee, it would destroy any hope he had for the music institute. So he was stuck. The money he'd worked so hard to save wasn't enough to help either one of them.

Colonel Clark leaned forward. "Sometimes little can become much. Seems as if I recollect reading about a young man who gave what he had, a small lunch, hardly enough to feed one person. And in the right hands, it fed thousands." He winked.

The door opened again. Walsh. So, he wasn't spending the night at Charlee's tonight.

The colonel motioned to him. "Noah, come join us. I was sharing the results of the concerts with Chance. Between ticket sales and donations, we raised over twelve thousand dollars." The colonel smiled like a proud dad who'd watched his son just hit a homer.

Noah walked over and stood between them. "Charity will be thrilled. She was already surprised at the number of townspeople who were willing to donate to her." He reached into the breast pocket of his jacket. "I'd like to add this to the pot, but don't let her know, please." He handed the colonel a folded check.

As Colonel Clark flipped open the check and read the amount, his eyes widened. He stood and shook Walsh's hand. "That's very generous, young man."

"I could never repay her for all she's given me. Knowing her has changed my life." He cleared his throat. "Good night, gentlemen."

Maybe Walsh was the man "Charity" needed. A few weeks ago, Chance would have never thought that, but now…maybe so. One thing he knew for certain, he wasn't the guy.

The colonel leaned over and held Walsh's check between the first two fingers of his right hand. "Loaves and fishes, Chance. Loaves and fishes."

30

Charlee sat in the reception area of the bank. The Vice President had called this morning and asked her to stop by today so they could work out the details of transferring the proceeds from the concerts into her account. Three performances with about two hundred people in attendance each at twenty dollars a person yielded around twelve thousand dollars.

That her friends and neighbors would donate that amount was humbling. But the reality was, despite their generosity, the donation was far from the total she needed to get her business back up and running. Maybe it was time to move on to something else. She should have thought more about this before she'd agreed to the colonel's idea.

Mr. Kemp came out of his office. "Good morning, Charlee. Thanks for coming on such short notice." He gestured toward his office. "Come on back."

Charlee followed Dad's friend and settled into one of the leather club chairs facing the massive oak desk.

The Vice President took a seat in the high-backed leather chair behind the desk. He folded his hands and leaned forward. His kind gaze calmed her. "I was sorry to hear about your shop. You've worked hard over the past few years to be successful. I'm sure it's heartbreaking to lose all your investment in a few brief minutes."

Please, please, no tears. "Thank you for being willing to take a chance on a young woman with a dream." As she answered, her voice shook. "You were the only one who believed in me in the beginning."

He smiled. "I doubt that's true, but even if it were, I'm not the only one anymore." He picked up a piece of paper from the credenza behind him and slid it across the desk toward her. "Here's what was deposited into your account this morning."

As she looked down at the deposit slip, her breath caught. "Surely there's been some mistake. The concerts couldn't have possibly raised this much. I don't understand." Her heart raced.

"I was told there was a sizable anonymous contribution in addition to the concert proceeds." He reached over and patted her hand.

The numbers on the slip blurred as her eyes filled, as she took another look at the printing on the paper.

Seventy-six thousand dollars was written on the deposit line.

"How can this possibly be?"

~*~

FOR SALE BY OWNER

The euphoria Charlee had felt at the bank dissolved into waves of nausea. That sign hadn't been there yesterday. Colonel Clark must have just put it up this morning. And it meant only one thing. Chance was leaving Crescent Bluff.

Slowly, Charlee made her way down to the lake. An abnormally gentle breeze rustled the bare branches overhead. As she passed the chapel, the memory of the first time she'd begun to see past the musician's exterior into Chance's heart replayed in her mind. His comment about Juilliard. Hers about men in tuxes. Then she could have never known he'd be the man who would revive the song in her heart. And now he was going away.

She grasped a sapling as she carefully slid down the path to the bank where she'd first heard the music of the spheres. She'd come to thank her Father, to apologize for her anger. She should have trusted Him. She should now, but Chance was leaving.

She dropped down onto the root-bench. She'd never loved anyone as much as she loved Chance, and losing him couldn't possibly be the best thing for her. But he'd been the one to reject her. Just as Jake had. And before long Chance would be gone, too. Just as Jake had gone. Maybe in a few years, she'd run into him in a store at Christmas time. He'd have another woman on his arm and wouldn't be able to understand why she didn't want to get together to talk over "old times."

Just as Jake had done.

So her impression of Chance that very first night she'd shared her table with him had been right—well, partially right. Unlike Jake, Chance had taught her that music was a blessing, created for worship, created to give joy. He'd removed that darkness from her heart.

Yet on the most basic level, when it came to love and commitment, he and Jake were the same.

Charlee took a deep breath, closed her eyes, and listened. No music today. She should pray, but no words would come. Her mind was running in a thousand different directions.

She should be grateful for the support of her friends. And she was. They'd accomplished something she would have never believed possible. Yet right now, she didn't even want to consider rebuilding her business. And then there was the sign, the "For Sale" sign. Today her future looked so different from the way it had a few weeks ago.

As the bushes to her right rustled, she opened her eyes to see the burnt orange sweatshirt emerging from the brush. Chance walked straight toward the lake and stared out across the water. He bowed his head.

Her heart burned within her. He was praying, and although unintentional, she was intruding on this very private time. But there was no place to hide. If she tried to leave, she'd interrupt him. All she could do was close her eyes in respect.

As the wind began to blow, the songs of the birds trilled in the distance. The symphony of creation sounded more loudly and clearly than she'd ever heard it. Their Father was rejoicing over him, over her, over them. The reality embraced her so firmly she could hardly breathe.

She opened her eyes in time to see him turn toward her, his face reddening.

"Hi." She should apologize. "I, uh, didn't mean to intrude. I'm sorry."

"You have just as much right to be here as I do. It's a free country." He stuck his hands in his pockets and looked back over toward the lake.

He could be so infuriating. "Oh, well, that's a very adult comment. I think the last time someone said that to me was in middle school."

"You're right. I'm sorry." He turned toward the path back to the inn.

"Wait, Chance. Please, don't go. Could we talk for a moment?" Her heart began to pound. "Please stay."

He ran both hands through his hair and then intertwined his fingers behind his neck. He looked up at the sky and then turned toward her. "Sure." He walked over to the root-bench and sat down beyond her reach, as close to the end as possible. As he folded his arms across his chest, he stared toward the lake. "Shoot."

She took a deep breath to steady her voice. The deliciousness of his cologne filled the void between them. "Thank you for donating your time the other night. I know the money should have gone to repay the Clarks for your room and board, and I appreciate the sacrifice you made."

"No problem." He lifted one hand and rubbed it against his cheek and across his chin. That hand should be hers.

"Look." She reached into her pocket, pulled out the deposit slip, and handed it to him.

As he opened it, his face softened, and he turned toward her. A slight smile warmed his face. "Charlee, that's great."

"I know. I was shocked." If only she could draw him close and kiss him, but instead, she put her hands in her pockets.

"That just shows how loved you are." He held out the slip to her and squeezed her hand when she took it. "I'm happy for you."

This morning's tears returned. "Mr. Kemp told me someone made a sizable anonymous donation. I wish I knew who it was, so I could thank them." Her words were barely more than a whisper.

He turned to face the lake. "I know who it was, and I'm sure he had good reasons for wanting to remain anonymous, but I'll relay your message to him."

He stood. "By the way, you may have forgotten that you're supposed to do vocals at church this week, but I'll understand if you don't want to sing. I just haven't had a chance to rework the schedule. See you around."

"Chance, wait. Please, can we talk?"

"Maybe another time. I gotta be someplace." He turned and walked away.

She would definitely sing Sunday. Definitely.

~*~

Chance tuned his guitar while the rest of the band set up. He'd forgotten Charlee was scheduled to sing this morning until he'd seen her at the lake the other day. She hadn't been to church since the last time they'd sung together, the Sunday after he'd seen her and Walsh kissing at her shop.

Memories of their first dinner together pierced his heart. If only he'd never sat at her table, life could have been so different. Different, but not necessarily better. As painful as her rejection was, he was thankful to have had her in his life if only for those few short weeks.

Some people weren't cut out for marriage. After two strikes, he now realized he was probably one of them. No more women. No more distractions. He'd come to Crescent Bluff with so many dreams. And maybe that was the problem. Maybe they were only his dreams, because now they were gone. No Charlee, no inn.

This morning a "Sold" placard was plastered across the "FOR SALE BY OWNER" sign. The inn had sold in less than a week. Unbelievable. Definitely a confirmation he'd been on the wrong track. A few months ago, the colonel had mentioned he'd had interest from a couple of perspective buyers, but he wanted Chance to have first crack at it. Well, he had, and he'd failed. If losing Charlee and the inn was God's plan for his life, so be it. He didn't understand it, and it sure didn't feel good, but he'd given his everything to his Father, and all he could do was trust.

The music today wouldn't be as dramatic as if he'd had a female singer, but he hadn't been able to come up with any other songs he felt led to do this morning. Besides, changing on such short notice wouldn't be fair to the rest of the band. He looked back toward the bass player. Maybe Jeff could do some vocals.

He leaned forward and spoke into the mic. "All right guys, let's pray, and then we'll start." He voiced the words in his heart. "Father, be glorified through our music this morning. Please remove all distractions from our minds, and keep our focus on You. Amen."

When he opened his eyes, movement to his right caught his attention. Charlee leaned toward the mic and turned back to face the band. "Sorry I'm late."

~*~

Charlee sat on the second row. Josh's sermon was from Jeremiah, the verses about God's plan to prosper and not harm us, to give us a hope and a future. She'd never asked God about His plan when she and Jake were dating. But Jake wasn't His plan. Then the business she'd started had been successful, so she'd been sure that was His plan. And now it was gone, too. And then Chance had come into her life when she wasn't even looking. She'd tried so hard to resist him, but she hadn't been able. She'd really prayed about Chance. And now he was gone. So if her Father had a plan for her life, why couldn't she find it?

Sitting across the aisle with Trey and Ally, Noah closed his recently purchased, and extremely huge, Bible. Definitely perfect for an English professor. His newfound faith was the one bright spot in this whole mess. His heart had changed, and she loved that. She just didn't love him. He wasn't the one who made her heart sing. Maybe no other man besides Chance ever would. As Josh prayed, she stood quietly, and slipped up to take her place on the platform.

The back set of songs was acoustic, contemplative. No drums, no bass. Only Chance's guitar and their voices. They drew stools up to the mics and settled onto them. Chance's eyes were closed, his head bowed. She leaned forward and slipped her hand into his. His fingers tightened. He didn't draw his hand away. She closed her eyes and prayed.

The first time she'd ever sung this next song was during rehearsal this morning. It was a redo of an old hymn entitled, "Satisfied." More than anything, that's what she wanted in her life right now. Satisfaction and the peace of knowing what Josh preached about. God's plans. Everything she'd put her hand to had failed.

Chance slipped his hand away and began the intro. As his fingers moved between the frets, her eyes fell on his forearm. Poema. Had lightning struck at that moment, it would have paled compared to her realization. That was it. All these years, she'd been trying to be the poet instead of the poem. *Help me trust You. Satisfy my heart.*

Chance's voice was warm as he began:

All my life long I had a longing, For a drink from some clear spring,
That I hoped would quench the burning, Of the thirst I felt within.

She added harmonies on the next verse.

Poor I was, and sought for riches, Something that would satisfy,
But the dust I gathered round me Only mocked my soul's sad cry.

As they transitioned into the chorus, her heart began to race.

Hallelujah! I have found Him, Whom my soul so long has craved!

Her soul had been craving the wrong things—success, true love. Not that they were bad. They weren't. She'd just expected them to provide something they alone couldn't. Genuine satisfaction. That could come from only one place.

Well of water, ever springing, Bread of Life so rich and free,
Untold wealth that never faileth, My Redeemer is to me.

31

Since they had no shop to go to, Charlee suggested they meet at The Perks for coffee this morning. She slid into the booth across from Ally. "Good morning."

"Morning." Ally picked up her yellow Perks mug and blew across the top of whatever flavored coffee concoction she'd ordered today. "The music was amazing yesterday, Charlee."

"Thanks, but I had nothing to do with it. Just showed up and sang…which was hard enough, don't get me wrong. It wasn't easy being that close to Chance."

Ally shook her head. "Trey and I are in agreement. You two are acting like a couple of spoiled kids."

"Don't blame me. I've tried to talk with him, but he refuses. Sometimes I just want to smack him."

"I think you've just proven my point." Ally laid her hand on Charlee's. "Don't be so hard on him. Look at it from his viewpoint. He's only doing what he thinks is best for you."

"Oh, right." She shook her head. "Breaking my heart is in my best interests?" That made no sense.

"He loves you, you know."

She knew he used to. "If that's true, then why won't he talk with me? Why is he avoiding me?"

"You know his past. He doesn't want to hurt you any more than he already has." Ally looked straight into her eyes. "That night when you missed each other at the chapel…he saw you with Noah. And he…he turned back to his old ways."

Tears filled her eyes. "I didn't know…" she whispered. He'd been fighting this whole thing alone. A lump filled her throat. "Why couldn't he trust me enough to tell me?"

"Maybe he thinks he's not good enough for you." She squeezed

Charlee's hand. "He loves you enough to let you go. Promise me you won't go down without a fight."

Charlee brushed away a tear. "I'm going to be a thorn in that man's side until he talks to me and we get this mess straightened out."

"That's my Charlee."

They sipped their drinks in silence for a few seconds. Poor Chance. Charlee wanted to draw him into her arms and kiss away the pain. To assure him she loved him…his heart.

"So, you said you wanted to meet about something this morning?" Ally raised her eyebrows in question.

"Oh, right." Charlee pulled the deposit slip out of her pocket and slid it across the table. "Look."

Ally smiled big, but with much less enthusiasm than Charlee had anticipated. "I know. I heard." The irrational guilt Ally had felt the night of the fire was gone. No one was at fault. The fire had just happened.

"You heard? How?" Charlee hadn't told anyone besides Noah and Chance. And Colonel Clark knew, of course. He'd given the donations to the bank.

Ally leaned forward, a serious look on her face. Her words were barely more than a whisper. "I have my source."

"Your source?"

Ally grinned. "Trey."

Chance must have told him. "Apparently, there was one anonymous donor who gave enough to meet the goal. Chance knows who it was, but he wouldn't tell me."

"Oh, really?" Ally's eyes shone with mischief. "Well, isn't that the definition of anonymous?"

"I want to thank the person, that's all."

Ally's face reddened.

"You know who it is, don't you?"

Ally looked down into her cup and then back up. Seriousness covered her face. "I promised Trey not to tell."

Oh, now Trey knew, too. "So, anonymous really means everyone knows but me. Please, Ally?"

Ally looked up to the ceiling and then back down. "I promised not to tell. But I didn't promise not to hint." She sighed. "The person who gave the donation did so because he cares for you. Because knowing you has changed his life. That's all I can say. Don't ask me again."

~*~

Charlee sat at the same table she and Chance had shared the night they met. She stared first at the menu and then up into her dinner-partner's face. "How was your week, Noah?"

"Lovely. I received a response from Baylor. They'll have an opening next fall, and I have an interview in a couple of weeks. If they offer me a contract, I'll begin searching for a place to live here." He'd come to Crescent Bluff every weekend since the first Sunday he'd attended church a few weeks ago. "Charity, I'll never be able to repay you for all you've done in my life. I'm truly happy."

She set down the menu and grasped his hands. "I'm happy for you, Noah. But I'm the one who needs to thank you."

His brow knit in confusion as he waited in silence.

"I know about your donation. Thank you. You shouldn't have given so much."

He looked first down at the table and then back into her eyes. "I didn't want you to find out. Who told you?"

She interlocked her fingers with his and pulled his hands up toward her. In time, perhaps she could come to love this man. Perhaps. "No one. I figured it out on my own." Well, maybe Ally helped a little. "You'll never know how much your kindness means to me."

"I wish I could have given more than three thousand dollars, and I would have if I hadn't had this possible move pending." His eyes were warm.

She didn't understand. Three thousand dollars was very generous, but even combined with the proceeds from the benefit, a huge shortfall would have still remained. She'd been so sure the donation had come from Noah. No one else she knew had extra money like that. Not even her parents anymore. Maybe Mr. Kemp at the bank, but she certainly hadn't done anything to change his life, as Ally had said.

Her throat went dry as the picture of the "For Sale" sign in front of the inn pushed its way into her mind. Surely not.

~*~

Noah had gone to meet Josh at The Perks for coffee and Bible study. Charlee stared at the door to room five as her heart pounded. Her eyes were on the verge of tearing up, so she took a deep breath. She refused to cry in front of him. Lifting her hand, she tapped on the door.

Chance's voice was muffled. "Just a minute." He opened the door slightly and peeked around the edge.

His hair was wet. The aroma of soap and shampoo drifted from the room. Through the small crack between the door and the molding, she could see a sliver of flannel pajama pants on the bottom and bare skin on the top. Behind the door he was shirtless. He must have just gotten out of the shower. His eyes were cold—no, filled with pain.

"Charlee."

She tried to swallow the lump in her throat. "Hi. Could I please come in?"

He looked down at the ground and then back into her eyes. "Afraid you can't do that, Charlee. It wouldn't be proper. Plus, I'm kind of busy right now going over some stuff for Sunday."

"What, you were doing that in the shower? Please, Chance. I need to talk with you." She wasn't giving in. "Just for a few minutes."

He raised up his arm and leaned against the doorjamb.

Poema.

He sighed. "I'll meet you in the parlor in about five minutes. I need to pull on some clothes."

"No, Chance. Not there. Someplace quieter, more private. How about the chapel?"

He shook his head. "Charlee, I don't think..."

"Please, Chance." She was begging, but she didn't care. "Either your room or the chapel."

He huffed out a breath. "The chapel."

~*~

Charlee drank in the beauty of his kind face. He dropped down onto the end of the pew. She closed her eyes and was in his arms watching stars racing across the sky.

He leaned forward and hung his head. "Well?" He gazed toward her.

"It was you, wasn't it?" She breathed slowly to steady her voice.

"Me?" He looked back at the floor. "I don't know what you mean."

"The anonymous donor. It was you." As he ran his hands through his hair, her heart ached with desire. Her fingers should be caressing the brown silk.

"Charlee, I told you I knew who it was, not that it was me."

Her face burned. "Chance, I know it was you. The day after the benefit, the inn went on the market. Why won't you give me a straight answer?"

He closed his eyes and leaned back in the pew.

"Why, Chance? Why did you give up your dream?" She wiped her tears away.

He turned and looked straight into her eyes. "It was the right thing to do. I never was able to come up with enough. I could have given you part of what I'd saved, but that wouldn't have helped either one of us. And after Walsh's donation, my savings was almost exactly the amount you needed." He shook his head, his next words barely above a whisper. "I wanted to do it."

She scooted toward him and grasped his hand. "I can't accept it. Take it back. Go talk to the colonel. Maybe you can get out of the sale."

He wove his fingers with hers. "The contract's been signed. It's too late, Charlee. I told you I didn't have a definite game-plan for the institute—that if God wanted it to work out, it would. And, now I know for sure. It's not in His plans." He withdrew his hand and stood. "But that's OK. I'm at peace, and I'm ready to get back on track."

"Please don't leave." She stood and stepped toward him. "I need to talk with you about Noah and me. I want to explain."

His face flushed. He drew her close. "No explanation's necessary. Really. I understand. And I can't say that I blame you." He stepped away. "I have to finish working on Sunday's service." He turned and strode toward the back of the chapel.

Adrenaline electrified her body. "Ashley Chance Jackson, stop. You owe me the courtesy of listening, at least."

As he continued up the aisle, her voice became strident, even to her own ears. "Don't leave. Don't you do it. Don't you dare walk out on me."

He looked at her with tired eyes. "I'm not the one you need." He turned his back to her and walked out the door.

~*~

No matter how hard Chance tried, he couldn't concentrate on the song arrangements. He didn't want Sunday, especially this Sunday, to be a failure, like so much of what he'd touched recently. But something else—someone else—had invaded his mind and heart.

He'd been such a jerk. Walking out on her was probably the hardest thing he'd ever done. He loved her, but sometimes love revealed itself in the most painful ways.

He'd wanted that money to do some good, and his heart was at peace with his decision. Some people would have thought he was stupid, and by the world's standards, he probably was. Over time, maybe she'd pay it back, but he certainly didn't expect that. The money had been a gift—no strings attached. But he knew her. She wouldn't want to feel indebted to him. That was the whole reason for anonymity. And that sure didn't work out too well. She was too smart, or Ally had told her. If that was the case, Trey was in big trouble.

He wasn't at peace, though. As much as he'd tried to tell himself he was ready to move on, that he was over her, he wasn't. The last thing he wanted was to love a woman who didn't return his feelings. But he did. Yet by walking away from her tonight, he'd smothered any hope they might possibly get back together. Listening to her explanation, her justification for choosing Walsh over him would have hurt too much.

But the truth was she'd made a wise decision.

He flopped back onto the bed and closed his eyes. The last few weeks had been a struggle, and he was so tired of fighting. Father, I surrender. Again. Take up the fight for me.

A soft knock sounded on the door. If he opened it, and she was standing there, he wasn't sure he'd be able to close it back, so he ignored it.

The knock sounded again. This time more loudly. "Chance? You in there?"

The colonel. Chance jumped up and opened the door. "Sorry, sir. I'm here."

The colonel smiled. "The prospective owners of the inn are out in the parlor, and they'd like to speak with you."

"It's kind of late. Plus, I'm really pretty busy." He wasn't up to putting on a happy face for strangers.

"They've made a special trip. You could give them five minutes, couldn't you, son?" The words were phrased as a question, but the command was implied.

"Yes, sir. I'll meet y'all in the parlor in a few minutes."

Colonel Clark smiled and nodded. He turned and walked down the hall.

Chance checked his hair, pulled on a leather jacket over his tee shirt and jeans, and then slipped on his boots. May as well try to look somewhat respectable. After turning off the light, he pulled the door closed behind him and headed down the hall to the parlor.

He recognized the gray-haired couple sitting on the settee talking with the colonel. "Mom, Dad…what are y'all doing here?" He scanned the rest of the parlor. No one else was there.

His parents stood and Mom stepped forward and gave him a hug. "Hi, honey. Surprise." She giggled.

Chance hugged her back. "Mom." Confusion swirled in his mind.

Colonel Clark stood. "If you folks'll excuse me, I have some paperwork to do."

His parents made appropriate responses, but Chance just stood there dumbfounded. "I don't get it. I was supposed to be meeting the people who are buying the inn." He laughed sarcastically. "That's not you, is it?"

Mom squeezed his hand. "Us?" She looked up at his father, smiled, and then looked back at him. "No, honey. Not us. Not really."

Elusiveness tinged her reply.

"Have a seat, son." Chance's father spoke for the first time.

As they sat on the settee, the logs in the fireplace crackled.

"AC," Mom began, "your father and I are so proud of the man you've become." She clasped his hand. "Years ago, when all that, you know, 'stuff' was going on, your agent contacted us and told us you'd decided to sell the rights to your music. We were heartbroken at the thought of you losing the fruits of your God-given talent. So…" Her voice began to quiver, and she bit her lip.

"What your mother's trying to say is," Dad continued, "we bought them. For the first year, we paid back our original investment. And then after that time, any royalty money was invested for you until the time was right."

Mom squeezed his hand. "So, no, honey. We're not buying the inn. You are."

~*~

Chance lay back in his bed, overcome with awe. Tonight's cloud-blanketed moon meant little light entered the room through the patio doors. The darkness of the room wrapped him in peace, a protective cocoon. He had no idea how much time had passed since his parents left. He'd been lying here in the dark trying to absorb everything that had happened. He should have been thanking his Father that a new line in his poem was being written and planning what his next step would be.

He searched for the joy he should be feeling. In a matter of minutes, he'd gone from a man who was unable to scrape together enough money to make the down payment on the inn to a man who could purchase it outright and have some left over to fund its development into a music institute. His heart burst with gratitude. But not joy.

Because something was missing. Over the past few months when he'd played this scenario through in his mind, Charlee had always stood beside him. But that part of the dream would never be a reality.

Mom and Dad's gesture was thoughtful, but it had come too late. He hadn't wanted to hurt them, so he hadn't said anything. If only he hadn't already talked with Josh. Tomorrow, he'd speak with Colonel Clark and see if he—his parents—could get out of the contract.

The French door to the patio rattled. The wind must have really kicked up. It rattled again. He sat up. No, it wasn't the wind. He could barely make out the silhouette of a person. Someone was trying to break in. He scooted out of bed, crept toward the door, and waited in the shadow. He was ready to jump if the intruder got in.

The glass panes flashed as the door inched open and a person wearing a ski mask or knit cap slipped into the room and stopped.

What if he was armed? Chance had no weapon, but he did have the element of surprise and size. The burglar was smaller than he was. And he'd learned some tricks living on the streets.

The trespasser turned to close the door. Chance's heart hammered in his chest. Time to rock and roll. Lunging toward the intruder, he grabbed him in a bear hug, threw him to the floor, and pinned him to the ground. "Speak."

"How dare you walk away from me earlier tonight! You will hear me out, Ashley Chance Jackson."

32

Charlee could hardly breathe. The weight of his body made pushing the words out almost impossible.

He rolled off her as quickly as if he'd fallen on a yellow jackets' nest. "Charlee, are you OK?" The concern she couldn't see on his face sounded in his voice.

The trunk of her body ached from him jumping on her and pinning her down. He'd stunned her. "If I was OK, I wouldn't be here."

Annoyance now replaced his concern. "Are you crazy breaking in like that?" He jumped up and groped for the desk lamp, his words biting. "What if I'd had a weapon? What if I'd hit you over the head with something?"

Light blinded her eyes. She sat up and shrugged her shoulders. She hadn't thought about that. She figured he'd be asleep by now.

"I could have hurt you."

"You've already done that." He was shirtless, wearing only flannel pajama pants. He was much more muscled than she'd realized. A warmth coursed through her as her heartbeat quickened.

His face reddened. He grabbed the sweatshirt from the top dresser drawer, pulled it over his head, and then offered her his hand and helped her up. "You really can't stay."

"I can, and I will." She cemented herself to the chair in front of the French doors. "I'm not leaving until you hear me out." Her heart raced.

He dropped onto the desk chair. Leaning forward, he placed his elbows on his thighs, and hung his head. His gaze focused on some undetermined spot on the floor between his feet. He looked so sad. "Charlee, I don't think…"

"I want to explain about Noah and me." Her voice quivered as sorrow rose into her throat. "I think I understand what's going on with you." She fought the impulse to jump up and pull him into her arms.

"Charlee, I…" His gaze crept up from the floor and found hers.

"I love you, Chance. No one else. Only you." She opened her eyes wide, but the tears washed her cheeks anyway. "And you love me."

"Loving you has never been the question. There's more to it than that." He drew in a ragged breath and rubbed his hand across his stubbled chin.

"Chance, we can do this. I want to do this."

He shook his head. "Everything's changed. Or maybe nothing's as I thought it was. Anyway, it's all different now." He stood. "I've tried to make a new life, but I failed. This is my last Sunday in Crescent Bluff. I'm moving back to Austin. I'll be working at the Hope House." His tone was flat, his words emotionless.

Her stomach heaved. This wasn't happening. He couldn't leave permanently. Maybe for a few weeks, but not for good. "No, Chance."

He stood and grasped her hand and brought it to his lips. "You may be able to do this, but I can't. I'm not the person you need…you deserve." He opened the patio door and led her outside. "I'll walk you to your car."

He wouldn't even listen to her. She wanted to scream, but instead she took a deep breath. "I don't need you to walk me to my car." Her words were deliberate. "I need you to listen to me. Five minutes, that's all I ask." She pulled her hand away. "You owe me that much."

She could hardly see him in the cloudy black of night, but a brief glimmer in his eyes told her he was at least looking toward her. She cradled his face in her hands and took a deep breath. "Chance, a person I love with all my heart once shared these words with me, and I think you need to hear them." She could manage only a whisper. "You're living in darkness, and the longer you stay there, the more distorted your vision becomes. What you think you've seen is not the truth. If you'll let me explain, you'll see how wrong your perception is."

She put her arms around him and rested her head against his shoulder.

He eased her away and stepped back into his room. "Whoever told you that was an idiot."

His words stabbed her heart.

~*~

Charlee shivered as the damp wind raced across the lake and swirled around her. She was freezing, and his icy words only intensified tonight's cold. Numbness had overtaken her…body, soul, and spirit. What had happened between the time he closed the door and now was a blur. But despite the blanket of darkness, she'd somehow made it through the brush to the root-bench. Though she stared ahead toward the lake, her eyes saw nothing. Her ears heard nothing. No shooting stars blazed overhead. No music of the spheres sounded tonight.

Their relationship was over. She'd thought she loved him, but she couldn't truly love a man who didn't respect her enough to listen to her. A man who doubted her. And for that reason, she would've never been able to trust him, to fully give herself to him.

She'd taken another chance with another musician because he seemed different. And this time, she'd even prayed about him. The heart she'd seen in the SDS letters had been so vulnerable, so gentle…so broken. The heart she'd come to love had seemed beautiful, generous, kind.

But once a poser, always a poser. He'd misled her and tricked her.

And she'd tricked herself. In the depths of her soul, she'd thought she felt a little voice asking for her trust, and she wanted their relationship to work out so badly she had blindly trusted and fooled herself into believing a lie. She'd been wrong…stupid. Never again. Never, ever again would a man cause her such pain.

Tears streamed down her face, sobs shaking her body. She'd lost her love. She'd lost her work. But she had one thing, the most important thing, left. Her Father. He'd been patiently waiting all along. *Father, please satisfy my longings with Your love.*

She stood and crept toward the lake on unsure legs. The wind unwrapped the clouds from around the moon, and tiny diamonds sparkled across the surface of the water. She pulled the knit hat Chance had given her for Christmas from her head and threw it out into the lake. The waves slowly carried it away. If only she could rid her heart of him that easily.

The wind rustled the brush behind her, and she turned. A white longhorn stared at her from the middle of a sweatshirt that in the moonlight looked more gray than orange. It came closer and closer until the arms of the shirt surrounded her and drew her in. Chance rested his cheek on the top of her head and rocked her back and forth. The warmth of his body and his hypnotizing scent enveloped her. She pulled him tight as their hearts beat in unison.

Chance placed his lips against her ear. "That idiot? The one I referred to earlier? He's so sorry." His whisper warmed her cheek. "You're right about my perception. I've been blinded by the darkness. Please forgive me, my love. If you'll still have me, I'm in."

33

As Charlee snuggled into the silken sheets, last night's memories brought a smile to her face. She scooted her hand over to the space beside her. Empty. She bolted up. Surely everything that happened wasn't a dream. No, the other side of the bed was warm. She gathered her husband's pillow to her nose and breathed in his delicious scent.

The sweet fragrance of jasmine greeted her as the spring breeze blended with a beam of sunlight and swirled its way through the sliver between the patio doors. She grabbed her robe from the floor and slipped it on. Then she tiptoed to the French doors and peeked out.

Chance sat in one of the patio chairs, a photo book about Kenya on his lap, inn stationery on the book, a pen in his hand. Her heart fluttered as the fingers of his left hand tapped the arm of the chair in time with a melody only he could hear. A song their Father had placed in his heart. Charlee glanced over his shoulder at the block printed words on the paper.

Last night was my wedding night. What's that trite phrase? "The first day of the rest of my life."

She tiptoed onto the patio, eased up behind him, and rested her hands on his shoulders. He leaned his head against her arm, and she brushed her lips against his satin hair. "What are you doing?"

He kissed her arm and then turned and smiled up at her. The amber flecks in his eyes sparkled golden. "Finishing the story."

This was the first time she'd heard his early morning voice—deep and gravelly. She loved it. And his first-thing-in-the-morning-look was just another version of his everyday-PR look. She loved that, too. "Really? So now that this is no longer an inn, who do you think will read it?" She hung her arms around his neck and nestled her cheek against his head.

"Oh, I don't know." He shrugged. "Maybe our children and grandchildren." As he drew away and turned toward her, his face reddened, and he smiled.

He was so cute when he was embarrassed. "Well, we've got several years until that time. Don't you think you could finish the letter a little later? Please?" She offered him her most innocent look.

He flashed his perfect grin. "Absolutely. Especially now that you're awake."

He set the book and stationery aside and stood. She grasped his left hand. A new tattoo in Hebrew, not Greek, encircled his ring finger. *I am my beloved's.* A matching one encircled hers. *My beloved is mine.* Just as with the other milestones in his life, he'd wanted a permanent reminder of their day—a wedding band that would never be removed, that would bind their hearts together forever. And so had she. Drawing his hand to her lips, she kissed it.

He brushed her hair aside and nuzzled her neck.

As she drew away, she looked up into her husband's face. His hair was longer than it had been when they first met months ago, and she ran her fingers through the chocolate brown decadence, just as she had many times last night. His embrace tightened around her, quickening her breathing.

His whisper tickled her to the soles of her feet. "I love you, Charity Bennett Jackson."

"I love you, Ashley Chance Jackson." She buried her head in his chest. "Will you play my song again for me?"

"Any time, any place, forever." He placed his fingertips under her chin and lifted her face. His gaze captured hers. "Except maybe right now." He rested his forehead against hers. "I kind of have something else in mind. After all, we don't have to catch that flight to London until tonight." He grinned.

His lips found hers and his tender kiss grew with passion as each second passed. Hunger filled her.

He drew away and eased open the door. "Come, my love." He turned toward her and offered his hand.

"Any time, any place, forever. I'm in." Grasping his hand, she looked down at the goose bumps covering her arms. A joy she'd never dreamed possible bloomed within her. He drew her close, and a special melody meant only for them filled her soul.

Chance swayed her back and forth. Then he rested his lips against her ear. "Listen," he whispered. "Do you hear it?"

"The Lord thy God in the midst of thee is mighty; He will save, He will rejoice over thee with joy; He will rest in His love, He will joy over thee with singing." Zephaniah 3:17

A Devotional Moment

The Lord is close to the brokenhearted and saves those who are crushed in spirit. ~ Psalm 34:18

Even Christians can become discouraged and disappointed when life throws them a curveball. They ponder and consider the ways of the Lord, sometimes going through doubt, anger, and pain as they contemplate how God can let bad things happen. Some realize that we live in a fallen world, and as such, evil and hurt will touch our lives. But as flawed humans, we still have to go through periods of grief, and with God's help, we can overcome all obstacles that keep us from Him.

In **A Time for Singing**, both protagonists have gone through a lot of pain and misery. As they fight their way out of the sorrows, they realize they must change their hearts and minds to allow God to work in their lives. Through their surrender, they find that God changes their lives and their love.

Have you ever felt so crushed by the trials of life that you felt like giving up or felt as if God was absent or didn't care? It's important during these low moments of depression, uncertainty, pain, and even a wavering faith, to make a conscious effort to let God help you—even if you're unsure He's there. It isn't easy to give up control of your broken life, but you are a work in progress, a work designed and loved into existence by God. Turn to Him and ask for help. Even when you are crushed, you will discover that in His compassion, you will be healed and brought to a better place than you've ever been before.

LORD, HELP ME TO WEATHER CRUSHING MOMENTS THAT BREAK MY HEART. HEAL ME FROM WITHIN. IN JESUS' NAME I PRAY, AMEN.

Acknowledgements

To the patient and perceptive Fay Lamb, thank you for working so hard with me over the years to make my writing the best it can be.

To the talented and creative Nicola Martinez, thank you for your encouragement and your beautiful cover designs. I have been blessed to serve together with you as a part of the Pelican family.

Thank you

May God's glory shine through
this inspirational work of fiction.

AMDG

You Can Help!

At Pelican Book Group it is our mission to entertain readers with fiction that uplifts the Gospel. It is our privilege to spend time with you awhile as you read our stories.

We believe you can help us to bring Christ into the lives of people across the globe. And you don't have to open your wallet or even leave your house!

Here are 3 simple things you can do to help us bring illuminating fiction™ to people everywhere.

1) If you enjoyed this book, write a positive review. Post it at online retailers and websites where readers gather. And share your review with us at reviews@pelicanbookgroup.com (this does give us permission to reprint your review in whole or in part.)

2) If you enjoyed this book, recommend it to a friend in person, at a book club or on social media.

3) If you have suggestions on how we can improve or expand our selection, let us know. We value your opinion. Use the contact form on our web site or e-mail us at customer@pelicanbookgroup.com

God Can Help!

Are you in need? The Almighty can do great things for you. Holy is His Name! He has mercy in every generation. He can lift up the lowly and accomplish all things. Reach out today.

Do not fear: I am with you; do not be anxious: I am your God. I will strengthen you, I will help you, I will uphold you with my victorious right hand.

~Isaiah 41:10 (NAB)

We pray daily, and we especially pray for everyone connected to Pelican Book Group—that includes you! If you have a specific need, we welcome the opportunity to pray for you. Share your needs or praise reports at http://pelink.us/pray4us

Free eBook Offer

We're looking for booklovers like you to partner with us! Join our team of influencers today and periodically receive free eBooks!

For more information
Visit http://pelicanbookgroup.com/booklovers

How About Free Audiobooks?

We're looking for audiobook lovers, too! Partner with us as an audiobook lover and periodically receive free audiobooks!

For more information
Visit http://pelicanbookgroup.com/booklovers/freeaudio.html

or e-mail
booklovers@pelicanbookgroup.com